SUFFER THE LITTLE CHILDREN

OTHER BOOKS BY AL LACY

Angel of Mercy series:
A Promise for Breanna (Book One)
Faithful Heart (Book Two)
Captive Set Free (Book Three)
A Dream Fulfilled (Book Four)

Journeys of the Stranger series:
Legacy (Book One)
Silent Abduction (Book Two)
Blizzard (Book Three)
Tears of the Sun (Book Four)
Circle of Fire (Book Five)
Quiet Thunder (Book Six)
Snow Ghost (Book Seven)

Battles of Destiny (Civil War series):
Beloved Enemy (Battle of First Bull Run)
A Heart Divided (Battle of Mobile Bay)
A Promise Unbroken (Battle of Rich Mountain)
Shadowed Memories (Battle of Shiloh)
Joy From Ashes (Battle of Fredericksburg)
Season of Valor (Battle of Gettysburg)
Wings of the Wind (Battle of Antietam)

Hannah of Fort Bridger series (coauthored by JoAnna Lacy):
Under the Distant Sky (Book One)
Consider the Lilies (Coming June 1997)
No Place for Fear (Coming September 1997)

SUFFER THE LITTLE CHILDREN

BOOK FIVE

AL LACY

MULTNOMAH BOOKS

SUFFER THE LITTLE CHILDREN
© 1997 by Lew A. Lacy

published by Multnomah Books
a part of the Questar publishing family

Edited by Rodney L. Morris
and Deena Davis
Cover design by D^2 Designworks
Cover illustration by Vittorio Dangelico

International Standard Book Number: 1-57673-039-5

Printed in the United States of America.

For information:
Questar Publishers, Inc.
Post Office Box 1720
Sisters, Oregon 97759

Library of Congress Cataloging-in-Publication Data
Lacy, Al.   Suffer the little children/Al Lacy.
   p. cm. -- (Angel of mercy series: no. 5)
      ISBN 1-57673-039-5 (alk. paper) 1. Frontier and pioneer life--
West (U.S.)--Fiction. 2. Orphan trains--West (U.S.)--Fiction. 3. Nurses--
West (U.S.)--Fiction. I. Title. II. Series: Lacy, Al. Angel of mercy series: 5.
PS3562.A256S8   1997   97-277
813'.54--dc21   CIP

97 98 99 00 01 02 03 04 05 06 — 10 9 8 7 6 5 4 3 2 1

To my sweet little niece,
Suzi Keller,
who is one of Uncle Al's most ardent fans.

I love you, Suzi!

And they brought young children to him,
that he should touch them:
and his disciples rebuked those that brought them.
But when Jesus saw it, he was much displeased,
and said unto them,
Suffer the little children to come unto me,
and forbid them not:
for of such is the kingdom of God.
Verily I say unto you,
Whosoever shall not receive
the kingdom of God as a little child,
he shall not enter therein.
And he took them up in his arms,
put his hands upon them,
and blessed them.

(MARK 10:13–16)

PROLOGUE

IN THE LATE 1840S, in New York City, a growing number of children lived on the city streets much like those depicted in *Oliver Twist*, Charles Dickens's 1838 novel about London's street waifs.

The shiploads of immigrants who had poured into New York from Europe found that the fabled New World was not the utopia they had dreamed of. Instead they had to cope with poverty and famine. With the scarcity of housing, and too few jobs, disillusioned and desperate parents were forced to leave their babies on doorsteps and their toddlers at the doors of police stations. They turned out their older children onto the streets to fend for themselves.

In a short time, entire "colonies" of street urchins had grown to unmanageable numbers. In 1848, New York City's chief of police, George W. Matsell, was quoted as saying, "There are some 10,000 children in the city who do not attend school. They live on the streets, for they have no other home night or day."

Many of the children were not abandoned, but became street waifs because their parents had either died or become so ill they could no longer provide the children food, clothing, or shelter.

Many of these children resorted to begging and stealing, but some found jobs selling newspapers, sweeping stores, restaurants, and sidewalks, and peddling apples, oranges, and flowers on the street corners. Others sold matches and toothpicks. Still others shined shoes. A few rummaged through trash cans for rags, boxes, or refuse paper to sell.

The thousands of children who wandered the streets were ill-clad, unwashed, and half-starved. They slept in boxes and trash bins in the alleys during the winter, many of them freezing to death. In warm weather, some slept on park benches or on the grass in Central Park.

At the turn of the decade, a New York minister, Reverend Charles Loring Brace, became deeply concerned about the growing numbers of hungry urchins. He realized they were bound to cause serious trouble or become victims of serious trouble, and decided to do something about it.

In February 1853, Brace led in establishing the Children's Aid Society, with a board of trustees comprised of laymen from churches of several different denominations. Judge John L. Mason was elected chairman; J. E. Williams of the Metropolitan Bank was elected treasurer; and Reverend Charles Brace was elected the society's secretary and would direct the work of the organization.

At first, the Children's Aid Society worked to get the children off the streets by providing food and shelter and establishing industrial schools to train them in a trade. The society also set up workshops. The boys worked at repairing shoes, and the girls learned to sew.

At some point the board realized they would have to find a different method of providing for the growing number of street children. The industrial schools and workshops were getting deeply in debt.

In 1854, after considering the alternatives, the board developed a "placing-out" program, sending forty-seven boys, ages seven to fifteen, and one supervisor to Dowagiac, Michigan. There the boys were chosen by farmers to help with the farm work. In return, the farmers promised to treat the boys as part of the family and to provide for their education.

This worked out so well that soon the Society was placing boys *and* girls at various farms in upstate New York. Within a few months, they were placing children on farms in the New England states. Though sometimes the farmers overworked the children to the point of slave labor, most of the time the children were treated well.

Before the end of the year in 1854, Reverend Brace had come up with the idea of taking the waifs west on trains and offering farmers and ranchers the opportunity to adopt them. The idea caught on quickly.

Thus, in 1854, what became known as "orphan trains" carried thousands of orphaned, abandoned, and destitute children from the slums of New York City into farm and ranch homes in the western states and territories. By 1857 the program was well underway. In that year alone, one thousand children between the ages of five and eighteen had been given homes in the West and put to work on farms and ranches.

By 1873, the total number of children sent west for adoption topped twenty-five thousand, and the farmers and ranchers were clamoring for more.

The biggest problem was the separation of brothers and sisters when the adoptive parents did not want the smaller children or could not afford to take all the siblings of one family. Both of these problems brought a great deal of criticism from the public.

Brace's orphan trains, however, were successful in spite of

the criticism as children were taken as far south as Texas and as far west as California.

In 1910, a survey concluded that 87 percent of the children shipped to the West had grown into creditable members of society, 8 percent had returned to New York, and only 5 percent had either disappeared, been arrested for crimes, or had died.

What's more, two of the orphans grew up to be governors, several became mayors, one became a Supreme Court justice, two became congressmen, thirty-five became lawyers, and nineteen became physicians. Many others became successful lawmen, farmers, ranchers, businessmen, wives, and mothers—those who made up the rest of the West's society.

1

February 1871

A HOWLING ARCTIC WIND whipped the eaves of the old tenement building and found its way through the cracks around the windows, making the thin curtains dance. A chill pervaded the room in spite of the fire in the kitchen stove.

Leah Hamilton's long black hair contrasted sharply with her pallid features, which were almost as white as the pillow that cushioned her head. Although she could barely see through the frostbitten windows, she could tell the gray sky over Manhattan Island was heavy with more snow.

The Atlantic coast of New York had taken a beating from ice, wind, and snow since late fall. Now it was early February, and the unrelenting winter was still punishing the land and the people without mercy.

Leah pulled up the covers around her thin neck. She was steadily losing weight, partially from lack of food in the cupboard, but mainly because the consumption had almost completely destroyed her desire for food.

Even when she did feel a little bit hungry, the meager food supply in the cupboard would hardly feed her three children. So she would tell them she wasn't hungry.

Leah rolled her head slowly and set her gaze on ten-year-old Susan, who was washing clothes and bedding in a galvanized tub. Six-year-old Nathan helped lift the wet clothes and wring them out.

Just then Susan looked up and saw her mother looking at her. "Are you cold, Mother?" she asked.

"No, honey, I'm fine, thank you." The purplish semicircles under Leah's eyes seemed to darken as she tried to smile at her daughter.

Susan dropped the wet clothing and dried her hands on a towel. She walked to her mother's bedside and touched her face gently. "Mother, you *are* cold. I'll hang something over the window. Let's see if I can keep the wind from coming in."

Susan went to the apartment's only closet and took out an old coat she had outgrown. She slid a chair across the floor from the kitchen table and climbed up on it to stretch the coat over the curtain rod.

"There, Mother, that will keep the cold air from blowing on you. I know it blocks the light, but it's better that you stay warm."

Leah reached out a shaky hand and Susan took hold of it and smiled again.

"Susie," Leah said, "I'm so sorry to be a burden to you and the boys."

"Mother, you're not a burden! Jared and Nathan and I love you very, very much. We just want you to get well."

Nathan came to stand beside his sister, a shock of sand-colored hair bouncing on his forehead. He had blue eyes like his siblings, but unlike them his face had an abundant supply of freckles. His brow furrowed as he said, "Please get well, Mommy. I want you to not be sick anymore."

Leah let go of her daughter's hand and took hold of

Nathan's. "I'm trying, honey. It makes me feel better when I see how you help Susie and Jared with the work around here. You're a good boy."

There was a pleading look in Nathan's eyes as he said, "Please let me hug you, Mommy."

Susan touched Nathan's shoulder as Leah's expression changed to sadness.

"Nathan," Susan said softly, "we would all like to hug Mother, but we can't get that close to her without maybe catching the consumption ourselves. She doesn't want us to get it. We couldn't help her get well if we had it, too, could we?"

Nathan's mouth quivered as he shook his head no.

"Come on, Nathan. We have to finish wringing out the wash."

It was all Leah Hamilton could do to keep from bursting into tears as she watched her children move back to the galvanized tub and pick up where they had left off. She was frightened for her children. She constantly wondered what would happen to them after she died. The little bit of money they had in the jar on the top shelf of the cupboard would play out quickly.

Even though her oldest son, Jared, brought in a small amount of money from the newspapers he sold and the odd jobs he picked up, he was only twelve years old and couldn't earn enough to keep them in the apartment.

The money in the jar was the end of the savings she and John had brought with them from Wales when they'd come to America in late 1866. John had taken it to a bank and exchanged it for U.S. currency.

The Hamiltons had not touched their savings when John was alive and Leah was working her cleaning job, but John had died of consumption in early 1870. From that time on, Leah had dipped into it once in a while to pay the rent. When the consumption in her own body had become so bad that she could no longer work, she was forced to keep dipping into the jar to pay the rent.

As she lay in the bed, listening to the wintry wind, she thought of the last $10—enough for ten more weeks if Mr. Girard didn't raise the rent. There had been talk in the tenement that he might raise it in March.

Leah watched Susan and Nathan busily wringing out the wash, and her mind drifted back to the day she and John and the children had arrived in New York harbor. The tall buildings—some as many as ten stories high—were awesome. The streets of New York City, teeming with people, the blue water of the harbor reflecting the winter sunshine, the seemingly countless stores and shops—all worked together to convey a warm welcome.

This was America. The New World.

People came from all over Europe to make their fortunes here. There was plenty of money, and all the emigrants were becoming wealthy, or so the Hamiltons had thought. But it didn't take long for the cold, hard truth to slap them in the face. John had found only part-time work at first. Leah had pitched in, picking up an office-cleaning job. After a few weeks, John found steady work driving a meat wagon, but the pay was far short of what they had been led to believe it would be in America.

And now John was dead, and she was dying. Her children would be orphans—waifs of the streets. Leah's heart was heavy within her, but there was nothing she could do.

She silently watched her children working. Susan scooped more coal on the fire in the kitchen stove, then began hanging clothes and bedding on the cords strung across the room from wall to wall. Nathan carried the wet pieces to Susan as she hung them up to dry.

Suddenly Leah began to hack and cough, covering her mouth with the sheet.

Nathan turned to look at her, and Susan hastily flopped a wet pillowcase over a cord and hastened to the bedstand. She quickly poured water from a battered metal pitcher into an equally battered tin cup and placed it to her mother's lips.

Leah coughed and choked as she swallowed the water in small sips. Susan could hardly stand to see her mother suffer this way, and she tenderly stroked a pale cheek, saying, "You'll get better when spring comes and the weather turns warmer, Mother."

Leah swallowed the last few drops of water and nodded. She wanted to weep, knowing that if she made it till spring it would be a miracle.

Nathan was standing by the bed again with tears in his eyes. "Mommy..."

"Yes, honey?"

"Please, could I have a hug?"

Leah's coughing had subsided, and she touched the sheet to her wet lips as she looked at her little son and said hoarsely, "Nathan, darling, I've told you so many times, this disease is very contagious. There is danger enough just because we're in the same room, but you would almost certainly get it if you were close enough to breathe in my breath. Mommy loves you, Nathan, and I don't want you to be sick like I am. Please try to understand."

Tears filmed Nathan's eyes, and he pivoted and ran to the other room, throwing himself on his bed as he burst into sobs.

Susan set the tin cup on the bedstand. "I'll talk with him, Mother. See if I can comfort him."

"Thank you, sweetie. He's so young to have to face all of this." Leah choked up briefly, then said with a tremulous voice, "I wish...I wish we'd never come here. I wish we'd never left Wales. Your father and I were both healthy there."

"I wish we'd stayed in Wales too, Mother," Susan said. "Father would still be alive, and you would be well."

Leah's eyes followed her daughter's movements as she went into the apartment's other room. So young, Leah thought. So awfully young to have such a load put on her shoulders.

The whine of the wind sent Leah's thoughts to Jared. Tiny ice crystals pelted the window. She pictured her oldest son on the street corner fifteen blocks away, selling his papers. His thin coat wasn't enough to keep him warm in this kind of weather. He must be freezing.

It was nearly nine-thirty in the morning. Jared usually finished selling his papers around ten o'clock. She knew that when the last paper was sold, her boy would go from store to store and business to business, asking for work. She hoped he found work that would bring him inside and out of the bitter cold.

2

THE STREET LANTERNS SWAYED at the corner of Thirty-eighth and Broadway, buffeted by the relentless wind. People passed by newsboy Jared Hamilton, turtling their heads into their collars, holding onto their hats, and bending their bodies against the cold.

Tiny pellets of ice stung Jared's face and whipped at his flimsy, tattered coat. His ragged stocking cap covered his ears. He switched hands periodically, keeping one hand in his coat pocket while he held up the morning edition of the *New York Tribune* in the other. Gloves were a luxury he couldn't afford.

"Get your morning pa-a-per! Read all about it! President Grant rejects tax bill proposed by Democrats in Congress!" Jared's breath puffed out in small clouds as he shouted above the howling wind.

One by one, men on the street stopped to buy a paper. When he had sold the one in his hand, he bent down and picked up another from between his feet. He shuddered as the cold attacked his joints and muscles, piercing his thin coat.

By 9:30, most of Jared's papers had been sold. He had only three left, but Leah Hamilton's devoted son would stay there in the cold until he had sold them all. He needed every nickel he could lay his hands on to take care of his mother, sister, and brother.

While stamping his feet to keep the blood circulating, Jared noticed a familiar carriage pass by with the words *New York City Children's Aid Society* emblazoned on its side. The carriage made a left turn and stopped at the corner diagonally across the intersection.

Jared had noticed four street children standing on the corner for the past half-hour. Faces red from the wind and heads dipped into their coat collars, they were begging passersby for money. A few people had placed coins in their hands, but most had ignored them.

A tall, slender man in a heavy overcoat and top hat emerged from the carriage and began talking to the children.

"Hey! Jared!" came the familiar voice of his friend Bodie Brolin from behind him. At the same time, a well-dressed man stopped in front of him and said, "I'll take two papers, Jared. My secretary likes to have his own copy."

Jared did a half turn and grinned at Bodie, then handed the man the paper in his hand and leaned over to pick up another one. When he had placed it in the man's hand, five nickels were laid in his palm. Jared shook his head and said, "It's only ten cents for two, Mr. Redmond."

The businessman smiled. "I know, Jared. The extra nickels are for your mother, sister, and brother."

"Thank you very much, sir," Jared said. "My mother, sister, and brother thank you, too!"

Redmond nodded, fixed his hat more firmly on his head, and hurried away to the warmth of his office building.

Jared then turned to his friend. "Hey, Bodie!" he said, smiling at the boy who was a year older and about an inch taller than himself. "How's business?"

Bodie Brolin made his living by selling small boxes of wooden matches and boxes of toothpicks. Bodie's mother was dead, and his father was an alcoholic. Louis Brolin only worked when he was sober, and much of what he earned he spent for more liquor. But he always managed to pay the rent each week. It was Bodie's earnings that kept food on their table.

Bodie pointed across the street and said, "I've seen that carriage picking up children before, Jared. You have any idea what happens to them?"

Jared nodded and stomped his feet. He was about to speak when a regular customer approached. "Hello, Mr. Wagner," Jared said. "Want your paper today?"

"Sure do." The small man smiled and clapped his gloved hands together against the cold.

Jared pocketed the nickel and waited for Mr. Wagner to walk away before saying, "The tall man with the carriage is Reverend Charles Brace, Bodie. He picks up homeless children and takes them to the Children's Aid Society building over on Fourth Street. His workers feed them and put them in new clothes."

"Must be a huge building!" Bodie said.

"Not so huge. They don't keep them there long—just until they have about a hundred children or so. Then they take them to Grand Central Station where the Society keeps three trains. They call them 'orphan trains.' Of course, all three trains aren't usually there at the same time. Most of the time, one of them is going to the West and the other is coming from the West—"

"Oh, yeah. I've heard about those orphan trains, but I didn't know they were connected to the Children's Aid Society."

Bodie was wearing a sandwich board that advertised on both sides the matches and toothpicks he had for sale. A man approached and said, "Hi, Bodie! The missus told me to get some more matches from you the next time I saw you."

Bodie angled his back to the wind and reached inside a small burlap sack slung over his shoulder. "How many boxes you want, Mr. Fleming?"

"I'll take five."

Bodie made his sale, pocketed the money, then asked Jared, "How do you know so much about the orphan trains?"

"I read about them in these papers I sell."

Bodie watched the tall man across the street who was loading the four urchins into the carriage. "So the children go out West for adoption?"

"Yes. The farmers and ranchers out there are glad to adopt them so the children can work for them. The children don't mind the work because they become part of the family, have a house to live in, and plenty of food to eat."

Bodie smiled, stamping his feet and working his arms against the cold. "Well, that's great. It sure beats starving on the streets of New York."

"I've read that most of the time it works out real good."

"Jared, has Reverend Brace ever stopped and talked to you to see if you have a home?"

"Yes. He's a very nice man. Since the first time he talked to me, he's stopped every once in a while. He always asks about my mother and how she's doing."

Two men approached Bodie and purchased matches. When they had moved on, Bodie said, "I think what Reverend Brace and his people are doing is wonderful. It really gets to me when I see these little kids going hungry and not having a home."

"There's only one thing about the orphan trains I don't like," Jared said, his hands jammed deep into the pockets of his thin coat.

"What's that?"

"One article I read said that lots of times brothers and sisters get separated from each other and adopted into different families."

"Oh, that would be bad." Bodie thought on it a moment, then said, "But I guess it would be better for brothers and sisters to be separated than to freeze or starve to death on these streets."

Jared had both hands to his mouth, blowing warm breath on them. "Well, Bodie, I need to go look for work now. I'll see you later."

Jared's first stop was Koehler's Grocery. Oscar Koehler had given him odd jobs on several occasions. The little bell above the door jingled as Jared moved inside. His cold body welcomed the sudden warmth.

Mr. Koehler was busy with customers at the counter, and a few people were moving about the store, picking up items from the shelves. Jared would wait.

While he walked about the store, wishing he had enough money to buy some foods he had never tasted, the little bell above the door jingled again, and Jared noticed four boys enter. He recognized them as the neighborhood toughs, led by Mike McDuff.

Jared watched the boys move among the rows of well-stocked shelves. They kept an eye on Oscar Koehler, who was busy with customers at the counter, and began stuffing items into their coat pockets. They hadn't yet seen Jared.

As one of the boys, Truxtun Gowen, paused at a shelf and picked up a small package of dried fruit, he spotted Jared, who was looking straight at him. Truxtun turned to his leader and whispered, "Hey, Mike! Lookee who's here!"

The foursome converged on Jared, eyeing him threateningly. McDuff was big for his age, and husky. He had a broad face with a wide nose, thick lips, and a mouthful of crooked teeth. He put his nose an inch from Jared's and hissed in a low tone, "You better keep your mouth shut, sissy-talkin' newsboy, or else!"

It always angered Jared when someone made fun of his accent. He fixed the bigger boy with a steady gaze and said, "Put back everything you stole, Mike, or I'll tell Mr. Koehler."

None of the boys noticed Koehler whispering to a male customer, who nodded and headed for the door in a casual manner, then moved outside.

A deep scowl framed Mike McDuff's thick features, and his eyes flared with anger. He kept his voice low as he said, "We ain't gonna put 'em back, Jared. And if you tell the old man we picked up this stuff, you'll be sorry. If you don't want your ugly face rearranged, you keep quiet!"

Jared glared at the toughs as they each picked out an inexpensive item to actually pay for and headed toward the counter where Oscar Koehler was waiting on an elderly woman. Jared eased up close to them.

When the silver-haired woman gathered her packages and headed for the door, Jared hurried past the elderly woman and opened the door for her.

"Why, thank you, young man," she said, showing him a toothless smile. "You are a gentleman."

"I try to be, ma'am."

Jared turned back and headed for the counter. The four thieves eyed him warily, wondering if he had the courage to tell on them, when the door opened behind him. Oscar Koehler shot a glance at the two men who entered. One was the customer who had slipped out a few minutes earlier. The other was a man clad in dark blue with a badge visible on his heavy overcoat.

Officer Dean Farone scowled at the four boys. "All right, fellas, empty your pockets."

"We ain't done nothin'," Mike McDuff protested. "All we're doin' is buyin' some—"

"I said empty your pockets!"

The boys looked a lot less cocky as they began pulling the stolen articles from their coat pockets and placing them on the counter.

An elderly man watched with interest, then said to the proprietor, "How'd you know they stole this stuff, Oscar?"

"Saw them from the corner of my eye. These thieves aren't as smart as they think they are."

When Officer Farone had made sure all the stolen goods were on the counter, he said, "You boys are under arrest."

"We didn't mean no harm, Officer," McDuff said. "We just took stuff we really need."

"You're supposed to pay for what you take, kid," Farone replied, "and you know it. Let's go. The jail's waiting."

When Officer Farone and the four boys were gone, Jared stepped up to the counter and said, "I was just about to tell you those guys had stuffed their pockets, Mr. Koehler, when the policeman came in."

Koehler smiled. "Thank you, Jared." He then turned to the customer who had gone after the law and said, "Thanks a lot, Murray."

"Glad to help," Murray said with a grin, and then picked up two stuffed paper sacks off the counter and left the bell jingling as he stepped outside and closed the door.

Koehler looked down at Jared. "You need some work today, Jared?"

"Yes, sir."

"Good! I just got in a shipment of fruit from the railroad. You can unload the crates and fill the empty spaces in the produce section. You know where everything goes, don't you?"

"I sure do, sir! I'll get right on it."

"Okay. The crates are over there, already opened. Take off your coat and stocking cap and go to work."

Jared worked steadily for the next hour, emptying the crates and putting the fruit in place, as customers came and went. There was a lull in business just as he finished his task, and Oscar Koehler came over to look at Jared's finished work. "You did a good job, as usual, son. How's your mother doing?"

Jared picked up his coat and put it on. "Not very well right now, sir. But she'll get better come spring when it's not so cold."

"I'm sure she will," the proprietor said. "You tell her I'm pulling for her, okay?"

"Yes, sir. And thank you for the work, Mr. Koehler."

"Well, thank *you* for doing such a good job, Jared," Koehler said, moving behind the counter. He opened the cash drawer and handed the boy a quarter.

Jared thanked him and said he would come by again tomorrow, just in case there was some more work he could do.

Moments later, Jared was back on the street with the powerful wind plucking at his clothing. It was no longer snowing.

In the next block was Stillman's Clothing Store. There were no customers in the place when Jared entered and found Peter Stillman at a desk behind the counter, working on his books. Stillman looked up and smiled. "Oh, hello, Jared," he said.

"Need the store swept out today, sir?"

"Not today. Come back day after tomorrow. You can sweep it then."

"All right, sir. I will. 'Bye."

Jared's next stop was the Manhattan Shoe Repair Shop, owned and operated by Luigi Olivetti, a balding, mustachioed man who had emigrated from Italy a few years before.

A tiny bell rang as Jared entered the shop. He could see Luigi at his bench, nailing a heel on an old boot. Seated on a wooden chair nearby was a man who wore a matching boot on his left foot.

Olivetti looked up and smiled, pausing in his work to say, "Allo, Jared. You look for a job today?"

"Yes, sir."

"I have no work for you today," Olivetti said, reaching into his pocket, "but I do have a nickel for you."

The customer on the chair smiled as he saw Jared's eyes widen. "You mean—"

"Yes, it is my gift to you because you are such a good boy. You work so hard to care for your mother and your sister and brother. Come back tomorrow, and I will have some cleaning for you to do."

Jared accepted the shiny nickel with a smile. "Thank you, Mr. Olivetti. Thank you very much. I'll see you tomorrow."

When the boy was gone, Luigi explained to the customer Jared's family situation.

"There is no father in the home?" the man asked.

"No. Mr. Hamilton died a year ago, and I'm afraid Mrs. Hamilton will die also. This boy, he is a fine one. He sells newspapers on the street every business day, then goes from place to place along these streets to see if he can earn money doing odd jobs. There is not a lazy bone in his body."

"Some lad," the customer said, reaching into his pocket. "When he comes in tomorrow, give him this dollar."

"Oh, that is nice of you," Luigi said. "This will make the boy very happy!"

The merciless wind continued its assault on Manhattan Island, whipping snow against buildings and swirling it into the faces of those who were still on the streets.

It was noon when Jared made his next stop at the local fire station. He could see that Chief Tom Stanwood and four of his firemen were about to sit down to lunch. Hot coffee steamed from their cups.

"Hey, guys," Stanwood said. "It's Jared!"

Jared pulled off his stocking cap. "Hello, everybody. Chief Stanwood, I was wondering—"

"Have you had lunch, son?" Stanwood asked.

"No, sir. I never eat lunch unless I'm here at noontime, sir."

"Well, tell you what. We'll put an extra plate on the table right now. You eat lunch with us, then I've got some work for you."

Jared smiled. "All right, sir!"

"You can scrub both fire wagons down and polish them like you've done many times before, okay?"

"Yes, sir!"

It was late afternoon as Susan Hamilton sat in a chair beside her mother, reading one of the schoolbooks a neighbor had given the Hamilton children.

Two lanterns burned in the room—one on the kitchen table where Nathan sat, trying to spell the words Jared had given him to learn, and the other on the bedstand next to Leah.

Susan's old coat was still hanging over the window to absorb some of the cold wind.

"What are you studying today, honey?" Leah asked.

"American history," Susan said, looking up at her mother.

"I'm reading about General George Washington at Valley Forge during the American Revolution."

"Valley Forge...that's in Pennsylvania, isn't it?"

"Yes. On the Schuylkill River in northeast Pennsylvania. What I'm reading right now is how cold it was when the Continental Army first set up camp there in December 1777. Sounds like it must have been about as cold as Manhattan Island is right now."

"Might have been," Leah said, and went into another coughing spell.

The door opened and Jared came in to see Susan standing over their mother as she hacked and coughed into a towel. He rushed over to the bed as if he could help, but there was nothing he could do.

"Has she been coughing a lot today?" Jared asked.

Susan looked more solemn than usual and nodded yes.

"I'm sorry, Mom," he said, looking into his mother's eyes.

Nathan ran up to Jared, who ruffled his thick locks and said, "Hi, little guy. You been studying those words I gave you?"

"Uh-huh. I'm learning 'em, too."

"Atta boy."

After a few minutes, Leah's coughing subsided. She slowly folded the towel and laid it beside her and tried to smile at her eldest son as she said hoarsely, "How did it go today, honey?"

"Fine," Jared said. "Sold all my papers and earned a dollar and ten cents on my odd jobs. Most of it came from washing and polishing the two fire wagons for Chief Stanwood. And guess what! Even though he didn't have any work for me today, Mr. Olivetti gave me a nickel!"

"Oh, that's wonderful honey," Leah said, forcing a smile past her pain. "I'm so proud of you. You're such a good boy."

"Nathan and I are proud of you, too, Jared," Susan said. "If you didn't work so hard, we'd starve to death."

"You're the bestest big brother in a-a-ll the world!" Nathan said.

Jared messed up Nathan's hair again. "And don't you forget it, pal!"

Susan laughed, and even Leah managed a smile.

"Well," Jared said, "it's time to get supper started. I had lunch at the firehouse, so I'm not as hungry as usual. The rest of you can have most of my share tonight."

An hour later, Jared helped his mother to the table. Leah brushed a lock of hair away from her eyes as she eased onto the chair. "Thank you, son. The food smells good."

"That's because Susie made the gravy, Mom," Jared said with a grin, patting his sister on the head.

"And don't you forget it," Susan replied.

During the meal, Jared told the family about seeing Mike McDuff and his three friends stuffing their pockets at Koehler's Grocery, and being warned that they would beat him up if he told Mr. Koehler. He explained that he was about to speak up and tell Mr. Koehler when he was interrupted by Officer Farone, who arrested the boys.

Leah set her tired eyes on Jared and said, "I'm so proud of you, son. You would have told the truth, even if it meant getting beaten up. I wish your father were here to see what kind of a man you're developing into."

"Well, Mom," Jared said, a bit embarrassed by her praise, "right is right, and wrong is wrong."

"True," she said. "But the Mike McDuffs in this world do the wrongs, and boys like you do the rights. I'm so thankful for you."

There was silence at the table for a few minutes as they ate their meager meal. Jared broke the silence by saying, "I saw the Children's Aid Society carriage today at Thirty-eighth and Broadway. Reverend Brace picked up four little children across the street from my corner. They will be going west on one of the orphan trains."

"Did Reverend Brace see you?" Susan asked.

"No. He was quite occupied with those children."

"How long has it been since he stopped and talked to you?" Leah asked.

"I guess he stops and chats with me about once a month, Mother. He always asks about you. Oh, and Mr. Koehler said to tell you he's pulling for you."

"Such a nice man," she said.

A worried look came over Nathan's freckled face. "Mommy…"

"Yes, honey?"

"Will me an' Susie an' Jared have to go on one of those orphan trains someday?"

Leah bit down on her lower lip.

"No, we won't, Nathan," Jared answered for his mother. "Mom is going to get well. When spring comes, she'll feel so good she can go back to her office cleaning job, and we'll do just fine."

3

EXCEPT FOR THE WHINE OF THE WIND in the pines, the tall man leading the black gelding down the snow-covered slope felt only the silence of the towering mountain peaks on every side. Any sign or sound of life, any movement or breath of living creature was muffled and stilled by the deep blanket of snow on the ground and snuffed out by the voice of the icy wind.

The man stopped when gray puffs of smoke came into view, rising above the trees at the bottom of the slope. Though he couldn't see any buildings, he knew a cabin of some kind was down there.

"We just might have them, Ebony," he said, patting the horse's neck. "We'll know soon."

The magnificent animal nickered as if he understood, and bobbed his head.

John Stranger had been on the trail of three outlaws for more than a week. Snowstorms had slowed his progress, but the man who wore a pair of identical jagged scars on his right cheek had an unusual talent for tracking outlaws—almost a sixth sense—and he knew he was slowly but surely closing in on his prey.

Chief United States Marshal Solomon Duvall, who was in

charge of all federal marshals from Colorado north to the Canadian border, south to Mexico, and west as far as the Arizona, Nevada, and Idaho borders, had often asked Stranger for help because he was always short of marshals to cover so much territory.

Duvall had found himself without a spare man on the force when the Duke Schelling gang robbed two Denver banks on March 19, leaving behind three dead bank employees and a teller with a fractured skull. The chief had asked John Stranger to track down the three men who were wanted for murder and bank robbery in three states and two territories. Duke Schelling, Harry Osmand, and Frank Sloan must be stopped and brought to justice.

A half-hour from the moment Stranger had spotted the rising smoke, he carefully led Ebony behind the barn, which was some forty yards from the cabin, and tethered the big black to a pine tree.

Eyewitnesses in Denver had given Stranger descriptions of the outlaws' horses. Now he swung his long legs over the snow-crusted split-rail fence that formed a small corral and crept up to the back door of the barn, listening to make sure no voices came from inside, and quietly flipped the latch. The three horses inside looked at him, and one nickered. Stranger smiled to himself and said under his breath, "Schelling and Company."

Ebony's ears pricked up as he watched his master emerge from the barn and inch toward a corner of the barn.

Stranger looked toward the cabin and studied the situation. Since he had no way of knowing where the men were inside, he dare not approach it in broad daylight. He glanced at the privy. Maybe all he would have to do was wait for them to come to him. If no one came out before dark, he would sneak up to the windows after the sun went down and take them by surprise.

✦

The three outlaws had whiled away the wintery afternoon playing poker.

When the sun was lowering toward the peaks, Duke Schelling picked up a nearly empty whiskey bottle and drained it. He belched and said, "You boys'll have to 'scuse me." He spoke over his shoulder as he moved toward the wall that held the coats and hats. "I'll be glad when they invent a way to put privies inside. Be back in a few minutes."

While Duke was putting on his coat, Frank started dealing a new hand. "We'll play one round without you. Don't get lost."

Duke laughed. "'Don't get lost.' Whattya think I am, Frank? A little kid?"

A blast of cold air entered when Duke left the cabin. He stepped onto the back porch and took a deep breath. His head was a bit woozy from the whiskey he'd put down a little at a time all afternoon, but the cold air helped to clear it some.

He tugged his hat tighter on his head and headed toward the small structure that already had a beaten path in the snow.

When Duke flipped the latch and swung open the door, he caught a glimpse of a tall man with black hat and black overcoat a split second before a rock-hard fist connected with his jaw. Pain exploded in his skull, and the world canted sideways.

He felt himself falling into a swirling black vortex…

Duke Schelling drifted up toward consciousness as if spinning through a dense gray fog. He was braced in a sitting position against an upright post inside the barn where he could not be seen from either door.

His head bobbed as if mounted on a spring as he blinked

and tried to focus on the man hunkered in front of him. He groaned and suddenly realized a gag was tied securely over his mouth. Part of the gag was stuffed inside his mouth, making it impossible to cry out.

His eyes widened as he tried to move his body and realized he was tied to the post and completely powerless.

"You'll wear yourself out trying to get loose, Duke."

Schelling's brow furrowed.

"You're wondering if we've ever met," Stranger said. "No, but I have your description, along with those pals of yours. Got them from the chief U.S. marshal in Denver. You boys are going back to Denver to stand trial for murder."

Stranger rose to his feet. "See you in a little while, Duke. I've got two more rats to trap."

Harry Osmand and Frank Sloan had been playing their two-man game for a half-hour when Sloan glanced toward the back door and said, "Maybe he *did* get lost."

"Maybe. He was almost tipsy when he went out there. Might be passed out, lyin' in a heap on the path."

"Let's give him a few more minutes. If he ain't back, I'll go check on him."

Ten minutes passed, and still no Duke.

Sloan laid his cards face-down and rose to his feet. "Don't cheat and look at my cards, pal," he said.

"Who, me?" Osmand said, and chuckled.

Sloan shrugged into his coat, put on his hat, and moved outside. He glanced toward the privy and called out, "Hey, Duke! You all right?"

A low moaning sound met his ears from inside the privy. He pulled open the door and caught a split-second glimpse of a man in black before he felt a sharp pain on his jaw and the lights went out.

When Frank had been gone nearly fifteen minutes, Harry drummed the table in irritation. "What on earth are they doin'?" he muttered.

He waited two more minutes. Still no Frank or Duke.

He scraped the chair on the hard wooden floor and stomped outside. Why would they stay out there so long in this sub-zero temperature?

Harry raised the latch to the privy, swung open the door, and found himself looking into the muzzle of a Colt .45 Peacemaker with the hammer cocked.

Marshal Solomon Duvall was at his desk, reading a report from the head office in Washington, D. C., when he heard a knock on the door and bid the person come in.

The door swung open, and the young deputy who served as Duvall's secretary said, "Sir, John Stranger is back, and he has all three fugitives in custody."

The silver-haired marshal smiled as he removed his half-moon spectacles and moved around the desk. "Sure didn't take him long to catch them. But that's John. I wish he'd let me pin a badge on him and put him to work on a regular basis."

"That's not liable to happen, sir," the deputy said with a grin.

"No. I suppose not."

The deputy stepped aside and allowed his chief to move through the door ahead of him into the outer office where two other deputies sat at their desks.

Duvall smiled when he saw the tall man standing over three sour-faced, unkempt, scraggly-bearded men on wooden chairs with their hands tied behind their backs.

Duvall gave them a contemptuous glance, then said to Stranger, "Good work, John. Where'd you catch up to them?"

"About ten miles west of Leadville. They were holed up in a cabin. Murdered the old man who owned it. Buried him in the dirt floor of his barn."

Duvall scowled. "Too bad we can't hang them once for each person they've murdered." He studied the men's faces a moment, recalling the description of each man on his wanted poster. Setting his hard gaze on the leader, he snapped, "Time to pay the piper, Schelling!"

Duke Schelling's truculent features reddened as he said, "Why'd you send a man who doesn't even have the authority to arrest us, Duvall? Who's he to track us down, pull dirty tricks on us to catch us off guard, and bring us in? He don't wear no badge!"

Duvall chuckled and leaned close to the outlaw leader, pinning him with his ice-blue eyes. "Well, Duke, if your feelings are hurt that you haven't been officially arrested by a man with a badge, consider yourself and your two pals officially under arrest. Feel better now?"

Schelling gave him a hateful look but said nothing.

The chief marshal turned to Stranger and said, "Let's take these killers to the 'Langan Hotel' together, John. The sheriff will need me to sign the papers so he can hold them in the county jail till they get their trial."

The Colorado sky was clear, and the sun was shining. Snow piled along the sides of the streets gleamed in the sunshine.

The three felons walked ahead of Stranger and Duvall as they moved along the street toward the sign that said Denver

County Sheriff's Office and Jail. People gawked when they saw the trio with their hands tied behind their backs. Someone shouted, "Hey, it's those dirty killers who robbed the two banks! John Stranger caught 'em!"

"Good for you, Stranger!" shouted a middle-aged man. "I think you oughtta be made assistant chief U.S. marshal!"

"I'll vote for that!" called a feminine voice.

"Chief Duvall would like that, wouldn't you, Chief?" another woman said loudly.

Duvall turned his head, smiled, and nodded vigorously. Some of the people applauded.

"Hear that, John?" the chief said with a chuckle.

Before Stranger could reply, Duke Schelling cut in. "What's this 'Langan Hotel' stuff, Duvall?"

"You don't know our sheriff's name, I take it," Duvall replied.

"No."

"Well, his name's Curt Langan. We call his jail the 'Langan Hotel.'"

When they reached the sheriff's office, Stranger stepped ahead of the trio and opened the door. Duvall followed them in. Sheriff Curt Langan and Deputy Steve Ridgway were talking with Stefanie, Langan's wife of three months, who was a Certified Medical Nurse at Denver's Mile High Hospital.

"Got some guests for the Langan Hotel, Sheriff," Duvall said.

"So I heard," Langan said with a smile. "Hello, John."

"Hello to you." The man in black towered over everyone else in the room. He turned to Stefanie and touched his hat brim. "Hello, Mrs. Langan. How's married life by now?"

Stefanie gave him a sunny smile. "Wonderful, John. I have no doubt the Lord saved the most marvelous, kind, and loving man in the world for me."

"Boy is she blind!" Deputy Ridgway said.

Curt showed his teeth in mock anger and said, "I'll deal with you after you lock these prisoners up."

"Okay, boys," Ridgway said to the outlaws, "right this way."

Duke Schelling turned and set fiery eyes on Stranger. "I wish I had you alone in a barn somewhere. I'd—"

"No you don't, and no you wouldn't, Schelling," cut in Duvall. "John could whip you in his sleep. Get them out of here, Steve."

When the deputy and the prisoners were gone, Langan turned to Duvall. "How long will I have them, Chief?"

"Not long. I'll go talk to Judge Carter right away. We can probably have their trial day after tomorrow…hang them the next day. We have plenty of proof that all three are cold-blooded murderers. We have enough witnesses to that fact right here in town."

Stranger turned to Stefanie. "Is Breanna in town?"

"Yes. She's working at the hospital today."

Langan went to his desk drawer, took out an official-looking paper, and laid it on the desktop. "Chief, if you'll sign this, I'll fill it in and file it so our three guests can stay here officially, even though they're your prisoners."

Duvall picked up a pen and dipped it in the inkwell, signing the paper as Curt and Stefanie looked on. The chief then said to Stranger, "I have another assignment for you if you're interested."

Stranger grinned. "You mean another one of those 'I need it done yesterday' kind?"

Duvall chuckled. "Well, sort of."

"Tell you what. I'll spend a little time with Breanna, then come to your office and let you fill me in on it. Probably tomorrow."

"Fine. That'll be soon enough."

Curt Langan put an arm around Stefanie as he said to

Stranger, "John, it seems to me that you ought to be made assistant chief U.S. marshal, since you do so much work for the head man of the office."

Duvall laughed. "Folks were saying the same thing on the street when we brought Schelling and his boys over here. When I retire in another year or two, I'm going to contact President Grant and recommend that he appoint John in my place."

"Now you're talking," Langan said.

John shook his head. "You two...I'm not cut out to wear a badge."

"John, you know I've already sent letters to President Grant, telling him of your volunteer work to track down outlaws, and of your unbelievable success in getting the job done."

"I appreciate your feeling that way, Chief. And I appreciate your writing the letters. But the president is far too busy to read them."

"I wouldn't say that, John. He knows who you are, believe me."

John laughed. "Look, Chief, enough with this 'retirement' stuff. You're too young to retire."

"I'll soon be sixty-five."

"I don't care. You're still too young. And besides, I'd go crazy sitting behind a desk."

Duvall snorted. "Well, I'll say this. If you did become chief U.S. marshal, you'd still be going after the outlaws yourself. Your desk would only gather dust."

"You've got that right."

"Well, like it or not, lady and gentlemen," Duvall said, "I've got to get back to my desk. See you tomorrow, John?"

"Yes, sir. Probably midmorning."

Deputy Steve Ridgway returned.

"See you later, Steve," Duvall said, heading for the door.

"You, too, Sheriff...Mrs. Sheriff."

Langan looked at his deputy. "Prisoners comfortable?"

"I hope not," Ridgway said.

Stranger chuckled. "Well, it's time for yours truly to head for the hospital and look in on my little gal."

Stefanie stepped closer. "John, I've been working the midnight shift. Breanna and I chatted a few minutes when she came in this morning. She said she sure hoped you'd get back sometime today, because she's leaving tomorrow morning."

Stranger's dark eyebrows arched. "Assignment?"

"Yes. Abilene, Kansas. She said she'll be gone for at least several weeks...maybe even three months."

"Abilene! That's the most dangerous town in Kansas! Why's she going there?"

"I really don't know. She said Dr. Goodwin told her it was a very important assignment, but we didn't have time for her to tell me what it is. She had to start work."

John nodded. "Okay. Thank you for telling me, Stefanie." He headed for the door and waved his hand. "See all of you later."

The tall man entered Mile High Hospital and smiled as he approached the receptionist. "You're new here, aren't you?"

"Yes, sir. Just started two days ago. But I already know who you are...Mr. Stranger."

John's smile broadened. "I suppose Breanna—"

"Yes, she did. And she described you perfectly. Are you really ten feet tall?"

"Just a smidgen under that," he said with a chuckle. "And you are—"

"Betty Donaldson. My husband is the new manager of the Grandview Hotel."

"Welcome to Denver, Mrs. Donaldson. Where are you and your husband from?"

"Chicago. I worked as receptionist at City Memorial Hospital. Jack—my husband—was with the Marquette Manor Hotel."

"Well, I hope you'll like Denver."

"We already do. I assume you're here to see Nurse Baylor?"

"Yes."

"I believe she's working the second floor this morning. I can go check for you."

"Thank you, but that won't be necessary. I'll find her."

John headed for the stairs. He was near the office of Dr. Matthew Carroll, the hospital's chief administrator—and husband of Breanna's sister, Dottie—when Carroll stepped through the door and saw John coming. "Hello, John!" he said, a smile lighting up his face.

"Howdy, Doc."

"You catch those outlaws?"

"Just finished putting them behind bars."

"Good. And I assume you're looking for the second-most-beautiful woman in the world."

Stranger grinned. "No. I know where Dottie lives. I'm looking for the first-most beautiful woman in the world. I understand she's on the second floor."

Carroll chuckled. "No. Dottie's at home. It's her sister who's up on the second floor."

"That's what I said!" John laughed and headed for the stairs.

Breanna Baylor was carrying a bundle of bedding when she spotted John coming toward her. "Oh, I'm so glad you're back!" she said, tossing the bedding onto a nearby cart.

John took her in his arms, and they both scanned the hall before stealing a sweet, tender kiss.

"Did you catch those killers, darling?" Breanna asked.

"Yes. They're in the Langan Hotel."

"Good."

"Sweetheart, Stefanie was at Curt's office. She told me you're leaving for Abilene tomorrow morning."

"Yes…and I'm so glad you got home so we can have a little time together tonight."

"Me, too. But why is Dr. Goodwin sending you to that horrible town? And what's to keep you there a possible three months? Doesn't he know it's the most violent town in Kansas? I don't care if Wild Bill Hickok *is* the marshal there."

Breanna stepped back a few inches as two nurses came down the hall. She smiled up at John and said, "Darling, don't get all upset. I'll be fine. I don't have time to explain it right now, but if you'll take me to dinner tonight, I'll tell you all about it."

"But…*Abilene.* I'm supposed to see Chief Duvall in the morning about another assignment. I'll just tell him I can't do it. I'm going to Abilene with you."

Breanna stroked his cheek as the two nurses passed, smiling at them. "You can't go everywhere I go. If Chief Duvall has another assignment for you, it must be very important. You must help him as you've always done. I'll be fine. We'll talk about it at dinner."

"Okay, I'll pick you up at seven."

"Seven it is. And darling…"

"Mm-hmm?"

"I love you."

"I love you, too. That's why I can't let you go to Abilene by yourself."

"I'm not going by myself."

"And who else is going with you?"

"His name is Jesus. He promised He would never leave me nor forsake me."

A grin spread over John's angular face. "Oh, so now you're preaching to me, eh?"

"Never. Just stating a fact. Jesus did say that, didn't He?"

"How do I argue with a Bible-quoting woman? See you tonight."

"You sure will," she said with a smile, and walked down the hall.

BREANNA LOOKED BOTH HEAVENLY and queenly in the candle-light as John seated her at a table in the fashionable restaurant at Denver's Grandview Hotel. The waiter stood by with menus in hand until John sat down. Then he told them what the chef's special was and left to give them a few moments to decide.

John only glanced at the menu and then laid it down and gazed at Breanna. She felt his eyes on her and looked at him over the top of the menu.

"I love you," he said softly, just as the waiter returned to take their order.

Breanna wore a floor-length black skirt and a white blouse with lace collar and ruffles at the neck and wrists. Her honey-blond hair was swept up into ringlets. A delicate gold chain around her neck bore a heart-shaped locket with a small diamond in the center. John had given it to her the previous Christmas.

After the waiter left, John took a sip of coffee and said, "Now, Miss Breanna, I want to hear why Dr. Goodwin is sending you to Abilene."

"I'm going there to help a young doctor by the name of David Cox establish a medical clinic. The town is growing and needs the clinic desperately."

"I know it's growing, but it's got a bad reputation for being a bloody place, sweetheart. Bullets fly every direction at any time of day. Maybe that's why they need the clinic—so many people are getting shot."

"It isn't just that, John. With the population growth comes all kinds of sicknesses and injuries, not to mention pregnancies…and babies who need medical attention."

John frowned. "But Abilene is wild and lawless. Some of the West's worst outlaws are there. I don't mean to be an old grandma, but I'm concerned for your safety."

"I assure you, darling, the Lord will take care of me."

An elderly couple threading their way among the tables stopped to chat for a moment. As they left, the waiter came with the meal. When the hot food was before them, John reached across the table and took Breanna's hand and thanked the Lord for the food.

They ate their meal in comfortable silence for a few minutes before Breanna said, "Tell me about Abilene, darling. I know you've been there on several occasions. You mentioned Wild Bill Hickok. Have you met him?"

"Yes, when he was marshal of Hays, Kansas, a couple of years ago. He's a tough hombre. He's only been marshal of Abilene for a couple of months."

"How did you meet him?"

"Well, he was attempting to disarm five outlaws in the middle of the street just as I was riding into town. I didn't know him by sight, but I knew he was marshal there, and I saw the badge on his vest. The outlaws had just gunned down another outlaw on the street. They'd had a run-in some time before that, I guess. Anyway, they shot the man in cold blood, as I later found out.

"Hickok had put them under arrest just before I rode in,

but they outnumbered him and were starting to resist. I could see it was going to get violent, so I sided with Hickok. With Hickok's odds strengthened somewhat, the outlaws decided to surrender quietly."

"I see," Breanna said. "So what caused him to leave Hays and become marshal of Abilene?"

"I don't know. He left Hays about a year before pinning on the badge in Abilene after Marshal Tom Smith was killed."

Breanna took a sip of coffee and then asked, "Any idea why Abilene has grown so fast?"

"It really started four years ago when the Kansas Pacific Railroad laid track through there, connecting the land east of the Mississippi River with the West. A wealthy man by the name of Joseph McCoy went there and established the Great Western Stockyards Company. After that Abilene quickly developed into a cattle-shipping center, and the town began to grow.

"Except in the dead of winter, cattlemen drive their herds from every direction to Abilene to market them, especially the Texans, who drive the hardy Longhorns up the Chisholm Trail."

"So it's become Kansas's toughest town because of the cattle market?"

"No. Because of its growth as a result of the cattle market. Money. It's money that brings the troublemakers. Of course, a lot of the trouble comes from drunken cowboys who like to let off steam after a long drive. But the money that changes hands there brings in outlaws, gunslingers, gamblers, and drifters.

"I can't disagree that the medical clinic is needed, Breanna. I just don't like to see you go there."

Breanna reached across the table and squeezed his hand. "Darling, don't worry. I'm not afraid. The Lord will protect me."

"I'm fully aware of His capability to do that," John said, and grinned, "but it wouldn't hurt if I went along."

"And you could be with me every hour of every day?"

"Well…not quite, but—"

"The Lord can, and He will. You must help Chief Duvall with his fight against lawbreakers, darling. He needs you. The West needs you."

John sighed. "So why could it be three months before you're back home?"

"While I'm there, I'll not only be assisting Dr. Cox with the medical work, I'll be training two young nurses for him. My length of stay will depend on how quickly they learn and are able to do the clerical work as well as the medical duties. Maybe I'll only be gone five or six weeks."

John took the last bite and placed his knife and fork at the top of his plate. "Well, when we get married, I'll talk to Dr. Goodwin about keeping your assignments shorter and farther apart."

"That will be fine with me, sir," she said, her eyes reflecting the love she felt for this man.

John was quiet for a moment, then said, "We've talked a lot about our wedding, Breanna. I hope the Lord gives the go-ahead soon. I have a feeling it's not too far off."

"I've felt the same way, John," she said in a steady voice. "But I know He'll speak to you in an undeniable way when His time is right for us."

"Yes, and yours truly has his ears open."

The next morning dark clouds were rolling toward Denver from the Rockies and the smell of snow was in the air.

John helped Breanna board the eastbound train, placed her hand luggage in the overhead compartment, and made sure she was comfortable. The conductor was calling for all passengers to board for the final time, and the engine's whistle echoed through Denver's Union Station as John bent over and kissed her tenderly.

"I'll be praying for the Lord to protect you in the hollow of His hand," he said.

There were tears in Breanna's eyes as she said softly, "And I for you."

When the tall man stepped from the train, he moved close to the window where Breanna sat and mouthed, *I love you.*

The train lurched forward and chugged out of the depot. When the engine and five cars had passed from sight, John climbed into the buggy and drove away. There was an ache in his heart as he headed for the federal building to learn about Chief Duvall's next assignment.

The pump organ was playing "Here Comes the Bride," and Breanna held Dr. Lyle Goodwin's arm as they walked down the aisle of Denver's First Baptist Church. In her free hand, she carried a bouquet arranged around a small white Bible. A delicate veil covered her face.

The building was packed to capacity, and everyone turned to watch the bride. Breanna could sense every eye on her.

She felt a touch of sadness that her parents had not lived to see this day. The sadness faded, however, when she set her gaze on the groomsmen, who stood in a fan shape. The tall handsome man next to the pastor attracted her gaze like a magnet. She smiled through the veil and felt tears well up in her eyes.

The organist let the music fade as Breanna and Dr. Goodwin approached the platform.

"Who gives this woman to be married to this man?"

"My wife, Martha, and I do, in place of her deceased father and mother," Dr. Goodwin said.

Reverend Bayless smiled. "Will you please place the bride's hand in that of the groom?"

The good doctor did so, then Breanna raised up on tiptoe to kiss his cheek through the veil.

She handed Dottie her bouquet, then looked up at John and slipped her hand into the crook of his arm. Bayless nodded, and Breanna lifted the front of her dress above her white slippers. She felt the iron strength in John's arm as they ascended the steps.

"Dearly beloved," Pastor Bayless began, "we are gathered here today to witness the joining together of this man and this woman in the holy bond of—"

"A-bi-lene! Ten minutes! Abilene, ten minutes!" came the voice of the conductor, yanking Breanna from her slumber and interrupting her dream.

She sat up, blinked, and felt keen disappointment that the wedding was the dream and her arrival in Abilene, Kansas, the reality.

She stretched her arms, covered a yawn, and looked out the window at the tawny Kansas countryside with a scattering of barren trees and bushes as far as she could see. In the distance, she saw a white farmhouse with a white barn and red silo, along with a few milk cows collected near the barn.

Soon farmhouses and outbuildings increased in number, and then the uneven rooftops of the town came into view. The train slowed as the conductor passed through the coach, calling, "Abilene! We're now arriving in Abilene!"

People began gathering personal items and the volume of voices, especially of the children, grew louder with excitement. Breanna heard two teenage boys say they hoped they would get to see a real quick-draw gunfight on Main Street before the sun went down. A man who sat across the aisle told them there were five hours of daylight left. They could easily see two or three gunfights before sundown.

The boys' mother, who sat on the seat behind them, leaned forward and said, "You boys won't be seeing any gunfights. Your father said our new house is at the east edge of town, nowhere near Main Street."

"Aw, Ma," one of the boys said, "can't we at least go walk Main Street for awhile? We want to see a gunfight."

"No," the mother said in a stern voice.

Apparently the boys knew not to argue, for no more was said. Breanna had seen enough gunfights to last her for the rest of her life. But she knew her chances of seeing plenty more while in Abilene were quite good.

The train chugged to a halt at the depot. As people scrambled from the coach, Breanna stood up to take her overnight bag from the rack. From behind, a young man said, "Here, ma'am, allow me."

"Why, thank you," she said with a smile, noting that he wore a low-slung, tied-down holster and bone-handled revolver on his hip. "You...ah, live here?"

"No, ma'am. I'm just here on some personal business. Once I take care of it, I'll head west again."

A middle-aged man pressed closer and set his gaze on Breanna over the young man's shoulder. "You ever hear of Billy Hampton, ma'am?" he asked.

The name rang a bell. Breanna had heard John speak of Hampton. Then she remembered that Billy Hampton was a young, upcoming gunfighter who was quickly gaining a reputation for his speed and accuracy. He was from up Montana way, or was it Wyoming?

"Yes," she said, and nodded. "I've heard of him."

"Well, you're a-lookin' at him, ma'am. This here young gentleman who just stepped up to help you is Billy Hampton, himself."

Breanna looked into young Hampton's cool eyes. "Billy, you're a nice young man. Why waste your life living by the gun?"

"I don't consider it a waste, ma'am. I like men to say my name with a quiver in their voice. Makes me feel important. And right now, I'm planning to put a little more fear in them. I'm here to square off with Tony Bianco. Ever hear of him?"

"Yes. Another gunfighter who's trying to climb the ladder. Are you telling me that Bianco is actually meeting you here for a shoot-out?"

"Sure. Shooting it out here in Abilene will spread the winner's name far and wide. That'll be me, of course."

Breanna shook her head. "What a waste, Billy. Even if it *is* you, this time, there'll be a man somewhere, sometime, who will walk away, leaving *you* lying dead in the dust. In the Bible, Jesus said, 'They that take the sword shall perish by the sword.' The same thing is true of a gun. Why don't you stop this foolish pursuit and do something worthwhile with your life?"

Hampton grinned and pushed his hat to the back of his head. "What are you, ma'am? Some kind of missionary or something?"

"No. I'm a nurse—a Christian nurse," she said, picking up her coat, preparing to put it on.

"Here, ma'am," Billy said, "let me help you." He held the coat for her as she slid her arms into the sleeves, then adjusted it on her shoulders.

"Thank you," she said, buttoning the coat. "I don't mean to stick my nose into your business, but you've shown yourself to be a gentleman. I just hate to see you waste your life as a gunfighter and die long before you have to."

Everyone else had left the coach, even the man who had informed Breanna of Billy Hampton's identity. Billy smiled and said, "Thanks for the sermon, ma'am. I know you mean well. But we must each follow our own destiny. So long, ma'am," he said, and hurried out of the coach.

Breanna picked up her overnight bag, moved through the door, and stepped off the train to the platform. The air had a bite to it. She pulled up her coat collar and watched Billy Hampton hurrying through the crowd. From the corner of her eye, she saw a young woman about her own age walking toward her.

"Miss Baylor?"

"Yes?"

The young woman extended her hand and said, "I'm Gloria Cox, Dr. David Cox's wife."

Breanna took her hand and squeezed it gently. "Well, hello. I'm happy to meet you, Mrs. Cox."

"Call me Gloria, please."

"All right. And you can call me Breanna."

The woman smiled even wider. "Welcome to Abilene, Breanna. I have a carriage hired...the driver will take care of your luggage."

Moments later, the two women sat in the rear of the carriage while the driver loaded Breanna's luggage. "David is looking forward to your expertise at the clinic, Breanna, but I'm a little worried now."

Breanna frowned. "Worried? About what?"

"You're too good-looking," Gloria said with a sly grin. "I'd rather have someone not quite so beautiful working with my husband."

Breanna laughed. "Gloria, I see you need spectacles."

"Oh, no, I don't. My eyes are perfectly good, and—"

The sound of gunshots from the center of town cut off Gloria's teasing.

Gloria turned her face toward town and said in a low tone, "Almost an everyday occurrence in Abilene, Breanna. Sometimes it happens several times a day. Some are buried and others are treated by my husband. And even some of those end up dead, too. We've been here five months, and hardly a day has passed that David hasn't had to work on men who have lived through gunfights or knife fights. Saloon brawls also give him a lot of business."

Breanna nodded silently.

Gloria looked back in time to see the grim look on Breanna's face, and said, "I hope working in such a tough and violent town won't be a problem for you, Breanna."

"No. In my work, I have to deal with violence and its results quite often. I…I was just thinking of a young man who was on the train with me. A gunfighter. He's here to challenge another man to a quick-draw. Really doesn't seem the type, but—"

"Hotel or clinic first, ma'am?" the driver asked.

"The clinic," Gloria said. "We'll have you wait while Miss Baylor meets my husband and the other nurses, then we'll go to the hotel."

Dr. David Cox was bent over the operating table, attempting to remove a lead slug from a man's chest, when he heard the door of the outer office open and close. Nurse Bonnie Rand was assisting Cox while Nurse Myra Dupree looked on. The strong odor of ether filled the room.

"I'll see who that is, Doctor," Myra said.

"Thank you," Cox replied without looking up.

Myra closed the surgery door behind her and smiled when she saw who stood in the outer office. "Hello, Mrs. Cox! This must be Miss Baylor."

Gloria introduced Breanna and Myra, explaining that Myra was eleven months into the twenty-eight-month program to earn her Certified Medical Nurse certificate. The other nurse, Bonnie Rand, would complete her C.M.N. work in seven weeks.

"Doctor busy?" Gloria asked.

"Yes'm. There was a gunfight a few minutes ago. One's dead, and the other is in surgery, barely hanging onto life."

Breanna's lips pulled into a thin line. "Do you know the name of the man in surgery?"

"Yes. It's Willard Metcalf."

"Oh," Breanna said, and nodded.

The door to the clinic opened and Bonnie Rand stuck her head out then looked back over her shoulder and said, "It is, Doctor."

They could hear Cox's voice say, "Tell them I'll be there in a moment."

Bonnie stepped into the office, closing the door behind her, and smiled at Breanna. "And this is Miss Baylor?"

Gloria introduced Bonnie to Breanna. Bonnie welcomed her warmly, then said, "Doctor will be out in a moment."

"The patient didn't make it," Myra said, knowing that the surgery would not be finished any time soon if the man were alive.

"No," Bonnie said. "Such a waste."

The door opened and Breanna was surprised at the youthful-looking man who came into the room. She knew Gloria was no more than twenty-nine or thirty, but she had expected the doctor to be somewhat older. He couldn't be more than thirty-one or thirty-two, Breanna told herself.

He walked toward her with an eager smile and said, "Welcome to Abilene, Miss Baylor."

"Thank you, Doctor," Breanna said, extending her hand. "I'm glad to be here."

"We've sure been looking forward to having you. The plan is this, unless you say otherwise. Gloria will take you to the hotel and feed you lunch. The two of us will take you to dinner tonight. We'll let you get a good night's rest, then the slavery begins at seven o'clock in the morning here at the clinic."

Breanna laughed. "The plan sounds fine to me."

The ride from the railroad station to the Cox Medical Clinic had been a short one, hardly giving Breanna any time to look at the town. As the carriage moved along Main Street through the business district, she decided it looked pretty much like most of the towns in Kansas.

There were the usual weatherworn clapboard buildings on both sides of the wide, dusty street, with their false fronts and faded signs. The saloons and casinos, however—except for a few older ones—were freshly painted, as were their signs.

Breanna didn't actually count the saloons and gambling places, but there were far more in Abilene than the average Kansas town. The air was too cold as yet for the doors to stand open, but she could hear the muffled, discordant sound of tinkling pianos coming from inside most of them.

In spite of the nippy weather, people milled about on the boardwalks and crossed the street anywhere they chose, but mostly at the intersections. Breanna noted the great number of hard-faced men who walked the street. It was evident that to them, life was just a day-to-day existence of drinking, gambling, and fighting, with no thought of God or eternity.

Breanna turned to Gloria and asked, "Are there any churches in this town? I haven't seen one."

Gloria shook her head. "None. There was a Methodist church over on Second Street when we first came, but they ran the preacher out of town three days after we arrived. I understand there have been other churches here at one time or another, but they didn't last. Maybe with the growth in population of decent people, some churches can get started here."

Breanna caught sight of a freshly painted sign at the corner of Main and Belmont.

MARSHAL'S OFFICE
and JAIL
JAMES BUTLER HICKOK, Marshal

Breanna wondered how "Wild Bill" had been derived from James Butler. Her eyes went to the open door of the office. She could see two men in conversation inside; one had his hand on the doorknob as if he was about to leave.

Seconds later, as they were passing a drinking and gambling establishment called *Tornado Tom's Saloon and Casino,* Breanna caught a glimpse of Billy Hampton laughing on the boardwalk with a group of men. Billy's face was toward the street, but he didn't see her.

O Lord, she thought, he's such a bright and congenial young man. If only he knew You...

As the carriage approached the Jayhawker Hotel, the women could see the Great Western Stockyards Company three blocks to the east, and a large herd of Texas Longhorns being driven into the corrals.

"So they're here," Gloria said.

Breanna looked puzzled.

"The Texans…we've been told the first herd this season would be arriving any day. They just came in off the Chisholm Trail. Now Marshal Hickok will have plenty more trouble on his hands."

Breanna nodded in understanding, and said, "Cowboys who have been on long drives are quite wild, I'm told."

"That's putting it mildly," Gloria said. "From what we've been told, this place almost becomes a battlefield when the cowboys come to town. There'll be hundreds of them when the cattle drives get into full swing this spring. We're just hoping that the new marshal and his team of deputies will be able to keep a lid on it."

"From what my fiancé tells me," Breanna said, "Mr. Hickok is a tough hombre. John met him when Mr. Hickok was marshal at Hays. I hope he's tough enough."

"Your fiancé! You're engaged, Breanna? Well, you'll have to tell me all about your husband-to-be. So he knows the famous Wild Bill Hickok, does he?"

"Yes."

"Is John a lawman?"

"Of sorts. He doesn't wear a badge, but he does a lot of outlaw tracking for Chief U.S. Marshal Solomon Duvall in Denver."

"Hmm. He sounds interesting. You can tell me all about him at lunch."

Breanna smiled, her heart warm at the thought of the man she loved. "I'll tell you a little, Gloria. It would take a long, lo-o-o-ng time to tell you *all* about him!"

5

AT 6:45 THE NEXT MORNING, Breanna entered the Cox Medical Clinic and found the doctor standing over an unconscious man who lay on the examining table. The two student nurses had not yet arrived.

Breanna wore a dark blue dress and her white nurse's pinafore. She had hung her coat in the closet in the outer office.

"Good morning, Doctor. Looks like you're getting an early start."

"Well, actually, this one has been here since just before midnight. Texas cowboy. Got into a fight at one of the saloons. His opponent broke a chair over his head. Some of his friends brought him here while one of them came to the house to get me. He's been unconscious ever since. I fear his skull may be cracked but there's no way to know."

"Well, Doctor, where would you like me to start?"

"With the books. I'll show you where everything is. I'm a horrible bookkeeper. Dr. Goodwin said you're excellent at everything you do, including keeping the books. As I said in my correspondence with you, once you get the books in order, I'll want you to teach both nurses how to keep them that way."

"Of course, sir."

They heard Bonnie and Myra in the outer office and called them to come on through to the surgery. Cox was explaining about the patient on the table when more sounds came from the outer office. Two cowboys were carrying a friend who had fallen off a saloon balcony the previous night. He was so drunk at the time, he didn't know he was hurt. As the liquor started to wear off about dawn he found the pain in his right leg so acute that he thought it was probably broken.

Dr. Cox had the cowboys lay their friend on a second table, saying he would examine the leg right away. He administered laudanum immediately to alleviate the pain.

Breanna went to work on the books, and Bonnie watched her while Myra helped the doctor set the broken leg, wrap it, and splint it.

The wild sound of drunken cowboys on the street filtered into the clinic while more patients came in. Some were local residents with normal aches and pains, colds and fever. Others were men who had been in fights and brawls.

Breanna had to leave the books for a while and work on patients while the nurses switched off working with her and Dr. Cox. By noon, Bonnie and Myra knew Breanna was going to be a great help to them. They could see that she knew plenty about medicine and was well experienced.

The patient with the cracked skull died just before one o' clock. Breanna was at the books in the outer office with both student nurses looking on when the undertaker came in to pick up the body. Only minutes after that they heard heavy footsteps on the boardwalk. The door opened and a man in black with a badge on his chest came in, half-carrying another man with his face a mass of blood.

"The doctor in?" the lawman asked.

"Yes," Breanna said, rising from the desk to look at the

bleeding man. "He's with a patient at the moment, but he'll be able to take care of this man momentarily. Let's get him back to surgery so I can get started on him. Bonnie, Myra, are there any towels here in the office?"

"Some right here," Myra said, opening a cabinet and placing a towel in Breanna's hand. She quickly pressed it to the man's bleeding face.

Her eyes caught the word *Marshal* on the badge, which told her this was not a deputy marshal but the man himself.

"You're Marshal Hickok?" she asked, pulling the blood-soaked towel away to study the deep gashes as Hickok carried the man toward the clinic door.

"Yes'm," Hickok said.

"I'm Nurse Breanna Baylor."

"You're new here, aren't you?"

"Yes. This is my first day. I'm actually a visiting nurse…the traveling kind. I work out of Dr. Lyle Goodwin's office in Denver."

"I see."

"I'm here to help get the clinic on its feet and to train these young ladies."

Myra rushed ahead and opened the door. As they passed through it, Breanna said, "Correct me if I'm wrong, Marshal Hickok, but from what I see here, this man had a broken bottle rammed into his face."

"Yep. Beer bottle."

Dr. Cox was working on a small boy who had fallen out of a tree and peeled skin off his arm. The boy's mother stood by him, looking on.

Cox looked over his shoulder, saw the marshal, the bleeding man, and Breanna dabbing at the gashes with the bloody towel. "Put him on the table over there, Marshal. Did I hear right? Broken beer bottle in the face?"

"That's right, Doc."

"Are the cuts deep, Breanna?"

"Very."

"Have Bonnie and Myra help you clean him up and make ready for stitches. He looks like he's pretty drunk, but go ahead and put him under. Use chloroform. I'll be done with Timmy, here, in a few minutes."

Hickok laid the man on the table, and the nurses went to work. He took a step back and said, "Well, I've got to get back out there, Doc. It's been extra wild since those Texans came in yesterday afternoon."

"Tell me about it," Cox said dryly.

The marshal set his keen eyes on Breanna, who was washing the victim's face. "Welcome to Abilene—is it *Miss* Baylor, or *Mrs.*?"

"*Miss* Baylor, Marshal. I'm engaged to be married, though— to a friend of yours."

Hickok, who was only thirty-four but was already graying, raised his salt-and-pepper eyebrows. "Oh? Close friend?"

"Not a familiar friend, but one who sided you in Hays when you were needing help. Big tall man with a pair of scars on his right cheek."

Hickok's jaw dropped. "Stranger?"

"Yes."

"Well, isn't it a small world? That's right. You did say you're from Denver. Well, let me tell you, ma'am, that date would be inscribed on my tombstone if John hadn't sided me. It was five against one, and those blackguards meant business. I might've gotten as many as three of them, but in the meantime, the other two would've pumped me full of lead. So you're engaged to John."

"Mm-hmm."

"Well, I'll say it right up front, he's one mighty fortunate man."

Breanna blushed but didn't reply.

"Well, I've got to get back out there. Doc, there's plenty of money in his pocket to pay you. Miss Baylor, you be sure to remember me to John when you see him."

"I'll do that, Marshal."

Suddenly a string of gunfire filled the air. "See what I mean?" Hickok said, and then he was gone.

By four o'clock, the man with the gashes in his face was back at his hotel room. Dr. Cox and Breanna—with the two student nurses observing—had treated two men for multiple cuts received in knife fights, a cowboy who had been gored by an angry bull at the stockyards, and had removed a bullet from a man named Bud Landrum, who had been the victor in a quick-draw shoot-out.

While they were working on Landrum, Breanna thought of Billy Hampton, wondering if he and Tony Bianco had shot it out yet.

When they finished patching up Landrum, he insisted he could walk to his hotel room on his own. He left, staggering some, after paying Dr. Cox his fee. Landrum was barely away from the clinic when two friends of the man Landrum had cut down in the gunfight shot him in the back and killed him.

When Marshal Hickok came to tell the doctor and nurses of Bud Landrum's death, Breanna asked him if the two gunfighters, Billy Hampton and Tony Bianco had shot it out yet.

Hickok grinned, stroked his handlebar mustache, and said, "No, ma'am. That one's set for high noon tomorrow."

Breanna gasped. "*Set* for high noon? You mean like a sporting event is set?"

"Well...ah...yes. Those two are famous gunfighters, Miss Baylor. Murder is against the law, but dueling isn't. Not in Abilene, or anywhere else I know of. There'll be all kinds of bets placed on the gunfight tonight in the casinos. You know Hampton and Bianco, do you?"

"I met Billy Hampton on the train yesterday. He told me he and Bianco had agreed to shoot it out here, but I didn't know the law had sanctioned it." She shook her head. "Marshal, this is barbaric."

"You're in a barbaric town, ma'am. I'm sworn to keep the law here, and I'll do it to the best of my ability. But as I said, dueling isn't against the law in Abilene, and neither is gambling. If I didn't let Hampton and Bianco shoot it out here, they'd just go someplace else and do it. Might as well let them do what they're going to do and get it over with."

It was almost midnight when Billy Hampton put the key in the door of his hotel room and unlocked it. He hadn't touched a drop of liquor while in the saloon promoting tomorrow's big gunfight. He wanted to be alert and ready when he faced Tony Bianco.

Movement in the hall caught his eye as he opened the door. He turned to see Breanna Baylor in the dim light that flowed from a single lantern near the stairs.

He touched his hat brim and smiled. "Well, if it isn't the little nurse! Are you staying in this hotel, ma'am?"

"Yes. I asked the desk clerk if you were registered here, and he said you were. I'm just a few doors down the hall."

"Well, ah...what can I do for you?"

"Marshal Hickok told me about the gunfight being set for noon tomorrow."

"Yes, ma'am," Billy said, throwing up a palm. "Now, please don't try to talk me out of it."

"Oh, I already learned that won't work," she said. "But I wanted to talk to you about dying, just in case you're the loser tomorrow. Billy, unless you have the Lord Jesus Christ in your heart and life, you'll go to hell when you die."

Hampton's face went rigid and his eyes turned cold. "I'm not going to be the loser, ma'am. Tony Bianco is."

"I have an idea I'd get a different viewpoint if I talked to Mr. Bianco tonight," Breanna said. "But let's say you do walk away from this shoot-out tomorrow, leaving Tony Bianco lying dead in the street. You're going to die sooner or later. I'd like the privilege of showing you from the Bible how—"

"Ma'am, I don't mean to be rude, but I'm not interested in what you want to show me." As he turned to enter his room, he grasped the knob so tight that his knuckles turned white. "Good night, ma'am."

He closed the door quietly in Breanna's face.

With heavy heart, she walked down the hall and entered her room.

It was close to noon and Breanna and her two students were in the outer office at the desk. The books were now in order, the records up to date. Myra and Bonnie were amazed at how simple the bookkeeping was, once Breanna had shown them some basic accounting principles.

Dr. Cox was in the back room ordering medicines from a drug representative from Kansas City. It had been almost an hour since he had treated a patient.

While the three women were bent over the desk in the outer office, Myra looked out the window and saw a crowd gathering. "Looks like another gunfight," she said.

Breanna felt a cold chill slither down her spine. Her conversation last night with Billy Hampton replayed in her mind. She was ready to present Jesus Christ to him, and when he shut the door in her face, she knew he was really shutting the door in Jesus' face.

"I don't understand why people like to see a person get killed," Bonnie said.

"The human race has been that way for a long time," Myra said quietly, "even like the Romans of old who gathered in the Coliseum to watch the Christians sawn in half, pulled apart on the rack, or torn to pieces by lions."

"You've studied some church history, I see," Breanna said. She had been praying for the proper opening to bring up salvation to her two new friends. "Do you know what being a Christian is all about, Myra…Bonnie?"

"Well," Myra said, "it has to do with belonging to a church in the Christian faith. At least, that's my understanding of it. I haven't really looked into it a whole lot. I—"

The outside door burst open. An elderly man came in, his face pale. "Is Dr. Cox in?" he asked, gasping for breath.

"Yes," Bonnie said.

"I need him bad! Well, that is, my *wife* needs him bad! It's her heart."

"Where is she, sir?" Breanna asked.

"On our farm a couple miles south of town. Our oldest daughter is with her now. I need the doctor to come with me!"

Dr. Cox was wrapping up his conversation with the salesman when Myra rushed into the back room to summon him. A minute later, physician and farmer dashed out the door, with

Cox carrying his black medical bag. The drug representative bid the nurses a hurried good-bye and left to join the crowd when he learned that a gunfight was about to take place.

The three women had turned back to the books when two gunshots echoed down the street, staccato fashion. There was a hum of voices, then all was quiet. When Myra opened the front door and looked out, Breanna turned so she couldn't see out the door.

"Well, it's all over," Myra said. "The crowd is scattering."

"Let's finish up here, girls," Breanna said, sitting down behind the desk. "There are a couple more things I want to show you."

Myra was still at the door. "They're bringing a man this way! Four men are carrying him."

Breanna's mouth went dry. "Just one?"

"Yes. The other one must be dead."

Breanna left the chair and looked through the partially open door past Bonnie and Myra. It was Billy Hampton! He was bareheaded and seemed to be unconscious, his head bobbing loosely.

As the men drew near, she could see blood on his shirt where his unbuttoned coat lay open. The crimson smear was in the center of his chest.

"Let's get the table ready, Bonnie," Myra said. "Breanna, it looks like you're going to be the doctor."

Breanna stepped outside and held the door open. "I'm Nurse Baylor, gentlemen," she said, as they squeezed into the office. "Dr. Cox isn't here. I'll do what I can for him. Please take him through that door. My assistants are getting the table ready."

Breanna looked down at Billy Hampton. His eyes were partially open. Before the men reached the table, she said, "Let's get his coat off."

Billy groaned as they removed the coat one sleeve at a time, then groaned again when they laid him on the table. Breanna picked up a pair of scissors from the nearby counter and began cutting the bloody shirt open.

"Thank you, gentlemen," Myra said. "We'll take it from here."

"Is the other man dead?" Bonnie asked.

"Yes," one of the men said. "He's on his way to the undertaker's parlor. We'll leave this one with you."

While the four men filed out the door, Billy looked up at Breanna with glassy eyes. "I...I won, ma'am," he choked. "I...killed him."

"He came real close to killing you too, Billy," Breanna said. "The slug is very close to your heart."

"Where's...the doctor?"

"You're looking at her." Breanna had the shirt out of the way and was studying the wound.

"But you're not a doctor. You...you told me you're a nurse."

"I'm all you've got, Billy. I've got to go after that slug immediately. Myra..."

"Yes?"

"Chloroform. Fast."

"Please, Nurse...don't let me die."

"I'll do everything I can, Billy."

"I should have listened to you."

"Yes, you should have. Now lie still and breathe deeply."

"Please don't let me die. I...I want to know more about...Jesus. I'm afraid to die! Please help me!"

"Lie still, Billy, and breathe deeply. If I don't get this slug out and stop the bleeding, you'll die for sure."

While the young gunfighter succumbed to the chloroform, Breanna and Bonnie scrubbed their hands in lye soap and running water from the well pump at the counter. Then Breanna had Bonnie tie a surgeon's mask over her mouth and nose.

She picked up a scalpel and began probing for the slug while Bonnie covered her own nose and mouth with a surgeon's mask. Myra was experienced in the use of chloroform, and kept the bottle close as Billy Hampton went completely under.

Breanna prayed silently for steady hands as she probed deeper and deeper. Finally, she felt metal against metal. Cold sweat beaded her brow. The slug was dangerously close to the heart. Keeping the tip of the scalpel against the slug, she said, "Pincers, Bonnie."

Breanna took them from Bonnie's trembling hand and carefully lowered the points into the wound. Once she had the pincers on the slug, she would have to remove it very slowly because of its position next to the heart.

"All right, Bonnie," Breanna said, "I want you to clamp the hemostats on the vessels and arteries one at a time. We've got to stop the bleeding as much as possible."

"I...I've never done this, Breanna," Bonnie said.

"But you've seen Dr. Cox do it. Just follow his procedure."

Once the clamps were in place, Breanna said, "All right, now I've got to remove this slug ever so carefully. Before I do, I want you to sponge away the blood from around the wound. Be careful not to touch my hand."

Breanna watched as Bonnie deftly soaked up the blood from the edges of the wound. "Excellent," she said. "You show a natural talent for this work."

"Thank you," Bonnie said.

Slowly and methodically, Breanna began to lift the lead slug. It was almost out when the rise and fall of Billy's chest stopped.

"Breanna," Myra said, "he's stopped breathing."

"Oh, no!" Breanna's voice barely squeaked out. "Please, Lord! He wanted to hear more about You! Please!"

It was too late. Billy Hampton had fought his last gunfight.

His words came back to Breanna: *"I...I won, ma'am. I...killed him."*

Breanna said in a half-whisper, "No. You lost, Billy. What shall it profit a man if he shall gain the whole world and lose his own soul?"

The room was quiet for several seconds, then Myra said, "That's from the Bible, isn't it?"

"Yes," Breanna said, keeping her eyes on the face of the dead man and fighting to control her emotions. "Jesus spoke them."

As the days came and went, Breanna taught Bonnie and Myra as much as she could each day. Quite often she had to work on one patient while Dr. Cox was working on another, as the student nurses observed and assisted both of them. Other occasions came when the doctor was making house calls, and Breanna had to handle problems large and small in his stead.

God provided opportunities for her to give her testimony of salvation through faith in the Lord Jesus. She made sure Myra understood that simply belonging to a church that was of the "Christian" faith did not make one a Christian.

It was almost eleven o'clock on Monday morning, April 10, when Dr. Cox arrived at the clinic. He had left a note for the nurses, saying he would be making house calls until late morning.

Myra, Bonnie, and Breanna were busy cleaning the examining and operating room. They looked up and smiled at him as he came into the room with a folded newspaper under his arm.

"Any patients while I was out?" he asked, placing his black medical bag on the counter.

"One man with a split lip," Breanna said, "and little Bessie Wyatt with a cut hand. I stitched them both up. Mrs. Wyatt will bring Bessie back on Friday so we can see how the cut is healing."

"Fine," the doctor said with a nod. "I guess you heard the gunfire about an hour ago."

"We did," Myra said, "and we were told it was another quick-draw shoot-out. The victor left his opponent lying dead in the street, mounted up, and rode out of town."

The doctor then took the *Abilene Courier* from under his arm and unfolded it. "Well, business will pick up this afternoon. I met Joe McCoy on the street a few minutes ago. He said there's a big Texas herd on its way in."

"Just think how bored we'd be in some small, peaceful country town!" Myra said.

Bonnie smiled. "Well, I guess you're right about that. Bring on the broken bones, cut-up faces, and bullet wounds!"

The doctor held up the newspaper so all three could see the headlines. "You ladies know about this?" he asked.

Big bold letters declared: *PRESIDENT GRANT TO VISIT ABILENE.*

"Oh, my," Myra said. "When, and why, is this going to happen?"

"Did you know anything about it, Breanna?" Bonnie asked.

"No. Let's hear about it, Doctor."

"I read all about it while eating breakfast this morning.

Didn't know if you ladies had seen the paper or heard the news. The entire front page is taken up with it, and there's another full-page article inside. The front page says the president will be coming through Abilene on a railroad tour in late April. The exact date of his arrival hasn't yet been established."

"So why is he coming through our town?" Myra asked.

"It's a whistle-stop, actually. Congress has been called upon to provide a large sum of money for roads and bridges as the West grows in population. The president wants to take a look at the territories for himself. Julia Grant will be accompanying her husband on the trip."

"She seems lovely by her pictures," Breanna said. "So, how long will President and Mrs. Grant be here, Doctor? Whistle-stops are usually just long enough for the president to make a short speech and move on."

"That's it exactly," the doctor replied. "The article says he'll make a short speech from the platform of his private coach. The chairman of our town council, Everett Varney, says he expects a large crowd. As word of the whistle stop spreads, and the exact date and time is set, people by the hundreds will come from other towns and from ranches and farms to see and hear the president. Mr. Varney is calling on the local band to play for the president and Mrs. Grant at the depot. He's asking the people to bring their American flags and wave them when the train pulls in."

The doctor opened the paper to page three. "Here's a picture of the president in front of the White House, flanked by his bodyguards." The photograph at the top of the page showed President Grant standing with eight men around him in army uniforms.

"The article says that since President Lincoln's assassination in April 1865, the U.S. Army has added to the number of men who serve as bodyguards to the U.S. presidents. Lincoln had three and despised using them. Andrew Johnson had six. And now, as per the United States Congress, President Grant has eight specially trained, uniformed men who hover near him wherever he goes."

"After what happened to poor Mr. Lincoln, that's as it should be," Myra said.

"I read an interesting piece of information in Denver's newspaper a few weeks ago about the 'scapegoat' engine," Breanna said. "When the president travels anywhere by train, the army has taken another precaution. What they call a 'scapegoat' engine precedes by some two hundred yards the train in which President Grant is riding. If would-be assassins should sabotage the track with explosives, or tear up the track with the intent of derailing the president's train, the scapegoat engine would come upon the spot first."

"Now that's a novel idea," Cox said.

Breanna sighed. "It's a sad thing that American presidents have to be so cautious."

"Yes," Cox said. "And President Grant has to be especially cautious. There are so many Southerners who hold a grudge against him because he led the Union to victory in the War."

Breanna nodded. "I know that's true for so many of the Southerners who can't accept that the War is over. In their hearts, they've never surrendered. I wish they would all just want to be Americans and go on to build this into an even greater country than it is. Even General Lee showed this to be his desire before he died last year."

"I hope, in time, we will all unite," Cox said.

"Well, I'll tell you this," piped up Bonnie, "I sure am excited about seeing President Grant...and his wife!"

"Tell you what," the doctor said, "on that day we'll close the clinic during the time the president is here so all four of us can go to the depot."

6

JARED HAMILTON WALKED ALONG Twentieth Street in Manhattan, enjoying the sunshine. The air still had a slight nip to it, but what few trees grew along the streets were in bud, and the small strips of grass around some of the tenement houses were turning green.

Clothing hung on wash lines between the buildings, dancing in the breeze, and children, after being inside all winter, were laughing and playing on the sidewalks.

Jared arrived at the office of Chester Whitfield, M.D., and pulled open the heavy door. The reception area was full of patients sitting on wooden benches, waiting their turn to see the doctor.

Dr. Whitfield had taken care of Jared's father, and Jared had come to this office with his mother two or three times before she had quit her janitorial job and become bedridden.

Jared looked toward the receptionist, Mrs. Halstead. She was plump and had rosy cheeks and a wide smile. He felt warmed by her smile now. "How's your mama doing, Jared?" she asked.

"Not so good, Mrs. Halstead." Jared moved closer to her desk. "She's getting worse. She can't get out of bed anymore, and she's very thin. I need to talk to Dr. Whitfield and ask him if he'll come and see her."

At that moment, the middle-aged physician was coming out of an examining room and overheard Jared's words. He stopped and walked toward the reception desk. "Hello, Jared. I'm sorry that your mother is worse."

Jared looked up at the doctor. "She's very sick, sir. Would you come see her?"

Whitfield cocked his head and rubbed the back of his neck. "Jared, I wish I didn't have to say this, but my coming to your apartment won't help your mother. I'll give you some more medicine for her, but it will only relieve her cough...nothing more."

The boy looked stricken.

Whitfield took in a deep breath and let it out slowly. "Son, I hate to be blunt, but I can't lie to you. There's nothing to be done to save your mother's life, any more than there was anything that could save your father's life. There's no cure for consumption. Your mother's life would be prolonged for a while if she could go to a sanitarium and be under constant medical attention. Since she can't afford to do that, she can't last long. I'm sorry, Jared."

Jared's lips trembled as he said, "Please, oh, please, Dr. Whitfield. Please come and see my mother. Maybe if you look at her you can help her more than you think."

Emily Halstead tried to swallow the lump in her throat and looked up at the doctor, hoping he would do as Jared asked.

Whitfield's heart went out to the boy and he laid a hand on his shoulder. "All right, son. I'll come by the apartment late tomorrow afternoon when I'm doing other house calls."

"Oh, thank you, sir!" Jared said. "I...I can't pay you anything right now, but I promise I'll pay you a little at a time."

Whitfield squeezed Jared's shoulder. "That won't be necessary, son. This visit will be without charge. I'll bring your mother some new cough syrup that will help her."

"Thank you, sir. Oh, thank you!"

Susan and Nathan were washing bedding in the galvanized tub when their big brother entered the apartment. Jared looked toward his mother's bed as he hung up his cap and coat. She was awake, and she looked at him with listless eyes.

"Is he coming?" Susan and Nathan asked in unison.

"Yes," Jared said, going over to his mother.

Leah's face was ashen and her sunken eyes looked at him dully. She tried to smile as she said, "When will Dr. Whitfield come, honey?"

"Tomorrow afternoon, late."

"Thank you for going after him," she said.

"I was glad to do it, Mother."

Nathan stood beside Jared. "The doctor will make you better, Mommy," he said.

"That's right," Susan said, stepping close, her hands dripping with soapy water.

Leah's lips curved slightly, and she nodded, though in her heart she knew she was about to die. Jared knew it, too, though he tried not to show it. It hurt Leah to see the hope in Susie's and Nathan's eyes. It would be so hard for them to face the reality.

When supper was cooked that night, it was Susan's turn to feed her mother, who could no longer get out of bed.

Later, when Leah was asleep, the children were sitting at the kitchen table, playing a game with used wooden matches. When the game was finished, Jared pushed back his chair and said, "I've got something for both of you."

They watched him go to his coat and reach into one of the pockets. He returned with three pieces of hard candy in each hand and laid them on the table. "Three for my little sister, and three for my little brother. You can only eat them if you promise to brush your teeth extra long before bed tonight."

"Oh, Jared!" Susan said, keeping her voice low so as not to disturb their mother. "How did you get this? I know you wouldn't spend grocery money on candy!"

Jared smiled. "You're right, Susie. Mr. Koehler gave it to me after I swept the store today. Not as pay, of course, but as a bonus above my pay."

The Hamilton children could not remember the last time they had eaten candy. As Nathan started to pop a piece in his mouth, Jared seized his wrist gently. "Wait a minute! Do you promise to brush your teeth extra long tonight?"

A smile curved Nathan's lips. "I sure do!"

"Okay." Jared released Nathan's wrist and looked at his sister.

She grinned. "I promise."

Susan happily looked at her three pieces then raised her eyes to Jared. "Where's yours? Did Mr. Koehler give you nine pieces of candy?"

Jared looked away.

"Jared…"

When he looked back he said, "I don't want any. Go on. Eat your candy."

Susan stared at him, love welling up in her eyes. "You like candy the same as Nathan and I do, Jared. It isn't fair that we get it all and you don't get any."

Since no one was paying any attention, Nathan quickly popped his other two pieces of candy into his mouth.

"It's all right, Susie," Jared said. "I don't want any. Really."

Suddenly they heard a slurping sound and looked at their

little brother. His cheeks stuck out like a chipmunk's, storing food for another day.

Susan giggled. "Hog. You made sure Jared didn't get any of yours."

Nathan stared back with a look of innocence on his face and wiped drool from the corners of his mouth.

The next afternoon, as soon as Jared finished polishing the fire wagons, he ran hard for home. The job had taken longer than expected, and it was getting near sundown. He wanted to be there to catch Dr. Whitfield before he went into the apartment.

Jared was puffing hard when he rounded his street corner and saw the doctor pulling up in front of the tenement.

Dr. Whitfield picked up his black medical bag and turned at the sound of running feet. "Well, hello, Jared."

"Hello, sir. I was cleaning and polishing the fire wagons at the fire station. Took longer than I thought. I wanted to talk to you before you go in to see Mother."

"Okay."

"Sir, I appreciate your being honest with me yesterday, but would you please not say anything to her or my brother and sister about how soon she's going to die? I want them to be as happy as possible until it…it happens. Do you understand?"

Whitfield was touched by the boy's maturity and courage. He laid his hand on Jared's shoulder. "It would probably serve a better purpose to just keep it between us, son."

Leah Hamilton looked up at Dr. Whitfield listlessly.

Whitfield glanced at the children and could see hope in their eyes, just from his presence. His heart was heavy for them, and for Jared, too. Soon he would have to be both father and mother to Susan and Nathan.

"Leah," the doctor said, reaching into his medical bag, "I'm going to give you some new cough syrup that will make you feel better. It just came on the market and is much better than anything I've given you before. Are you coughing a lot?"

Whitfield held up the large dark bottle so all could see.

Leah nodded as Jared said, "She has, Doctor. It seems to hurt her more than ever when she does, too. Will this cough syrup make it so she doesn't hurt so much?"

"It just might do that, son," he said. "It's really good stuff."

Whitfield went through the motions of listening to Leah's heart and lungs with his stethoscope, checked her eyes, ears, and throat. "Well, I've seen a lot worse," he said.

Jared looked up and gave him a secret smile.

The doctor turned to Susan and said, "If you'll get me a spoon, I'll give her some of it right now."

Susan hurried to the cupboard and brought back a spoon, fixing her eyes on the bottle.

As the doctor poured out the black liquid, he said, "She is to have two of these three times a day—morning, noon, and night."

Susan nodded.

"And Jared, when it's running low, you come by the office, and I'll give you another bottle."

When Leah had swallowed both doses, the doctor said, "There. That'll make you feel better, and make it so you don't cough so much."

Leah looked into his eyes, trying to thank him with her smile.

When the doctor was gone, Nathan stood close to his mother and said, "See, Mommy? Dr. Whitfield is gonna make you well! Could I hug you, now?"

"No, honey. Only...only when I get better."

"Okay. Pretty soon, huh?"

"Yes, honey. Pretty soon."

Later that night, Jared lay awake in bed, staring at the faint glow on the ceiling from the gaslight on the street. His mother had experienced a bad coughing spell about two hours after Dr. Whitfield left. She told the children it didn't hurt quite so much when she coughed, which made Jared feel better.

Jared could hear Nathan's even breathing beside him, and he could hear his mother's rattled breathing from the other room. There were muffled sounds coming from Susan, who was in her own bed across the room. He quietly turned and looked toward her, listening intently. Then he heard again the sound of weeping.

Jared left his bed and leaned over her. She had the covers over her head and he took hold of a corner of the blanket. "Susie…"

She pulled back the cover and Jared sat down on the edge of the bed. "What is it?" he asked.

"It's Mother. She's not going to get well. Doctor Whitfield talked like she is, but I know it was only to make everybody feel better." She sucked in a sharp, quivering breath. "Oh, Jared, what are we going to do?"

Jared hugged her tight and let her weep.

Finally he said, "Susie, I'll take care of you and Nathan. I don't want you to worry. I'll work hard and make enough money to keep food on the table."

"We won't have a table," she said. "When the money in the jar is gone, and we can't pay the rent, Mr. Girard will make us leave."

"I'll find a way to make enough money to pay the rent," Jared said. "Don't be afraid. I love you, and I love Nathan. I'll take care of you."

81

Susan grew quiet, and Jared let go of her and brushed the hair out of her eyes. "You lie down and go to sleep now, Susie."

As he padded back toward the other bed, Susan whispered, "Jared…"

He stopped and looked over his shoulder, "Yes?"

"You're the best big brother a girl ever had."

Ninety miles south of Abilene, Kansas, at Wichita, three grim-faced men waded their tired horses across the Arkansas River. The sun was shining from a clear azure sky. There was a slight breeze, and the sweet smell of spring was in the air.

The trio drew up in front of the Bulldog Saloon and dismounted, shuffling wearily across the boardwalk. The interior of the saloon was relatively dark, and it took a minute for their eyes to adjust. They waited just inside the door for a moment and noted that the place was about half full. A few men stood at the bar; the rest were at various tables. The tallest of the three men headed toward the bar. The other two followed.

"Howdy, gents," the bartender said. "What'll it be?"

"Just a little information," the tall one drawled.

"Oh?"

"We're lookin' for a fella named Scott Logan. He was a colonel in the Union Army durin' the War. We knew him and heard he was livin' in Wichita. As long as we're passin' through, we'd like to see our ol' friend and say hello."

The bartender was about to reply when a husky voice from a nearby table said, "Send 'em over here, Willie. We'll tell 'em how to find Logan."

"You heard the man," the bartender said, and turned to a couple of new customers.

The trio ambled to the table and stood looking down at the two men who occupied it.

"Have a seat," the one who had spoken up said. As the three men sat down, the man said, "I think I detect that you're from the South, my friend."

The tall one nodded. "You got it right. Tennessee."

The man offered his hand and said, "I'm Clyde Tripp. My pal, here, is Walt Sparrow. Walt's from South Carolina, and I'm from Louisiana. We were both in the Confederate Army in the War. Fought mostly under Stonewall Jackson. We own farms just outside of town."

The tall one shook Tripp's hand, then Sparrow's. "My name's Monty Drake. This is George Macon and Jake Brawmer."

"All three of you boys from Tennessee?" Sparrow asked.

"Sure are," Macon said.

There was iron in Clyde Tripp's voice as he frowned and said, "I'm thinkin' mebbe you boys are wantin' to see Logan for another reason than to say hello to him."

"I was thinkin' the same thing," Sparrow said. "We know Logan but we don't like him."

"We don't like *any* man who wore a blue uniform in the War," Tripp said.

Drake looked at his partners and said, "Looks like we found the right men to talk to, fellas."

Tripp glanced at the whiskey bottle on the table. "Hey, you boys want a drink?"

"No, thanks," Drake said. "Maybe some other time. Right now, we want to know where to find Logan."

"Oh? Mind tellin' us what you want with him?" Sparrow asked.

"Not at all," Drake said. "The three of us were captured at the Battle of Chicamauga in September '63. They took us to a filthy Yankee prison camp near Cairo, Illinois."

Tripp nodded. "Yeah. We know about that. Colonel Scott Logan was in charge of the camp."

"Yeah," Jake Brawmer said. "And treated us and all the other prisoners like animals. We watched hundreds of our comrades die from Logan's brutality, and from lack of proper food and water. We want revenge, and we're gonna get it!"

Tripp wiped a hand over his mouth and glanced at Walt Sparrow, then cleared his throat. "Fellas, I'm sure Walt will concur with this. What Logan did at the prison camp was wrong, but if you're gonna murder him, we don't want no part of it. Murder is out."

"That's right," Sparrow said. "I don't cotton to cold-blooded killin'."

Monty Drake was quite obviously the trio's spokesman. "Hey, we don't intend to kill him. All we want is to give him a lickin' for what he did at the prison camp. Right, guys?"

"Right," they said in chorus.

Drake and his friends located the Logan place easily and drew up in a cluster of cottonwood trees about a hundred yards from the farmhouse.

Drake peered at the house and outbuildings. "Nobody movin' around; maybe they're not home."

"How about one of us goin' in closer?" Macon suggested. "They could just be inside the house."

Drake shook his head. "I don't want Logan to see even one of us. Don't know if he'd recognize us, but if he did, he'd know why we were here. Let's be patient and just watch the place for awhile."

Two hours passed. At sundown, even Drake began to get

antsy. "You don't suppose Tripp and Sparrow sent us to the wrong place, do you?" he said.

"Naw," Macon said. "They know we'd come lookin' for 'em."

Drake rubbed his chin thoughtfully. "Well, we're stayin' right here till Logan comes home."

The half-moon shed a faint silver light on the three Southerners who ate beef jerky and hardtack for supper. An owl hooted high up in one of the cottonwoods as Macon said, "It must be nine o'clock, Monty."

Suddenly the sound of a rattling wagon met their ears. Seconds later they saw the wagon in the dim light as it slowed down near the narrow trail leading to the house and turned in.

"It's him!" Macon whispered. "Let's go get 'im!"

"Hold on," Drake said. "Not now."

"Huh?"

"We'll wait till mornin'."

"Wha—? Why?"

"'Cause I want that dude to *see* who's killin' 'im."

7

DRUSILLA LOGAN SAT ACROSS THE TABLE, watching her husband devour biscuits and gravy. She smiled with satisfaction and said, "It's so good to watch you enjoy my cooking."

"Twenty-four years I've enjoyed your cooking, Drusilla." Scott Logan paused and shook his head. "No, *twenty* years. The War robbed me of four."

Drusilla watched him mop up the last of the gravy on his plate and then asked, "You going to begin spring plowing today?"

"Uh-huh. Have to get it harrowed and seeded right away. What will you do today?"

"Well, I owe letters to our daughters-in-law, so I'll write them first. Then I've got sewing to do. I'm making me a summer dress. Couple of your work shirts need buttons, too, if you recall."

"Mm-hmm."

"Which field are you going to plow first?"

"The one right out there to the west of the toolshed."

Drusilla nodded. "I'll have lunch ready at straight-up noon."

✦

Scott Logan was whistling "The Girl I left Behind Me" as he headed for the barn. The four horses in the corral watched him move in their direction, and the two saddle horses nickered.

"Not today, boys," he said. "You get to rest. It's Dick and Bess today."

The early morning sunlight seeped through the knotholes and cracks in the barn walls, and a long, bold shaft of light came from the open door in the hayloft overhead. Logan climbed the ladder and pitched an ample amount of hay into the trough below for the horses. Then he descended the ladder and distributed the hay more evenly in the trough. As he headed for the back door of the barn to let the animals in, three figures emerged from the shadows under the hayloft.

Logan squinted. "Who are you? What do you want?"

Monty Drake grinned evilly. "You don't remember us, Colonel? Cairo? A year and a half of your brutality?"

Each man had a long-bladed knife in his hand. At first Logan's lips moved soundlessly, then he found his voice. "Now, whoever you are…I ran that prison camp under the orders of General Ulysses S. Grant. I just did my duty as an officer of the Union Army."

"Duty?" Drake said. "It was your duty to torture your prisoners when they dared ask for decent food and clean water…and warm clothing in the winter?"

Logan tried to focus on their faces and remember their names.

"Sergeants Monty Drake, George Macon, and Jake Brawmer, Colonel," Brawmer said raggedly. "Now do you remember?"

"Well, I…ah…yes. I remember you. Now listen, I don't

know what you want, but—"

"Revenge, I think it's called, *sir*," Macon said, waving the knife in a threatening gesture.

"Now, look. My camp was no different than dozens of those you Confederates had. Our men were mistreated too. Starved. Beaten."

"That's hearsay, Colonel!" Drake said. "What we're talkin' about isn't hearsay! We were there."

"That's all a part of war," Logan said, slowly backing away.

Macon gripped his knife tightly. "Yeah, Colonel? Well, this is part of war, too. What you did during the war has its consequences!"

A chill spread through Scott Logan's veins, and his heart hammered in his chest. He pivoted and dashed for the pitchfork he'd left at the feed trough.

Drusilla finished cleaning up the kitchen after breakfast and glanced toward the field her husband was going to plow. He wasn't there yet.

She had been at the sewing table for an hour or better when she leaned against the window and looked toward the field again. Still no sign of Scott.

Drusilla lay down her sewing and stepped out on the back porch. Her head bobbed with surprise when she saw all four horses standing at the corral fence. "What's going on?" she murmured to herself, as she stepped off the porch and headed for the barn.

The rusty hinges complained when she opened the door and stepped inside. "Scott…"

She moved deeper into the shadowed old structure and mumbled, "Well, where in the world can he be? Scott…!"

A high-pitched scream escaped her lips when she found Scott with the pitchfork buried in his chest.

The killers were ten miles away, headed for El Dorado. They laughed and joked as they replayed the frightful look on the colonel's face when he ran.

"Sure slowed him up when your knife buried itself in his back, eh, Jake?" Macon said.

"It'll do it every time!" Brawmer replied.

"Well," Drake said, "it'll be a pleasure when we get to Emporia and tell our two old prison mates that we took care of Logan!"

"How far did you say Emporia is from El Dorado, Monty?" Brawmer asked.

"About forty miles. We'll make El Dorado in time to eat supper this evenin', and by the same time tomorrow we'll be eatin' supper with our old pals!"

The last glow of sunset ebbed away and shadows moved across the land as the three riders dismounted in front of the El Dorado Café. While drinking coffee and waiting for their meal, they overheard four men at a nearby table saying something about President Grant.

Drake looked at his friends. "Did either of you catch what they said?"

Both shook their heads.

Drake leaned toward the neighboring table and said, "Excuse me, gentlemen. I'm a great admirer of President Grant. Did I hear one of you say he's comin' to Kansas?"

"You sure did, stranger. He's making a railroad tour of the

West to see if we really need the money for roads and bridges that Congress is being pressured to provide. He's going to make only one whistle-stop in Kansas…at Abilene."

"Oh, really? How come Abilene?"

"Newspapers say it's because Abilene's the fastest growing town in Kansas. He'll be there this coming Saturday, the twenty-second."

Drake thanked the man and turned back to Brawmer and Macon, his eyes glinting.

"Can we make it to Abilene in two days, Monty?" Brawmer asked.

"Sure, if we bypass Emporia."

"It'll be worth it," Macon said. "We can head for Emporia after we shoot Grant. Then we'll have two items of good news for our old pals!"

"Tell you what," Drake said. "We've been sleepin' on the ground ever since we left Tennessee. Let's celebrate our good fortune and get ourselves hotel rooms for tonight. Tomorrow we'll stop in the Western Union office and wire our pals in Emporia about our change in plans."

On Tuesday, April 18, Jared Hamilton climbed the stairs to the apartment after an exhausting day. When he opened the door and stepped inside, he saw both Susan and Nathan standing over their mother as she coughed and gagged. Susan was holding a towel to her mother's mouth and speaking to her in soft tones.

"She's coughing up blood again, Jared," Nathan said.

Jared put an arm around his little brother and pressed him close as Susan continued to help their mother. After a while, Leah's coughing subsided and Susan wiped the blood from her mouth. After spending a few more minutes at the bedside,

Jared and Susan began cooking a meager supper while Nathan stayed by the bed. Leah's eyes were closed, and she was barely breathing when the children sat down to eat.

Suddenly Nathan laid down his fork and began to cry, saying, "Mommy's gonna die, Jared! Mommy's gonna die!"

Both Jared and Susan left their chairs and tried to comfort him. Soon, all three were weeping as they clung to each other.

Finally, Jared said, "Nathan, you go sit by Mommy and take care of her while Susie and I wash the dishes and clean up the kitchen."

Nathan moved up quietly beside the bed, glad to see that his mother was sleeping. She didn't cough and hurt when she slept. He knew he wasn't supposed to touch his mother but he couldn't help himself. He wanted to hug her but would settle for just holding her hand for a moment. When he touched her hand it felt cold. His eyes went to her face, then settled on the covers where he was used to seeing her chest rise and fall.

A tightness gripped Nathan as he turned toward the kitchen and forced the words past the constriction in his throat. "Jared! Susie! Mommy's cold, and she's not breathing!"

On Thursday, April 20, the Hamilton children rode through the streets of Manhattan in a carriage provided by the city. Their mother's body had been picked up by men from the coroner's office on Wednesday morning. She would be buried in a potter's field on Manhattan Island's north side at the expense of the state.

Clarence Dickson, one of the coroner's staff, drove the carriage. Though there would be no minister to even say anything over the wooden box that held Leah Hamilton's body, the coroner felt that her children should be allowed to see where she was buried and to look at the coffin before it was lowered into the ground.

"Jared," Nathan said in a small voice, "are they gonna let us look at Mommy before they bury her?"

"I don't know," Jared said. He spoke to the man driving the carriage. "Mr. Dickson, can we see our mother before the coffin is lowered into the ground?"

"I don't think so, son," Dickson said over his shoulder. "I'm sure the lid has already been nailed down. The only persons who will be there are the gravediggers."

Jared put his arm around Nathan and pulled him close. "I'm sorry, Nathan," he said.

The little boy started to cry. "But I wanted to tell Mommy good-bye."

"Me, too," Susan said, fighting back her tears.

"Tell you what," Clarence Dickson said, "there's a toolbox in the back of the carriage. I'll pry off the lid so you kids can say good-bye to your mother."

Soon the carriage was off the road and moving slowly through the paupers' cemetery. Two gravediggers stood beside the coffin, watching as Dickson pulled up and set the brake. "You kids wait here just a minute," Dickson said.

The children looked on as Dickson said something to the gravediggers and they nodded. Dickson hurried back to the carriage. "All right, kids," he said, opening the small trunk space at the rear of the vehicle. "Those men are willing to wait a few minutes."

Moments later the lid of the cheap box was off. Dickson backed away several steps to allow the children some privacy.

Leah Hamilton's pale hands were crossed over her chest. Her peaceful face reminded the older children of the good days before their father and mother got sick.

Jared picked Nathan up and held him in his arms. After several minutes, Jared sniffed and said, "Tell Mommy good-bye, Nathan." He lowered his little brother over the coffin so that he could stroke her hands.

"Good-bye, Mother. We love you," Susan said.

As the days passed, Jared was able to find enough work to keep him busy thirteen and fourteen hours a day. He even tried to find night work, but there were no night jobs for twelve-year-old boys.

Two days after their mother was buried, Susan and Nathan watched their big brother take the last dollar out of the jar in the cupboard. It was Saturday, and the rent was due for the next week.

It had taken every penny Jared could earn to keep food on the table.

"Jared," Susan said. "We'll have to move out a week from today. Where are we going to go?"

"I've been thinking," Jared said, holding the dollar bill in his hand. "Maybe Mr. Girard would let me do work around the tenement building to pay for our rent. I could work nights."

"I could help you."

"Me too," Nathan said.

Jared descended the stairs to the ground floor and knocked on Lloyd Girard's door. He extended the dollar bill. "Here's next week's rent money, Mr. Girard."

Girard accepted it. "How are you kids doing since your mother passed on?"

"It's a little tight, sir, but I'm able to earn enough money most days to keep food on the table. Sometimes we don't eat breakfast."

"Oh. Uh-huh."

"Mr. Girard, I wanted to ask you something. It's going to be real hard for me to earn enough money to pay the rent and buy food, too. Would you let me do work for you around the building to earn our rent? It would have to be nights, mostly."

Girard shook his head before Jared had finished speaking. "Nope. Can't do it, kid. I'm sorry, but I have to have cash money for the rent. If you can't pay me a dollar next Saturday, you'll have to move out."

During the next few days, Susan took Nathan with her and knocked on doors all over their neighborhood, asking for work. She was given a cleaning job now and then, and Nathan was allowed to help her. By Friday she had accumulated only forty-one cents. All of Jared's earnings that week had gone for food.

After supper on Friday evening, Jared knocked on Lloyd Girard's door. "Oh, hello, kid. You wanting to pay the rent tonight instead of in the morning?"

Jared lifted up his hand and displayed the forty-one cents. "This is all I have, Mr. Girard. Would you accept it in place of a dollar?"

The pot-bellied man switched a cigar from one side of his mouth to the other. "Can't do it, Jared. I have my own bills to pay. I've got to have a dollar from you by tomorrow morning, or you're out."

Susan and Nathan were waiting just inside the door when Jared returned. He shook his head. "He wouldn't accept the money. Said it has to be a dollar by tomorrow morning, or we have to get out."

"What's going to happen to us?" Susan asked, her voice quavering. "Where are we going to live?"

"Are we going to die?" Nathan asked.

"We're not going to die, Nathan," Jared said. "We...we'll just have to find a spot in an alley like other children who have no home. I'm glad the weather is getting warmer. We'll take our pillows and blankets with us."

"What about when winter comes?" Susan asked.

"I'll figure out something by then. We have about five months before the cold weather comes back." Jared paused, then added, "I can't leave the two of you in the alley while I'm out selling papers and doing my odd jobs. You'll just have to go with me."

The next day, the Hamilton children left the apartment with nothing but their coats and the bedding they would need. Susan and Nathan stayed with Jared as he sold his papers. When he did his odd jobs, they helped him as much as they could. Late in the afternoon, they carried their bedding into an alley behind a large clothing store where many crates and boxes were stacked. Jared had bought food from Oscar Koehler, who also gave them a bottle of water.

They placed three boxes side by side to sleep in. When their "beds" were ready, they sat on a wooden crate and ate their cold supper, washing it down with water.

That first night in the alley they lay in the boxes, talking just to hear each others' voices. Nathan was afraid of the dark shadows cast by the street lamps at the ends of the alley. Susan had her own fears but masked them to help Jared calm Nathan. When little brother was convinced that neither Jared nor Susan were afraid, he finally drifted off to sleep.

When Nathan was breathing evenly, Jared rolled over and listened to see if Susan was asleep. He could barely see the top of her head. She was still, but he knew she was awake.

"Susie," he whispered.

"Yes?"

"Are you all right?"

There was a long moment of silence. "Jared, I'm scared. What if some hoodlums come down this alley and stumble onto us? Maybe they'll kill us!"

"You mustn't think like that. Nobody's going to bother us here. I'm not going to let anybody hurt you or Nathan."

"You promise?"

"I promise. Now go to sleep."

8

THE HAMILTON CHILDREN SLEPT FITFULLY, waking several times during the night. Morning came with a cloudy sky and a chill in the air. Before leaving the alley, the children stashed their bedding in a wooden crate.

When Jared's papers were all sold, he started his routine of going from door to door in the business district, asking for work. He was stocking shelves for Oscar Koehler with help from Susan and Nathan. When noon came, Mr. Koehler took them into the back of the store and fed them lunch. Jared assumed this would be his pay for the day. He was pleasantly surprised when Koehler paid him in full.

Jared got two other brief jobs, and by three o'clock he was sweeping the boardwalk in front of Luigi Olivetti's shoe repair shop. Susan and Nathan sat on a bench near the shop's door.

Jared noticed Bodie Brolin walking toward him. He hadn't seen Bodie in over three weeks, which was not uncommon. Bodie had several areas where he peddled his toothpicks and matches.

"Bodie!" Jared said, pausing in his work.

Bodie smiled. "Hi. How's your mother doing?"

Jared's grin faded. "She...died, Bodie. Two weeks ago last Tuesday."

"Oh, I'm so sorry." After a pause Bodie said, "Are you still living in the apartment?"

"No. We ran out of rent money."

"You're living in an alley?"

"Yes, behind Boxler's Clothing Store on Thirty-seventh Street."

"Where are your little sister and brother?"

Jared pointed with his chin toward Susan and Nathan on the bench. "Right over there. I keep them with me all the time."

"Sure," Bodie said with a nod, moving toward the younger children. Jared followed and introduced them.

"I've heard a lot about you two," Bodie said. He turned back to Jared. "I...I wish I could take all three of you home with me, but my father would throw a fit. Even if I took you in when he was passed out drunk, he'd be really mad when he sobered up and knew you were living with us."

"That's all right, Bodie," Jared said. "I understand. We'll make it all right in the alley."

"Till cold weather comes," Susan reminded him.

"Yes. Well, I'll think of something by then."

"Well, it's good to see you again, Jared. And it was good to meet you, Susan and Nathan. I've got to go to work now."

Jared carried the broom back to where he had left off, and was about to start sweeping again when he saw four boys headed toward him. It was Mike McDuff and three of his pals. Jared didn't like the look in their eyes. He threw a quick glance over his shoulder, but Bodie had his back to him. If he called for help, McDuff and his friends would pounce on him for sure.

Susan saw the uneasiness in her brother's eyes and took Nathan by the hand to go stand beside Jared.

"Well, lookee who's here, guys," McDuff said, fixing Jared with piercing eyes. "These your bodyguards, Jared?"

"My sister and brother," Jared said.

McDuff glanced at Susan and Nathan, then fixed his eyes on Jared. "Miss us?"

"I noticed you weren't around."

"We've been in jail. But here we are again, back on the streets. I don't mind tellin' you, Jared, I'm feelin' pretty ill toward you, and so are my buddies. You were gonna tell old man Koehler 'bout us stealin' that stuff."

Jared set his jaw. "Stealing is wrong," he said.

"We gotta eat. And we need things. The old man wouldn't have missed what we took."

"You wouldn't have to steal if you'd work and earn money like I do."

"Only reason you don't steal is 'cause you're scared to," McDuff said with a sneer.

"You're crazy! I don't steal because it's *wrong* to steal!"

"Aw, that ain't it," Truxtun Gowen said. "You're just a panty-waist sissy."

"You leave my brother alone!" Susan said. "He doesn't steal because stealing is *wrong!*"

Archie Boyle snorted. "What's this, Jared? Your little sister really *is* your bodyguard. Panty-waist!"

McDuff laughed. "Yeah, I bet this little guy here with all the freckles is tougher than you are!"

Jared set his jaw. He had no desire to mix it up with the young toughs, but his own anger was rising. "You boys had enough fun yet? I think it's time you found something else to do. I've got a job to finish."

McDuff took a step closer. "Maybe before we go we oughtta black your eyes and bloody your nose!"

Susan's eyes blazed. "My brother is a lot more man than you are!"

McDuff spat out a curse and slapped Susan. She staggered back and touched the burning spot on her cheek.

Jared leaped toward McDuff with the broom in his hand and drove the handle like a ramrod into his stomach. Mike doubled over, breath whooshing from his mouth.

"You dare hit my sister!" Jared shouted. He dropped the broom and punched the bigger boy on the nose. McDuff tried to fight back, but Jared peppered him with stinging blows.

"Jared, look out!" Susan cried, as the other boys lunged at him.

Jared turned to meet them but was knocked off his feet. Susan leaped on Truxtun Gowen's back, digging her fingernails into his eyes. Gowen began howling, trying to free himself, when Bodie Brolin grabbed Marty Lukacher by the shirt collar and yanked him off Jared.

Suddenly Police Officer Dean Farone came charging in. "What's going on here?" he demanded, while pulling a scratching, clawing Susan off Truxtun Gowen's back.

"These hoodlums were going to beat up my brother!" Susan said.

Luigi Olivetti had suddenly appeared along with one of his customers.

"I can believe that, Susan," Olivetti said.

"It's a lie!" Mike McDuff said, still wiping blood from his nose and lip. "We weren't gonna beat up on Jared! We were just talkin' to him. *He* started it. He hit me in the stomach with that broom, then punched me in the face!"

"Yeah!" Marty said. "We didn't start nothin'!"

"Besides, we happen to know that Jared steals from stores!" Archie Boyle said. "We seen 'im do it!"

Farone set hard eyes on Boyle. "I don't think you ought to be pointing your finger at someone else stealing, lad."

"Well, we learned our lesson," McDuff said. "We don't steal no more since we got outta jail."

Susan could barely contain her indignation. "You were calling my brother a sissy because he said it's wrong to steal, and he won't do it!"

"Hold on, now!" Officer Farone said. "Let's quiet down. So this is your sister, Jared?"

"Yes, sir, and this is my brother, Nathan. My sister's name is Susie."

"I assume you have the broom because you were sweeping the walk for Mr. Olivetti here?"

"He was," Luigi said.

"And why are Nathan and Susie with you, Jared?" Farone asked.

Jared explained why he had no choice but to take his sister and brother with him while he did his jobs.

Farone turned to young Brolin. "And what is your part in all of this, Bodie?"

"I was just getting started peddling my matches and toothpicks up there on the corner, Officer, when I happened to look this way and see these three guys jump Jared. Jared's my friend. I came to help him."

"I see."

Hatred flashed in Mike McDuff's eyes. "I'll tell you somethin' else, Officer," he said. "Bodie's a thief, too. I've seen him take stuff lots of times. He's just like Jared. They're two of a kind."

Bodie set his steady gaze on McDuff. "If you've got proof I'm a thief, produce it. If you don't, then shut your mouth."

McDuff's face flushed but he didn't reply.

"Well, I'm telling all of you," Officer Farone said, "there'd better not be any more fighting *or* stealing in my territory. I'll be watching you. Get out of line just once and you'll be looking at the world through bars."

McDuff held a finger on his cut lip and looked at the policeman. "Can we go now, Officer?"

"Yes. But you'd better remember what I said. And I don't want any retaliation on Jared over this incident, either. Understand?"

"Sure. We'll drop it right here."

"Fine. You can go."

When they were out of earshot, Officer Farone said, "I know their kind, Jared...Bodie. They're troublemakers. And I know you're not. Best thing you can do is steer clear of them. In this situation, it was their word against yours, so I had no grounds for punishing them. Do you understand?"

Both boys nodded.

"All right then. I'll be on my way."

Luigi Olivetti laid a hand on Jared's shoulder as the officer walked away. "Jared, if all the boys in this city were like you, these streets would be a lot safer. And you, too, Bodie."

Breanna Baylor had put in many hours every day at the Cox Medical Clinic and filled in for Dr. Cox when he was making house calls or was away from the clinic for other reasons. When he was there, she helped him with various surgeries, broken bones, bullet and knife wounds, as well as the normal sicknesses, injuries, and pregnancies of the nonviolent citizenry.

She had also been teaching Bonnie Rand and Myra Dupree how to order supplies and stock the medicine cabinets, keep the books, make and file patient records, handle the mail, and make the bank deposits, as well as how to improve their medical work in every way. The sooner they could handle things the sooner she could leave Abilene and return to Denver.

It was late morning, and Dr. Cox was taping a farmer's broken finger, when they heard gunshots from some distance up the street. "Could be more patients for us out there," Dr. Cox said.

Breanna shook her head. "So far there's been at least one gunfight or knife fight a day since I've been here."

"Well, this is Abilene," Cox said.

Myra excused herself when she heard footsteps in the outer office. Seconds later, she returned with Marshal Hickok and a wounded deputy marshal. Blood ran between Max Dillard's fingers where he gripped his upper left arm.

"Come over here and sit down in this chair, Deputy," Breanna said. "Dr. Cox will be with you shortly. My name is Breanna Baylor. I'll see what I can do for your wound until we can get you up on the table."

While Breanna guided Dillard to the chair, Dr. Cox looked at Marshal Hickok. "What happened, Marshal?"

"Some half-drunk fool pulled his gun and started shooting in the street in every direction. Max tried to disarm him and got himself shot. I had to shoot the man."

"Dead?"

"'Fraid so."

Breanna used a pair of scissors to cut away the cloth from around the wound. "It's not too bad, Doctor," she said over her shoulder. "The bullet went through the fleshy part of the upper arm near the shoulder. Didn't touch the bone."

Hickok and Breanna assisted a watery-kneed Max Dillard to the table. As Dr. Cox went to work on the wound, he glanced briefly at Hickok and said, "We were just talkin' about the president stoppin' here to make his speech tomorrow, Marshal. Are you plannin' to take any precautions when he's here?"

"I'll have my six...well, *five* deputies with me at the depot. I doubt Max will be up to it. With the president's eight body-guards, that'll make fourteen men standing ready in case of trouble."

At the same time the conversation was going on at the Cox Medical Clinic, three hard-faced, unkempt riders drifted into Abilene. Monty Drake, George Macon, and Jake Brawmer went virtually unnoticed, for the town was full of men of the same description.

George Macon was humped over the pommel of his saddle feeling lightheaded and sweating profusely.

As their horses carried them slowly up Main Street, Drake and Brawmer eyed the saloons right and left. Suddenly Drake pointed into the next block. "There it is, Jake."

Moments later they reined in at the hitch rail in front of the Broken Spur Saloon. Drake and Brawmer dismounted and stepped up to Macon, who was still slumped over.

"C'mon, George," Drake said. "A good stiff belt of whiskey will set you right."

Macon looked at him with fever-dimmed eyes. "I jus' want to get me a room and hit the bed. You an' Jake can go on in and take a look."

"You'll feel better if you get a drink under your belt," Drake insisted. "C'mon."

Brawmer looked up the street and saw a big sign in front of the Jayhawker Hotel. "Hotel's right up there, George. You'll be there shortly. Right now, do as Monty says. Come on inside with us."

Drake and Brawmer helped Macon inside the Broken Spur and eased him onto a chair.

✦

Breanna and Myra were cleaning up the table and cupboard in the operating room after working on Deputy Marshal Max Dillard.

At the outer door, Hickok had an arm around Dillard to support him. "Just put this on the town's bill, Doc," Hickok said.

"Will do. Max, you take it easy for a few days. That wound will slow you down."

"I'll see that he takes whatever time off he needs," Hickok said. "See you later."

Hickok and Dillard started down the boardwalk and had to make way as four cowboys carried one of their own toward the clinic. Cox saw them and held the door open.

As they passed through the door, one of the cowboys said, "He fell off the balcony over at the Rosebud Saloon, Doctor. His leg's busted up pretty bad."

Cox saw blood oozing through the half-conscious man's pantleg. Bonnie left the desk and hurried to open the examining room door. When Breanna cut away the pantleg, she saw splintered bone protruding through the skin. Both student nurses looked on as Breanna administered chloroform to the cowboy, helped Dr. Cox set the compound fracture, take stitches, and splint it.

One of the cowboys took the injured man's wallet from his pocket, pulled out enough money to pay the doctor, and carried their friend away.

When the operating room was clean once again, Breanna told Dr. Cox that since it was quiet for the moment, she would go over to the general store and see if the supplies had come in.

As Breanna entered Anderson's General Store, Hazel Berry

and Maude Wilcox were coming out; both were patients of Dr. Cox.

"Oh, Breanna," Hazel said, "isn't it exciting? Just think of it…tomorrow we get to see President Grant! Is Dr. Cox going to close the clinic so all of you can go to the depot?"

"Yes, he is. We're going to close up just before noon."

"Oh, that's good. Nobody should have to miss such an event."

Maude and Hazel moved through the door, and Breanna headed toward the counter, where proprietor Miles Anderson was waiting on two well-groomed men. She could hear them saying they had been riding through town on their way to Nebraska when they saw flags and banners at the depot. People on the street told them the president was coming through Abilene tomorrow.

Breanna smiled to herself as the two strangers spoke. Their heavy Southern accents were unmistakable. She was impressed by the way they were dressed. They were much cleaner and neater than most men who rode into Abilene.

"We've decided to stay over and see the president, Mr. Anderson," the taller one said. "We noticed there are three hotels in town. Do y'all recommend any one over the others?"

Miles Anderson smiled. "Well, gentlemen, I've never stayed in any of them, but from what I'm told, the Jayhawker is the best."

"All right. We'll stay at the Jayhawker."

Anderson handed the men their purchases and then saw Breanna standing behind them. "Oh, hello, Miss Baylor," he said, smiling warmly. "What can I do for you?"

Both men turned to look at her.

"The supplies I ordered a couple of weeks ago from Kansas City…have they come in yet?"

"Yes, they have. I'll get them for you in a moment, but I

think I should introduce you. Gentlemen, this is Miss Breanna Baylor. She's a nurse in the Cox Medical Clinic in town."

Both men tipped their hats. "Honored to meet you, ma'am," the tall one drawled. "My name is Davis Claymore, and my friend here is Cleve Holden. We're from Atlanta, Georgia."

"I'm happy to meet you both," Breanna said, and smiled.

"I have to admire a lady who will work as a nurse in this tough town, ma'am," Claymore said. "You must stay pretty busy with all the violence I've heard goes on here."

Breanna tilted her head. "Well, Mr. Claymore, I'll have to admit that Abilene has its share of violence, and then some. It's enough to keep the doctor, two other nurses, and myself quite busy."

Cleve Holden ran his gaze back and forth between Breanna and the proprietor, and said, "I understand you have a pretty tough marshal here—the famous Wild Bill Hickok."

"That we have," Anderson said. "He's *plenty* tough, let me tell you. Why, a couple days ago there were four hard cases rode into town, figuring to have themselves a big time. They began shooting up one of the saloons. Wild Bill was summoned, and before it was over those four men lay dead on the floor, and Wild Bill—"

Anderson's words were cut off by the sound of gunfire. It went on for about ten seconds, then stopped suddenly.

The Southerners looked toward the door. "That sounded pretty close out there," Holden said. "I half expected bullets to come flying through those windows over there."

"Happens like that sometimes," Anderson said. Then to Breanna, "I'll be right back, Miss Baylor. Your order is in the back."

While the proprietor hastened to get the supplies, Holden

said, "I've long admired Ulysses S. Grant. Tremendous general, even if he was on the wrong side. And he's a good president."

"I couldn't agree more," Claymore said. He smiled at Breanna and said, "How did a pretty lady like you—"

Anderson set four heavy boxes on the counter. "Do you have someone to help you with these, Miss Baylor?"

"No, I was just going to carry them one at a time. The clinic really isn't that far away."

"Tell you what. My sons will be here in a few minutes. I'll have them carry the boxes for you."

"That won't be necessary, Mr. Anderson," Claymore said. "Cleve and I will carry them to the clinic for Miss Baylor right now."

"Oh, I don't want to impose on you gentlemen," Breanna said.

"It won't be an imposition, ma'am. It will be our pleasure."

"Well, if you're sure…"

"All right, Miss Baylor," Holden said, grinning, "lead the way."

As Breanna headed toward the door, she said over her shoulder, "Thank you for the good service, Mr. Anderson. Just put these items on Doctor's bill as usual."

"Will do," Anderson said with a wave of his hand. "See you at the depot tomorrow."

9

MARSHAL HICKOK DELIVERED the wounded deputy to his wife and headed back to the office. Another herd of cattle had arrived in Abilene the day before and the Texas cowboys were taking a few days off before making the long ride back.

The Texans wandered up and down the boardwalks and dusty streets, checking out the town's numerous saloons and gambling establishments. They had a few drinks in each one, and the more they drank the rougher they got, even fighting among themselves.

As Hickok made his way up Main Street, boisterous laughter shared the afternoon air with loud, sometimes angry voices coming from the saloons and casinos. Tobacco smoke drifted through the doors above the batwings, and piano music followed it. Cheap liquor was served inside the noisy places under expensive mirrors and fancy glass chandeliers.

Near the Alamo Saloon, Hickok heard glass shatter, punctuated by coarse laughter. A heavy voice boomed, "You'll pay for that mirror right now, mister, or I'm going after the marshal!"

The bartender's harsh words were answered with two more shots and a loud crash and tinkle of glass.

Hickok barged through the batwings to find a Texas cowboy

holding a smoking revolver. A glass chandelier lay shattered on the floor.

"Marshal," the bartender said, "this fool just shot my bar mirror, then shot the chandelier off the ceiling!"

The cowboy blinked as he turned to see Wild Bill Hickok moving toward him, saying, "I'll handle him, Harry."

The bartender caught the eye of a man at a nearby table and mouthed, *deputies!* The man got up quickly and left the saloon.

"Give me the gun, cowboy," Hickok said, extending his hand.

"You ain't takin' my gun, Marshal."

Hickok moved closer. This time his words came out sounding like a growl. "I'm taking your gun, and after you pay Harry for the damage you've done, you're going to jail."

A wild look flared across the cowboy's face. "You ain't takin' my gun, and I ain't payin' that dude nothin'…and I ain't goin' to no jail!"

Hickok's gun was still in the holster. He grabbed the cowboy's gun hand and twisted the weapon from his grasp, then cracked him over the head with it. The cowboy went down like an uprooted tree.

The marshal found the man's wallet and checked it for currency. "Harry, what's it going to cost to put everything back like it was?"

"I'd say about two hundred dollars, Marshal."

Hickok extracted the bills, counted out three hundred and said, "Here's some extra for the trouble he caused."

After handing Harry the money, Hickok rolled the unconscious cowboy onto his belly and clamped cuffs on him.

In his peripheral vision, he saw a man moving toward him. He looked up at a hulking form and held the cowboy's gaze as he rose to his feet. The man was at least two inches taller than Hickok with thick shoulders and a massive chest.

"You wanted to say something, cowboy?"

"Yeah. That was my pal you just cold-cocked. We rode all the way from Austin together."

"And?"

"You ain't takin' him to jail."

"Oh?"

"Take the cuffs off him."

The crowd of men waited in awe. The cowboy outweighed Hickok by at least eighty pounds, yet the marshal showed no fear.

"What's your name, cowboy?" Hickok asked.

"Big Zack McCluskie."

"Well, Big Zack, you just back off and mind your own business."

"I can mash you, take the key off your limp body, and remove the cuffs myself, Marshal. Now do it or else."

For a brief moment there was deathly stillness in the Alamo Saloon. Then before the huge Texan could throw a punch, the marshal's ironlike fist whipped McCluskie's head sideways. His legs gave way, and he dropped to his knees, shaking his head. There was a roaring in his head as he worked his way to his feet and staggered toward the marshal. Hickok cracked the cowboy savagely on the jaw again. This time, McCluskie hit the floor with a loud *whump*. The batwings flew open and three deputies bolted into the saloon, guns drawn.

"Everything's under control, boys," the marshal said with a grin. "These two cowboys who're taking naps are going to jail. Chuck, put your cuffs on the big one."

Moments later the two Texans were being ushered through the batwings on wobbly feet.

In a back corner of the saloon, one Texan whispered to another, and the man nodded, malevolence showing in his eyes.

George Macon's face was shiny with sweat and he was shaking with chills. Monty Drake and Jake Brawmer helped him from the saddle and half-carried him toward the door of the Jayhawker Hotel.

"We'll get you into bed, George," Drake said, "and maybe by mornin' you'll feel better."

The desk clerk looked up as two men helped a third man to a chair in the lobby then stepped up to the desk.

"We'd each like a separate room," Drake said.

The clerk was a small, thin man. He flicked a glance at Macon and said, "What's the matter with him?"

"Just a little fever," Drake said. "He'll be all right."

The clerk frowned. "I think it would be best if he didn't stay here. You ought to take him to Dr. Cox down the street. Let him put your friend up in the clinic."

"It ain't a disease, pal," Brawmer said. "Just a little fever. Like Monty said, we'd like three rooms."

The clerk bristled and was about to speak again when Drake reached across the desk and grabbed him by the front of his shirt. He pulled the man halfway across the desk and said, "Three rooms, mister! Now!"

The little man's eyes bulged. "Y-yes, sir."

"That's better."

"H-how long will you gentlemen be staying?"

"Just tonight."

"All right. I...I have three rooms in sequence available on the second floor."

When the men had registered and the rooms were paid for, Drake and Brawmer carried Macon up the stairs. "You just lie here and rest, George," Drake said. "Jake and I are going to check out the railroad station. Okay?"

Macon nodded, sleeving sweat from his face.

"Tell you what, George," Brawmer said, "when we get back we'll stop at the desk and order up some hot water so you can take a bath. Maybe a good long sit in hot water will make you feel better."

Drake and Brawmer smiled at the clerk as they passed through the lobby and out the door. The little man smiled weakly in return.

They were riding toward the west end of town when they heard gunshots split the air. They could hear loud voices, more gunshots, then all went still.

"Nice town," Brawmer said, grinning. "Lots of gunplay."

As they drew near the depot, Drake said, "Let's leave the horses in front of the land office and walk the rest of the way. Don't want to draw any attention to ourselves."

Moments later they arrived at the railroad station on foot, threading their way through a large crowd of people. Some had just arrived on the train from Chicago, and the others were there to meet them.

Drake scanned the surrounding buildings and said in a low tone, "Grant's coach has to be the last car on the train so that he can stand on the platform and make his speech. So the train will have to pull ahead far enough to leave Grant's coach at the west edge of the depot."

Brawmer nodded.

Drake continued to talk through logistics and finally said,

"We need to position ourselves on the roofs of that coal shed, the back end of the office of the lumber yard, and the station building, itself."

"Sounds good to me," Brawmer said, "except for one thing."

"George?"

"Yeah. The team's gonna be a mite smaller if he ain't feelin' a whole lot better in the mornin'."

The sun was going down when Drake and Brawmer boarded their horses for the night and headed for the hotel. When they entered the lobby, the clerk was registering a man and his wife who had come in on the train from Chicago. They were talking excitedly about President Grant's speech the next day.

"It's the biggest thing to ever happen to this town," the clerk said.

"If he only knew!" Drake said.

When the couple had picked up their luggage and headed for the stairs, Brawmer stepped up to the desk and said, "Our ailin' friend needs hot water so he can take a bath. Can we get that brought up to him some time soon?"

"Why, ah…yes. Within half an hour, sir."

"Fine. Thanks."

They found Macon lying in a pool of sweat, yet shivering from cold. His face was a sickly gray.

"I…I don't know what's the m-matter with me," he said. "Maybe I'm gonna die."

"Naw," Brawmer said. "It's just one of them fevers everybody gets now and then. It'll be gone soon."

"You've got to get better fast, George," Drake said. "We need you on one of those rooftops tomorrow."

"I...I guess you're right, Jake. Maybe the hot bath will m-make me better."

"You bet."

Drake moved to one of the two overstuffed chairs. "See that finger? It's going to put that lowdown Yankee in his grave! You boys can take your 'just-in-case' shots, but Grant'll be dead by the time your slugs hit him!"

"Who cares which bullet gets him—"

Brawmer's words were interrupted by a knock on the door. "Probably the hot water, Monty," he said, heading for the door.

In spite of his chill, it took Macon a few minutes to adjust to the heat of the water.

"How's that feel, George?" Brawmer asked.

"Good. Feels good."

"All right," Drake said, "Jake and I are going to eat supper at one of the cafés, then go back to the Broken Spur. When the water cools off, you get in bed. We'll look in on you when we get back."

Night had fallen when Brawmer and Drake finished their meal. They weaved their way up the boardwalk through milling cowboys to the Broken Spur Saloon.

They eased up to the bar and ordered drinks, then turned around to look the place over. They noticed two well-dressed men talking above the noise. Their Southern accents left no doubt on which side of the Mason-Dixon line they had been born. Drake and Brawmer walked over to their table.

"Well bless my old Southern heart, if we don't have some real gen-yoo-wine sons of the South here!" Drake said. "Where you gentlemen from?"

"Atlanta," the taller one replied. "And you gentlemen?"

"Tennessee."

"Well, put 'er there, brother!"

Drake shook hands and said, "Name's Monty Drake. And my partner here is Jake Brawmer."

"I'm Davis Claymore, and this is Cleve Holden." Claymore pointed to two empty chairs at the table. "Sit down, fellas."

The dim light of the street lamps left large patches of dark as Marshal Hickok and two of his deputies walked Main Street. Hickok's other deputies were patrolling a block away on the opposite side of the street.

"So how close to the president's coach do you want us to stand, Marshal?" Erwin asked.

"I'll talk to the bodyguards before the president appears, and see how they want us to position ourselves. Main thing is to keep a sharp eye for anything suspicious."

"Hope I get to shake his hand," Erwin said.

"I doubt you'll be able to get that close," Hickok said as they continued along the boardwalk, greeting people with a smile and a nod of the head.

Five Texans waited in the shadows between the Anderson General Store and the *Abilene Courier* building. A sixth man stood on the boardwalk, leaning against the front wall of the general store. His thoughts seethed with revenge. After what Hickok did to Leroy and Big Zack...

Suddenly he hurried into the dark void between the buildings. "Hickok's comin', fellas! Get ready! He's walkin' between two of his deputies."

✦

While the Texans were plotting, Deputies Keeton, Suttle, and Linn walked across the street toward Hickok and the other two deputies. As they drew up, Keeton said, "Marshal, you want to put a little variety in your life and switch sides of the street?"

"Sure," Hickok said. "No trouble so far?"

"Thought we had some in the alley over there a few minutes ago, but it turned out to be a couple of old men in a fist fight. Both were accusing the other of cheating in a card game. How about you?"

"Not so far. Well, c'mon, fellas, let's move to the other side. See you later."

The deputies waited till the marshal and Kymes and Erwin were on the other side, then headed up the street toward the general store.

As Marshal Hickok and his two deputies drew near the Wagon Wheel Saloon, Hickok stopped at the batwings and looked inside. The sound of a tinkling piano and the babble of voices filled the night air. After a few seconds, he turned back and said, "Everything seems quiet in—"

Hickok's words were cut short by the staccato sound of gunfire behind them.

"C'mon!" Hickok said, breaking into a run. "Our men may be in the middle of that!"

Several people had gathered in front of the general store and newspaper building as Hickok, Kymes, and Erwin came running up. The people quickly made an opening for the marshal

119

and his two deputies. One of the townsmen shone a lantern on the bodies.

All three deputies had been riddled with bullets from behind. Their guns were still in their holsters.

Hickok drew in a shuddering breath. "No way we can track them in the dark," he said, "and we have to be here for the president tomorrow. But when the president's gone, we'll go after them!"

Deputy Erwin rubbed his chin and said, "You know what it looks like to me, Marshal?"

"What?"

"Dave was in the middle, and he's got the most bullets in him. They must've been lying in ambush and didn't see us switch routes with…with our three pals here. They were gunning for you!"

Hickok lifted his hat and rubbed his temples. "You could be right, Floyd. Maybe a result of my jailing those two Texans tonight."

"Probably," Kymes said. "And whoever did it might not even leave town. They could be right here under our noses, and we'd never know it."

"Well, all we can do is wait till daylight and see if we can find a clue," Hickok said.

10

G<small>EORGE</small> M<small>ACON WAS FAST ASLEEP</small> when Monty Drake and Jake Brawmer returned to the Jayhawker Hotel.

"He still has a fever but he's not sweating like he was," Drake said. "Maybe he'll be lots better by morning."

"Sure hope so," Brawmer said. "He'll be glad to hear about those three deputies being gunned down tonight. Makes our job easier."

"Yep, and we'll tell him about Holden and Claymore in the morning."

Saturday, April 22, arrived with a clear sky and a brilliant sun peeking over the eastern horizon.

George Macon awoke, dripping with sweat. His fever was higher than ever. His mouth felt as dry as a sand pit, and the whole room seemed to be spinning around him. He forced himself to a sitting position on the edge of the bed and planted his feet on the floor. He waited for the dizziness to subside a little, then rose to his feet and stumbled toward the water pitcher on the dresser. He didn't bother to use the tin cup, but lifted the pitcher and gulped water, spilling it down the front of his long johns.

When the door opened behind him, he couldn't turn around without clutching the dresser to keep from falling. Drake and Brawmer exchanged worried looks.

"Hey!" Drake said, crossing the room. "Are you worse?"

"Yeah...you gotta get me to a doctor. My fever's higher than ever."

As Drake guided Macon to the bed, Brawmer said, "I guess you won't be in on the killin' today, George."

Macon wiped his face on the sheet and spoke with a slur as he said, "I'm sorry, fellas."

"Well, it's not quite the task it might have been," Brawmer said. "Three of Hickok's deputies were gunned down last night. He's got another one down with a gunshot wound. So that'll leave us only Hickok and the other two."

"Good," Macon said, licking his lips. "You...you've still got Grant's bodyguards—"

"We'll handle it, George," Drake said. Then to Brawmer, "We'd better take him to that clinic we saw yesterday."

"I doubt it's open this early. Let's you and me go eat breakfast. We'll take George to the clinic as soon as we get back."

Breanna descended the stairs at the Jayhawker Hotel and was surprised to see Gloria Cox seated in an overstuffed chair. Gloria smiled and rose to meet her.

"Good morning, Breanna."

"Good morning. To what do I owe this pleasure?"

"Doctor asked me to tell you that he won't come to the office until about ten. He delivered a baby just before midnight and didn't get home until almost six o'clock. He's trying to get a little sleep."

"Oh, of course," Breanna said. "The girls and I will take care of things."

Gloria laid a tender hand on Breanna's arm. "You are such a dear. I wish you were going to stay and work for David on a regular basis."

"I can't do that, but thank you for feeling that way."

Together they stepped outside into the early morning sunshine. "See you at the depot," Breanna said.

"You sure will. I wouldn't miss seeing the president for anything."

Bonnie Rand and Myra Dupree, who shared an apartment together, were just unlocking the door of the clinic when they saw Breanna hurrying toward them up the boardwalk.

It took the nurses only a few minutes to prepare the clinic for another day's business. Myra looked at the clock and said, "Breanna, we've got about twenty minutes before time to open up. Could we talk with you about something?"

"Of course."

"Well, Bonnie and I were up until one o'clock this morning talking about what you've told us about being saved, having our sins forgiven, and going to heaven."

Breanna's heart skipped a beat. She'd sown a lot of Scripture seed in their hearts since coming to Abilene.

Myra continued speaking. "Both of us were raised in formal churches back east and were taught that to go to heaven we have to live by the church's decrees and regulations. What you've told us is so different."

Breanna nodded and said, "Myra, nobody makes it to heaven by following the decrees and regulations of a religious system. Paul wrote in the Book of Ephesians that salvation is 'not of works lest any man should boast.' It's by grace." She opened her purse and pulled out a small Bible and handed it to Myra. "Here, honey, let's look at it. Read Ephesians 2:8–9 to us."

Myra read: "For by grace are ye saved through faith; and that not of yourselves: it is the gift of God: not of works, lest any man should boast."

"Do you see what God is telling us?" Breanna asked. "The very faith that saves the sinner is a gift from God, and we get that gift by hearing the Word of God. The Bible says that all of us started out in spiritual darkness. But when we hear the Word of God, it dispels the darkness.

"When God's light comes into our darkened hearts and minds, we see ourselves as sinners before a holy and righteous God. We could never pay the penalty for our own sins—nothing we could do would ever be enough. So Jesus came from heaven specifically to pay for our sins. On the cross He shed His precious blood and died. But if He had stayed in the grave, He couldn't save us. So on the third day, He rose from the grave and is alive to save every sinner who will come to Him in repentance, ask for forgiveness, and receive Him into his or her heart."

Bonnie's eyes glinted. "So Jesus did all that was needed by His death, burial, and resurrection. It's not religious ceremonies and rituals that save a sinner, it's Jesus Himself."

"That's it, honey. It's called grace. There's just one thing to do, ladies. Romans 10:13 says, 'For whosoever shall call upon the name of the Lord shall be saved.'"

"I'm ready," Bonnie said.

Myra nodded. "Me too."

Afterward, Breanna's student nurses wrapped their arms around her with tears flowing down their cheeks as Breanna thanked God for their salvation.

Only seconds after Breanna's "Amen," they heard heavy footsteps at the front door. Breanna rushed to unlock it. Two men stood there, supporting a man between them.

"Is the doctor in, ma'am?" Monty Drake asked. "Our friend, here, is real sick."

"Bring him in," Breanna said, stepping aside. "Take him through that door back there, where the nurses are standing."

Bonnie and Myra preceded the men into the examining room. "Put him on the table," Myra said.

Breanna followed and stepped up to feel the man's brow. "Bonnie," she said, "take his temperature."

While Bonnie went to the cupboard for the thermometer, Breanna asked, "Are you three friends?"

"Yes'm," Drake replied. "My name's Monty Drake. This here's Jake Brawmer. Our sick friend is George Macon."

Breanna nodded. "Well, Mr. Drake, Dr. Cox isn't here right now, but I'm a certified medical nurse. I can probably handle the problem."

"What do you think's wrong with George?"

"I'll have to ask some questions and examine him to find out."

"What kind of questions?" Brawmer asked.

"Well, for starters, how long has he had the fever?"

"About three days. It's worse now. Last night we thought maybe he was gettin' better, but he was worse than ever when he woke up this mornin'."

Breanna looked at Macon. "Mr. Macon, do you have a sore throat? Don't try to answer around the thermometer. Just nod or shake your head."

Macon shook his head no, his teeth chattering against the thermometer.

"Ears feel plugged up?"

Again he shook his head no.

"Pain in any part of your body?"

He shook his head for the third time.

125

"All right. As soon as we have your temperature, I'll have to do a thorough examination and see if I can find some sign of what's causing your fever."

Macon's eyes widened. *"You?"* he said, forgetting to keep his lips tight around the thermometer.

"Yes."

"I'll wait for the doctor!"

"Sir, I'm a professional nurse. I do examinations on men all the time."

Macon shook his head.

"Mr. Macon," Breanna said with a sigh, "you're a very sick man. If that temperature goes much higher, you could be in real trouble. The quicker we know what's wrong with you, the quicker we'll know how to treat you."

Suddenly there were wild shouts on the street, followed by sporadic gunfire.

"More cowboys whooping it up," Myra said. "A new herd came in from Texas late yesterday afternoon."

Breanna removed the thermometer and angled it toward the light. "Mr. Macon, your temperature is dangerously high. We can't wait for the doctor to get here." To Drake and Brawmer, she said, "You men wait in the outer office. I'll be out to talk to you as soon as I know what we're dealing with."

"Now, Mr. Macon, I want you to relax," Breanna said. "Let's see what we have here." She took off his shirt and carefully checked his chest, back, abdomen, underarms, wrists, feet, and ankles.

"What're you lookin' for?" Macon asked.

"Rash. Do you have diarrhea?"

"No. What do you think it is?"

"Well, I was checking for typhoid fever, but you have none of the symptoms except for fever. You have rash under your arms and on your wrists and ankles. Rash always goes with typhoid, but this rash is the wrong color. So we rule out typhoid."

"Whew! I'm glad for that!"

"My next guess would be cholera. High fever always goes with cholera, but you have none of the other symptoms. So we rule out cholera, too."

Breanna picked up a stethoscope and fitted it into her ears. "Could be influenza. I'll know in a minute."

The student nurses watched with interest as Breanna listened to Macon's chest, checked his respiratory tract, looked in his throat and ears, and thumped his abdomen. "Not influenza either."

Macon's teeth continued to chatter as Breanna stood back, scratched her head, and thought on the situation. "Mr. Macon, let me ask you this. While riding from Tennessee, have you slept on the ground much?"

"Yes, ma'am."

To the student nurses, Breanna said, "We've got to bathe his wrists and neck with cool water and see if we can get his temperature down before I examine him further."

"Do you think you know what it is?" Myra asked.

"I might."

"Well, tell us," Bonnie said, as she set a bucket of water next to the table.

"I think it's tick fever. If I'm right, we've got to get it out pronto. First let's undo his belt. A tick's favorite place to burrow under the skin is in the small of the back, right at the belt line."

Breanna touched Macon's shoulder and said, "All right, Mr. Macon, I want you over on your belly."

Breanna and Bonnie helped him roll over. Breanna immediately saw the inflamed area with a tiny dark spot beneath the skin in the small of his back. She nodded at Bonnie and said to Macon, "We found your problem, Mr. Macon. It's a tick, all right."

"Can you get it out?"

"Yes. Bonnie, I'll need alcohol and a pair of tweezers."

"Will…will I be all right, then, ma'am?"

"Getting the tick out will be a major step in the right direction, Mr. Macon, but the infection is already in your bloodstream. It's going to be a battle to get your fever down, and that's what we've got to concentrate on."

While Bonnie was collecting the alcohol and tweezers, Breanna went to the outer office and told Drake and Brawmer what she had found. When they asked if Macon would be all right, she said he was still in danger. She suggested they come back later in the day and check on him.

As Drake and Brawmer walked back toward the hotel, Drake said, "We don't have a choice, Jake. We'll just have to do the job on Grant without George."

"I understand that," Brawmer said, "but as soon as we kill Grant, we've got to ride hard and fast. People are bound to see us on those roofs when we open fire. There's no way we can ever come back for George. We just gonna leave him here?"

"Well, there's another alternative."

"What's that?"

"We could forget killing Grant."

Brawmer's eyes widened. "Oh, no! I hate leavin' George, but I hate Grant alive a whole lot more."

"Okay. Now, let's take us a walk over to the depot and make sure everything's set up like we figured. Don't want any unexpected problems."

11

WHEN DR. COX ENTERED THE CLINIC he found George Macon sitting in a galvanized tub of tepid water while the nurses poured more water over him.

"What's going on?" he asked, still looking sleepy after his long night.

"Keep it up, girls," Breanna said, as she told the doctor about Macon's condition.

Cox glanced at the man in the tub. "What's his temperature?"

"It was a 103.8 before we put him in the tub. We tried wood alcohol first, but it did absolutely nothing."

"Were you able to get all of the tick out?"

"Yes, sir."

"By what you're telling me, he's had that infected tick in his body for quite awhile."

"I'd say so, Doctor. Maybe better than a week."

Cox moved away and motioned for Breanna to follow. "Breanna, it may be too late for him."

"I realize that, Doctor."

"Well, you've done everything for him that you can. Just keep doing what you're doing."

✦

As the presidential train rolled westward past Bonner Springs, Kansas, Ulysses S. Grant stood in the swaying coach, combing his hair in front of the washstand. He would turn forty-nine in five days, and he noted the increase of gray strands in his sandy brown hair, especially at the temples.

His wife, Julia, sat in an overstuffed chair, looking out the window. "This is beautiful country, Ulys," she said. "So many hills, trees, and brush."

"Not like the part of Kansas you've never seen, dear," he replied. "The farther west you go, the flatter it becomes, and with comparatively fewer trees."

Julia was quiet a moment, then she said, "Bloody Kansas."

"What's that, dear?"

"I said *Bloody Kansas*. That's what they called it when John Brown and his men were killing pro-slavery people here before the War."

"Mm-hmm. You know, Julia, I've been thinking about shaving off my beard."

This brought Julia's head around. "Ulys, you're joking."

He turned with the comb in his hand and smiled. "Yes, I'm joking. I thought that would get your attention."

"Why, you wore a beard through the entire Civil War. You were elected president while wearing your beard."

"Far be it from me to ruin my image," he said with a chuckle, and lay down the comb. He crossed to her chair and kissed her tenderly.

There was a knock at the front door of the coach. Grant strode to the door and called, "What's the password?"

"Appomattox!"

The president opened the door and smiled at the leader of

his bodyguards, Lieutenant Randall Jeffries.

"Good morning, Mr. President," Jeffries said. He had fought under Grant the last year of the War. "Your breakfast is here, sir."

Just behind the lieutenant was a smiling black man in white shirt, jacket, and chef's cap, bearing a tray with covered plates and a steaming coffeepot. "Mornin', Mistah President."

"Good morning, yourself, Josiah."

Josiah carried the tray to the table and gave Julia a big smile. "Good mornin', Miz Grant." Then he turned to the president and said, "I fixed the favorite breakfast of the first lady—scrambled eggs, bacon, shoestring potatoes, an' pineapple slices."

Grant made a face. "Pineapple?"

Julia patted her husband's arm. "You don't have to eat the pineapple, Ulys."

"Oh, I forgot, Mistah President. There *is* a dish of strawberries on this tray somewhere."

"Well, now you're talking!" Grant said. "I was going to have Lieutenant Jeffries throw you off the train, but since you also thought of me, I'll refrain."

Josiah laughed and moved toward the door. "Hope y'all enjoy your breakfast."

"We will!" Grant said.

Randall Jeffries let Josiah through the door, then said, "I'm right outside this door if you need me, Mr. President."

While the Grants ate their breakfast, Ulysses glanced out the window and saw the shadows of the four bodyguards atop the coach reflected against the grassy slope, and two more on the platform. He looked at Julia and shook his head. "Sure doesn't leave a man much privacy, does it?"

Julia lowered her coffee cup, meeting his gaze. "But you're still alive, Ulys. You know how Mr. Lincoln often slipped away from his bodyguards. And that night in Ford's Theater, he ordered them to stay some distance away from his private box."

"His private box," Grant said, with iron in his voice. "The one you and I would have been sharing with him and Mary if we'd accepted their invitation."

Julia's thoughts went back to April 1865. She and Ulysses were in Washington, and the Lincolns had hosted them for dinner at the White House on Monday evening, April 10. During the meal, both the president and Mrs. Lincoln had invited them to Ford's Theater on that Friday night to see the play, *Our American Cousin*. The Lincolns were excited about seeing the play and urged the Grants to attend it with them.

Julia spoke out loud. "Ulys, I'm so glad we already had other plans. You remember, we tried to change them, but it turned out that we couldn't."

Grant nodded. "Yes…it was bad enough just hearing about it. How horrible it would have been to have actually seen it."

"Well, Ulys, darling, I would rather have less privacy and have my husband alive. Please promise me you won't ever order your bodyguards to give you space like poor Mr. Lincoln did."

Grant drained his coffee cup and wiped his mouth with a napkin. "I promise, dear."

"Thank you," she said softly. Then, "Ulys, you didn't eat much. Don't you want some more eggs and potatoes?"

"No, thank you. I've had enough. The strawberries are excellent but I just can't eat any more."

He left his chair and walked to the windows on the other side of the coach. Julia's heart warmed with love for him as he stood there, watching the grassy fields roll by.

He was a small man, standing five-feet-five inches, and was quite thin. Julia wished she could make him eat more. But since they were first married he had been a light eater and had never weighed more than a hundred and thirty pounds.

She smiled when she remembered what General Oliver O. Howard had said in his memoirs of the War about the first time he met Grant: "I had never seen a photograph of the general, and had never heard a physical description of him. From all I had heard of his military genius and courage in battle, I had conceived him to be very large, and of rough appearance, and was astonished by his small size—no larger than George McClellan—rather thin in flesh and very pale in complexion."

But what a giant he is inside! Julia thought.

She left the table and stepped up beside her "giant," who stood barely two inches taller than she. He turned and gathered her into his arms and kissed her. "I love you, Julia," he said.

"And I love you, darling."

Ulysses kept an arm around her, and they stood looking out the windows together. On a long, wide curve the "scapegoat engine" came into view some two hundred yards ahead.

"I'm really excited about seeing Abilene, Julia. The *real* Wild West, the newspapers call it. And it must be, or they wouldn't have hired Wild Bill Hickok to be their marshal."

Julia caught some of his enthusiasm and said with a giggle, "Who knows? Maybe we'll even get to see a real gunfight!"

It was nearly eleven o'clock when Davis Claymore and Cleve Holden left the Jayhawker Hotel and strode toward the railroad station. People were already heading that way to get a good vantage spot to see the president. Wagons, buggies, carriages, surreys, and riders on horseback created heavy traffic in the dusty streets—all converging on the depot.

Flags and banners decorated buildings on both sides of the track. Adults and children alike carried small American flags.

Abilene's brass band had been given a special spot on the station platform. They wore their brilliant red-white-and-blue uniforms, and their instruments glistened in the sun.

"They're really goin' all out," Holden said.

Claymore and Holden took note of Bromley Cook, chairman of the town council. A group of people were gathered around him, examining the large wooden "key to the city" in his hands.

When they had taken in the whole scene, Claymore said, "Let's go get our horses, Cleve."

Hostler Ray Carlton collected the money for the board of Monty Drake and Jake Brawmer's horses. "Thank you for the business, gentlemen," he said. "I know there are two other stables in this town, and I appreciate that you came here."

"Just looked like the right place when we rode into town yesterday," Brawmer said with a grin, slipping his rifle into its boot. "You brushed 'em down good, and they look well-fed."

Drake eased his long-barreled weapon into the saddle sheath and said, "Keep our friend's horse here till he gets better. He knows which stable."

"Of course, Mr. Drake."

Drake took the reins of his horse and swung into the saddle. Brawmer did likewise.

"You gentlemen aren't going to leave town before President Grant arrives, are you?"

"'Fraid we have to," Drake said. "Got some pressing business down the trail."

Brawmer touched his hat brim. "Thanks, Ray."

They were about to guide their horses through the stable's corral gate when two men on foot appeared.

Ray Carlton smiled. "Hello, Mr. Claymore...Mr. Holden. You wanting your horses?"

"Yes," Claymore said.

"Okay. I'll saddle them up for you."

Claymore looked up at the men on horseback. "Well, if it ain't our Southern cousins! How're you doin', Monty...Jake?"

"Fair to middlin'," Brawmer replied.

"I see you gentlemen know each other," Ray said. "I guess that shouldn't surprise me. I'm told you Southerners are all kin in one way or another."

"You got that right," Cleve said. He squinted against the sun, which was almost at its zenith in the sky. "You boys ain't leavin' town before the president gets here, are you?"

"Have to," Drake said. "Got important business up the trail."

"Well, that's too bad. Hate to see you miss the excitement."

"Life does have its little sacrifices," Brawmer said. "Looks like our sacrifice today is not gettin' to see the most important man in the country."

Ray Carlton still hadn't moved. "How come you're here to get your horses, Mr. Claymore, if you're stayin' for the big doin's?" he asked.

"We have to leave as soon as the train pulls out. Best thing is for us to have our animals ready."

"Makes sense," Brawmer said. "Maybe we'll see you fellas down below the Mason-Dixon line sometime."

"Just could happen," Claymore said.

With that, Drake and Brawmer rode into the broad, dusty street as if they were heading out of town. At the next corner, they took a side street and made their way to the rear of the railroad station building. There were several other horses tethered there.

"Hey, this is better than we'd planned," Drake said. "This way, our horses won't be noticed at all."

A buggy drove in and parked near the saddle horses before Brawmer and Drake had dismounted, but the family left the buggy and headed around the station building without even glancing their way.

"Okay," Drake said, scanning the area and slipping his rifle out of its boot. "I'm going up. Be careful nobody sees you over there."

Brawmer grinned and lifted his rifle from its sheath.

In spite of the nurses' efforts, George Macon's temperature climbed to 104.8 degrees. His head hung low, and most of the time he seemed unaware of his surroundings.

Doctor Cox finished taking the latest thermometer reading and shook his head. "This is getting us nowhere," he said. "We might as well put him back on the cot. The infection is well-saturated throughout his system. The only thing we can do is keep putting cool water on his wrists and neck."

Breanna looked at the clock. "Doctor, you and the girls go ahead to the depot. I'll take care of George."

"No," Cox said. "All of you go; I'll stay with him."

"Doctor," Breanna said, "just help me get him dried off and onto the cot. I'm staying with him. I insist."

Before the others could protest, Breanna threw up her hands and repeated, "I insist!" and then added, "If you don't get going, you'll miss the speech."

Breanna watched the door close behind the doctor and student nurses. She felt keen disappointment that she would miss seeing the president and first lady, but *somebody* had to stay here, and it might as well be her. As she knelt beside her patient she could see a deathly pallor beneath the sheen of sweat. He looked at her with glassy eyes.

"Am...am I goin' get well?" he mumbled.

She took the thermometer from a tin cup of alcohol next to the cot and placed it under his tongue. "Don't talk now, George. I need to get your temperature again. We're doing everything we can to make you well."

She dipped a heavy towel into the water bucket and applied its coolness to both sides of his neck. She bathed his wrists and then his neck again.

When she glanced up again the clock read 12:07. The train must be late since she hadn't heard the brass band and the cheering crowd.

She pulled the thermometer from Macon's mouth and almost gasped...105 degrees. The man was going to die. She wished there had been an opportunity to give him the gospel.

Macon's breathing was shallow. His eyes were closed and his mouth sagged. Breanna lightly slapped his cheeks. "George..."

No response.

She slapped him harder this time. "George!"

He opened his eyes slightly.

"George, don't go to sleep on me. You must stay awake."

"Huh?"

"I said you must stay awake!"

His eyes drooped but didn't close.

Breanna worked feverishly, continuing to press cool water to vital spots. Suddenly she heard the shrill blast of a train whistle drowned out by the blare of the brass band and the loud cheering of the crowd. There was another blast, followed by more chugging, then Breanna remembered that they were probably greeting the "scapegoat engine."

✦

Marshal Hickok and his two deputies moved toward the rear coach of the train as it chugged to a stop. Each of the lawmen carried a Winchester .44 repeater rifle. The president's eight bodyguards were stationed on both sides of the presidential car, each wearing a sidearm and carrying lever action repeater carbines.

The noonday sun glinted off the badges of Hickok and his deputies, and one man moved forward to meet them. He nodded in strict military fashion and said, "I'm Lieutenant Randall Jeffries, chief of the president's bodyguards."

"We're here at your bidding, Lieutenant," Hickok said. "What would you like us to do?"

"My men and I will station ourselves in a semicircle around the platform, Marshal. If you will flank them on one side, and your deputies on the other, you can help us search the crowd and the surrounding area, not to mention give us more firepower, if needed."

"All right," Hickok said. "Deputies, you take that side over there, and I'll take this one. That all right, Lieutenant?"

"Yes, sir. But before we set up, President Grant has asked to meet you."

"Really? I...I didn't realize he knew who I am."

Jeffries smiled. "We all know about the famous lawman Wild Bill Hickok, sir."

"Well, I'm deeply honored. But won't this delay the president's speech? The train's already late."

"It will only take a minute; he's waiting right now. Shall we go in?"

The band continued to play patriotic marches, and the crowd cheered loudly as Jeffries led the marshal up the steps of the coach. Grant had been watching through the curtain, and opened the door. The crowd roared louder at the sight of the door opening, even though they hadn't yet seen the president.

Inside, a smiling Ulysses S. Grant shook Marshal Hickok's hand in greeting, and Julia watched him as she stood a step behind her husband. The look in her eyes and the smile on her face reflected the excitement she felt at meeting the famous marshal.

George Macon tossed his head from side to side and began mumbling incoherently. His delirium didn't surprise Breanna after such a high fever. She could pick up bits and pieces of what he was saying, but none of it made sense.

"Roofs…train…"

"George," she said, squeezing his cheeks between her thumb and fingers. "What are you trying to say?"

"Roofs…train…"

"Train roofs, George? What about train roofs?"

Grant…"

"Grant? President Ulysses S. Grant?"

George Macon did not respond to her question but continued to speak disjointedly.

Breanna cupped his face in her hands and shook his head. "George, what are you talking about? What do you mean by all this?"

"Rifles…shoot…Monty, Jake…shoot…"

Suddenly Breanna's stomach clenched with fear, and she bolted out the door.

12

BREANNA HELD HER SKIRT ANKLE HIGH and ran as fast as she could for the depot a block and a half away.

Breathless, a stitch knifing at her side, she ran. They were going to shoot the president right in front of hundreds of people!

She ran...thinking of Ford's Theater in Washington...of John Wilkes Booth.

She ran. Horror was a living thing inside her, crawling and hissing with the whisper of death if she didn't get there in time!

She ran, her heart pounding so hard her chest hurt.

Stragglers were leaving their buggies and saddles as she drew nearer the depot unnoitced. The roar of the crowd and the loud blare of the brass band thundered in her ears and seemed to fill the whole world.

She pressed her legs for more speed and somehow found the strength.

Just a little farther. She could see the crowd waving their flags. Now the rear of the president's private coach was in view. There were eight uniformed men in a semicircle around the coach's platform. She recognized Deputies Wally Kymes and Floyd Erwin on her left and Marshal Hickok on the right.

The president had not yet put in an appearance. Now she

was shoving people out of the way, gasping, "Excuse me! Excuse me, please!" Some paid her no attention, while others looked at her askance.

Roofs! They were on the rooftops. But which buildings? If these people would only get out of my way...

Suddenly the rear door of the coach opened. At the same time, Breanna saw movement atop the station building.

The roar of voices and the blare of the band increased as Breanna drew within forty feet of the coach. "Mr. President, no!" she yelled. "Riflemen on the rooftops!" The deafening din drowned out her voice.

Breanna slipped past a bodyguard who was thrown off because the runner was a woman and obviously unarmed with her hands holding up her skirts. She was able to charge up the steps of the platform and catch a glimpse of a dark-headed woman behind the president before she lunged. Grant's attention was drawn to the blond woman coming at him, but his only reaction was to flinch a split second before she dived for his legs and knocked him over.

The president fell on top of Breanna as a bullet zinged above them, plowing into the carpeted floor of the coach. Julia Grant had already jumped out of the doorway.

The instruments abruptly stopped playing, and screams filled the air as the bodyguards scanned the buildings and the crowd for a rifleman.

Marshal Hickok found him first, atop the station building, and was bringing his carbine to bear as a second shot split the air from the opposite side of the tracks. The second bullet came lower and ripped through the sleeve of Breanna's dress before splintering the doorway.

Monty Drake swore, worked the lever of his repeater rifle, and raised up to fire again. Just as Drake squeezed the trigger,

Marshal Hickok's bullet hit him in the forehead, killing him instantly.

Drake's slug chewed into the back wall of the coach, missing Breanna and the president by inches.

Lieutenant Jeffries spotted Jake Brawmer on the roof of the lumber yard office and pointed him out to his men as he darted onto the coach platform to shield the president.

The crowd panicked and began to run in every direction. The band members dropped their instruments and ran for cover.

Brawmer was so intent on killing Grant that he was like a madman, tossing all caution aside. He raised up, steadied his weapon, and took aim just as a staccato of rifle shots echoed among the buildings and railroad cars. He slumped over the low wall, hovering there momentarily before falling headlong to the ground below.

Hickok and his two deputies dashed to the rear of the station building and began climbing onto the roof to make sure the other would-be assassin was dead, even though all firing had stopped.

Some thirty yards away, Davis Claymore backed away from the thick-bodied cottonwood tree where he had stationed himself as a back-up for Drake and Brawmer.

Cleve Holden rushed to join Claymore behind a small shed. He could hardly contain his anger. "That nurse messed it all up, Davis!" he said. "I couldn't get a clear shot once she knocked him down."

Davis Claymore swung a fist through the air and ejected a string of profanity, ending with, "I wish they'd killed *her!* There's nothing we can do now. That stinkin' Grant is still alive, and we're cold meat if we try to take him out now."

"We best get outta town," Cleve said.

They walked slowly toward their horses. The uniformed men were still looking in every direction for any sign of more assassins, and Hickok and his deputies were now on the roof of the station building. The stunned crowd was just beginning to move from their frozen positions.

Davis and Claymore leisurely trotted out of town so as not to attract attention. When they were out of sight, they put their horses to a gallop and rode hard for a half-hour then hauled up at a small creek to let the horses drink.

Holden looked back toward Abilene and said, "It eats my innards out to know that ol' Useless S. Grant is still breathing."

"Mine, too," Claymore said. "That day we got the telegram in Emporia from Monty, telling us to meet them in Abilene at the Broken Spur, I didn't know what to expect. Then when they told us the news about Grant coming to Abilene…"

Holden spit in the dirt. "If it hadn't been for that stupid nurse—what's her name?"

"Breanna Baylor."

"Yeah. If it hadn't been for her, Grant would be dead now. Instead, Jake's dead for sure. No man could live with that many bullets in him. And Monty's probably dead, too. It looked to me like he got it in the head. And George. Sick as he is, he'll probably die, too." Holden rubbed his chin. "Hey, I just thought of something."

"What?"

"I saw that nurse come running from Main Street when she headed for Grant's coach. She must've been at the clinic taking care of George."

"Yeah! George must've got cold feet and told her about the setup!"

Holden's eyes darkened. "They both gotta die, Davis. Him for blabbing it, and her for interfering."

Lieutenant Jeffries rolled off the president and gave him a hand up. A shaken Ulysses S. Grant then took both of Breanna's hands in his and lifted her, saying, "Young lady, you just saved my life. I—"

"Oh, Ulys!" Julia cried, wrapping her arms around her husband. "Thank God you're still alive!" She burst into tears and great racking sobs shook her body.

Grant held her close, patting her back. "It's all right, now, honey. I'm fine, and it looks like our bodyguards have killed the men who did the shooting."

"Sir, let's move you and Mrs. Grant inside the coach until we know there's no more danger," Lieutenant Jeffries said. Then to Breanna: "You, too, Miss. There could be more assassins."

Breanna saw Dr. Cox and Myra and Bonnie in the crowd. They were looking directly at her. She started to tell the lieutenant that she would go to her friends, but he was already ushering her into the coach.

"I'll be right back, sir," Jeffries said, and closed the door.

Grant started to speak to Breanna, but Julia beat him to it. She hugged Breanna and said, "You wonderful, brave dear! You saved my husband's life!"

"Yes, young lady," the president said, "you could have been hit just as easily as I!"

Julia kept hold of one of Breanna's hands and looked at her admiringly. "That was a very unselfish thing you just did."

"Mrs. Grant, I didn't give the danger any consideration. All that mattered was that I warn the president."

"How did you happen to see the shooters?" the president asked.

"I didn't, sir. I learned about the assassination plan just a few minutes before you stepped out on the platform. I knew the shooters were on the roofs, but I didn't know *which* roofs."

"How? Who told you? Was it someone in the crowd?"

"No. I was a block and a half away. You see—"

The door opened and Lieutenant Jeffries looked in. "Excuse me, sir. Both riflemen are dead, and my men have secured the area. A Mr. Bromley Cook is chairman of the town council and wants to know if he should send the crowd home."

"No, I'll still make my speech, if the people will give us a few minutes to collect ourselves."

"I'll tell him, sir. I'm sure the crowd won't care if they have to wait."

Jeffries moved back onto the platform and closed the door. They could hear the town council chairman tell the crowd that the president would appear with Mrs. Grant and make his speech in a few moments. There was a rousing cheer, and the band struck up a happy tune.

While the crowd waited and the band played, President Grant looked at Breanna's attire. "You must be a nurse."

"Yes, sir."

"And I see by the rip in your sleeve that you almost took one of those bullets."

Breanna looked down and her face blanched.

Julia rushed forward and hugged Breanna impulsively again. Then holding her at arm's length, she said, "How can we ever thank you, Miss— Oh! We don't even know your name!"

Grant shook his head. "Forgive us. You can see we're a bit rattled. Please. Tell us your name."

"Breanna Baylor."

"What a lovely name!" Julia said. "And it is *Miss* Baylor?"

"Yes, ma'am."

Outside, the band continued to play, and the crowd noise was gaining in volume.

"Well, Miss Breanna Baylor," the president said, "how can I ever thank you? If you hadn't knocked me down—"

"There's no need to thank me, sir. The fact is, the president's life is more important than my own."

"You leave me without words, Miss Baylor," Grant said.

"I'm just glad you're alive and unharmed, sir."

Grant then turned toward the door. "Well, Julia, I think we'd better go out there now."

The first lady dabbed at her eyes with a hanky and nodded.

Grant opened the door a crack and found himself looking at Lieutenant Jeffries's back. The lieutenant turned and smiled. "You ready, sir?"

The bodyguards were back in place, as were the lawmen.

Grant turned to Breanna and said, "Julia and I would like to have a little more time with you after I make the speech, Miss Baylor. Maybe some tea?"

"I would be honored, sir, but don't you have a schedule to keep?"

A soft smile graced the president's lips. "Miss Baylor, if it weren't for you, I wouldn't be going anywhere except back to Washington in a coffin. The schedule can be changed. Besides, I'm very curious to learn how you found out about the assassination plot. Please come out and stand with us on the platform."

Breanna blushed. "Oh, no, sir. I couldn't do that. I—"

"I insist."

"Here, dear," Julia said, taking Breanna by the hand. "Stand next to me."

While the applause and cheering went on, Julia pulled Breanna along with her and stepped up beside her husband.

Grant did not try to quiet the crowd. They had been through a shock, and he wanted them to let it out.

Breanna looked down and saw Dr. Cox and her coworkers edging their way up to one of the bodyguards. Dr. Cox said something to him, and the soldier turned and looked at Breanna, asking with his eyes and hand signals if she was all right. Breanna nodded, then said to Julia above the din, "That man is Dr. David Cox, who owns the clinic where I work. It's important that I speak to him."

"Of course, dear. Just hurry back before Ulys starts to make his speech."

Breanna stepped down from the platform under the watchful eyes of the nearby bodyguards and moved up to Dr. Cox and Myra and Bonnie.

"You were marvelous, Breanna!" Cox said above the roar of the crowd.

Myra and Bonnie shook their heads emphatically. Then Myra said, "Breanna, we just saw the bodies of the assassins. They were the two men who brought George Macon into the office."

"Yes, and George was in on it, too," Breanna said. "That's how I learned about it. He became delirious and began to mumble things that I soon put together. I ran here as fast as I could. The Grants have asked me to stand with them on the platform while he makes his speech, then spend a little time with them in the coach before the train pulls out. One of you needs to go see about George."

"Okay, Breanna," the physician said. "Gloria's over here with some of our friends. I'll go back to the clinic and leave her here so at least part of the Cox family is represented. Myra...Bonnie, you stay here and take in the speech. I'll see all three of you later."

Cox went to his wife, spoke to her briefly, and hurried toward the clinic.

When Breanna turned around, Bromley Cook was speaking to the president from the bottom step of the platform. Grant nodded, and Cook ascended the steps, carrying the wooden "key to the city." Julia motioned for Breanna to hurry.

Julia and Breanna stood behind the president and the council chairman as Cook raised his hands for silence. It took a few seconds to bring the crowd to order. When all was quiet, Cook welcomed the president and Mrs. Grant to Abilene and presented him the key, and the people cheered and applauded as the band played.

Grant raised his hands. Instantly the crowd grew quiet. "Ladies and gentlemen," he began, "Mrs. Grant and I were very excited about stopping here in Abilene. We wanted to meet all of you people, and we were especially interested in meeting your famed marshal, Wild Bill Hickok."

Flags waved and people cheered. Hickok looked a bit embarrassed, and nodded at the crowd.

"I want to express my deep appreciation to Marshal Hickok and his men, and to my personal bodyguards under the leadership of Lieutenant Randall Jeffries for how quickly they reacted when the shooting started a little while ago. The assassins were quickly disposed of, and the area rendered safe for all of us.

"Julia and I met someone else today—a gallant little lady who literally risked her life to save mine, as all of you witnessed a while ago. Most of you know her, I'm sure."

Julia urged Breanna forward and the president took Breanna's hand, smiling warmly at her. "Ladies and gentlemen, I present to you the heroine of this day, Nurse Breanna Baylor!"

The crowd went wild, applauding and whistling their

approval. Breanna's features tinted as she smiled modestly, wishing she could somehow melt away.

"In my career as a soldier," Grant said, "I have learned the meaning of such words as valor, courage, bravery, boldness, and gallantry. All of these words fit this lady who saved my life today. She learned of the assassination plot only minutes before it was to take place and risked her own life to save mine. She gave no thought to her own safety." He turned to her then and said, "Miss Breanna Baylor, you have grit! Thank you for what you did."

While the band played and the crowd roared their approval, a photographer from the *Abilene Courier* hastened to a spot between the tracks with a tripod and camera. The president motioned for Julia to move up beside him.

"Smile and hold it!" shouted the photographer, ducking his head under the camera's cloth and raising the powder stick.

The powder flashed, and the crowd broke into applause. Then President Grant made a short speech, telling the people of Abilene of the great plans he had to expand the West and encourage people to move there. He felt sure he would be able to recommend to Congress that funds be provided for roads and bridges.

The people gave Grant a long ovation, then he waved and said, "Let's go inside, Julia."

Grant's personal secretary, who rode in another coach, was standing at the bottom of the platform. As the women moved inside, Grant leaned down and said, "Charles, make a note." Then the secretary scribbled in a little notebook as the president talked to him.

When the president was finished, Charles Broadman nodded and put away the notebook. "She deserves whatever you do for her, sir," he said.

"And Charles, will you alert Josiah that we want hot tea in

our coach as soon as possible?"

"Yes, sir," Broadman said, and hurried away.

Ten minutes later, Breanna was seated comfortably in the presidential coach with the president and first lady, holding a cup of tea. Outside, the crowd drifted away, but the eight bodyguards continued to surround the coach.

Grant took a sip of tea and set his eyes on Breanna. "All right, Miss Baylor. Tell us how you learned about the plan to assassinate me."

Breanna kept it as brief as possible, closing by telling the Grants how she had felt, trying to reach the depot in time.

"Miss Baylor, you are indeed a woman of great courage and grit."

Breanna smiled. "Let me tell you where my grit comes from, sir...Mrs. Grant."

Both leaned forward to hear what she would say.

"I am a Christian," Breanna said. "The Lord Jesus Christ has lived in my heart now for several years. Ever since I came to know Him, I've had a boldness of life that I never had before. Not only in telling others about what He did for me at Calvary but in all other facets of my life."

"I see," Grant said, and nodded. "You sound exactly like my long-time friend, Oliver Howard, Miss Baylor."

"*General* Oliver Howard, sir?"

"Yes. He was under my command for about two years in the War. Never missed a chance to put in a word for the Lord. Quite often quoted Scripture to me, trying to get me to become a Christian, too."

"I recall hearing that General Howard is a Christian. But you have never opened your heart to Jesus, sir?"

"No, though I've thought a lot about it."

"And you, Mrs. Grant?"

"The same," Julia replied. "I have a cousin who's a preacher. He's talked to both of us about it on several occasions."

Breanna scooted forward in her chair. "I urge both of you to take care of it before it's too late. "

The president looked at Breanna kindly. "Thank you for the admonition, Miss Baylor. Oliver has admonished me in the same manner. Julia and I will seriously consider what you've said. Won't we, dear?"

"Yes," the first lady said, nodding.

"Now, let me ask you, Miss Baylor," the president said, "is Abilene your home town?"

"I was born in Kansas, sir, but my home is now in Denver, Colorado."

"I see. So what brings you to Abilene?"

"I'm a traveling certified medical nurse. I work out of Dr. Lyle Goodwin's office in Denver. When I'm at home any length of time, I work at Denver's new Mile High Hospital. My brother-in-law, Dr. Matthew Carroll, is chief administrator there."

"Any plans to marry, dear?" Julia asked.

"Yes, ma'am. Let me tell you about my fiancé…"

Breanna set her gaze on the president and said, "Sir, you will recall that Chief U.S. Marshal Solomon Duvall has written to you often, telling you of volunteer work being done for him by a man called John Stranger…"

"Of course! I'd like to see Duvall pin a badge on that man, but so far he hasn't been able to get it done."

"You'd have to know John to understand, sir. He likes the freedom of volunteering. And he's independently wealthy. He doesn't need a deputy marshal's salary."

Julia's eyes widened. "Are you telling us you're engaged to this John Stranger, dear?"

"Yes, I am."

The president's face had taken on a sharp interest at the mention of John Stranger. "I've wanted to meet the man you're engaged to for a long time, Miss Baylor. I hope someday I will."

"I hope so too, sir."

Grant leaned forward in his chair. "Tell me. His real name isn't *Stranger*, is it?"

"That's what everybody calls him," Breanna said.

Grant chuckled. "Mm-hmm. Just what I thought. That's what they *call* him, but he has another name, doesn't he?"

Breanna set her cup in her saucer. "Mr. President, you and Mrs. Grant have honored me greatly by letting me spend this time with you. I'm sure you need to be moving on down the track, so I really should let you do it."

Grant shook his head and grinned but decided not to press her on the subject. He rose to his feet and said, "My deepest gratitude, Breanna Baylor, for saving my life."

Julia wrapped her arms around Breanna, saying, "My deepest gratitude, also, Breanna."

The three of them moved to the door and stopped. Grant said, "Miss Baylor, would it be all right if the president of the United States gave you a hug?"

She smiled warmly. "Of course."

After Grant gave her a gentlemanly embrace, Breanna stepped out on the platform and found Lieutenant Jeffries waiting for her. She noticed a small group of people near the rear of the coach. Town council chairman Bromley Cook was with them, as was the photographer who had taken her picture with the president earlier. At the same time she saw Bonnie Rand, heading her way.

"Ma'am," Jeffries said "Myron Wells, editor-in-chief of the *Abilene Courier* is here, along with two reporters and his photographer. They would like to talk to you and get another picture of you standing near the coach. Would that be all right?"

"All right, Lieutenant," she said. "But first I think my friend Bonnie, here, wants to say something to me."

Bonnie came close and said in a low tone, "Breanna, when Dr. Cox arrived at the clinic, George Macon was dead."

13

ON FRIDAY EVENING, MAY 5, young Bodie Brolin sold his last packet of toothpicks and box of matches a few minutes after dusk. A cool breeze was coming off the Hudson River, but compared to the icy winds of the past winter, Bodie told himself it wasn't bad at all. He pulled up his sweater collar and headed for home.

Bodie dreaded going home. His father was staying drunk for longer periods of time, and he was making life a nightmare for his son. Bodie had turned fourteen on April 26, and Louis Brolin had not even mentioned it. Maybe it hadn't even crossed his mind, or if it did, he didn't care enough about his son to wish him a happy birthday.

When Bodie came within a couple of blocks from where Jared Hamilton and his sister and brother lived in the alley, he found himself envying them. They had to sleep in boxes, but at least they didn't have a drunken father to put up with.

Bodie was glad that Jared had a steady job working afternoons in Koehler's grocery store. This assured him of regular income, along with his morning job selling newspapers, and made it easier for Susan and Nathan. They stayed with Jared all day, but at least now they were at the grocery store in the afternoons instead of walking the streets while Jared looked for work.

Bodie spoke to the lamplighters who were slowly working their way down the street. One of them called after him, asking how his day had gone. He called back that he'd sold everything he was carrying. The lamplighter responded by saying that someday Bodie would be a millionaire.

Bodie laughed and moved on.

Soon he was approaching a dark alley. Its black maw looked like a living thing that wanted to swallow him whole. He grinned to himself, thinking, Bodie, you pass alleys all the time. Nothing has ever swallowed you yet.

Suddenly, Bodie thought he saw a movement at the edge of the alley. His heart slammed against his ribs and he hastened his pace.

He was almost past when he heard a shuffle of feet behind him. He wheeled to see several shadowed figures coming at him on the run. He could just make out the faces of Mike McDuff and his three pals, Marty Lukacher, Truxtun Gowen, and Archie Boyle. There were three toughs with them whom Bodie had seen around, but he didn't know their names.

It wasn't in Bodie Brolin to run, though their demeanor sent an icy prickling down his spine. He turned to meet them head-on. When they skidded to a halt, he asked, "Something I can do for you, boys?"

Without a word, they seized Bodie and dragged him toward the alley. He struggled, but there were too many. When they had him in the darkness, away from the street, they flung him down on the ground and pinned him in a spread-eagle position, face-down.

Mike McDuff knelt beside Bodie and dug his fingers into his hair. "I've been nursin' a grudge, Brolin."

"About what?"

"That day you jumped in to help Jared Hamilton. You shoulda stayed out of it."

"Jared's my friend. He'd do the same for me."

"Well, you're gonna be sorry you interfered. You're gonna pay now."

Anger rushed through Bodie like a river of fire, replacing his fear. "You can't make me pay by yourself, though, can you, Mike?"

"Whaddya mean?"

"You've got to have your pals help you."

"Oh, yeah? I ain't scared of you!"

"Then send your cronies away and fight me one-on-one, just the two of us."

McDuff didn't reply.

"Well?"

"Shut up." McDuff stood up, mumbling under his breath. He looked around in the deep shadows and found a length of broken fence post. He gripped it snugly in both hands as he stood over Bodie. "You're gonna be sorry for shootin' off your mouth, too, Brolin."

Bodie's heart tripped against his ribs as McDuff brought the post down on his head.

When Bodie came to, the dark objects of the alley looked like formless blurs on the edge of his vision. It hurt to raise his head. He wondered how long he had been unconscious.

A trickle of blood ran down his face. He hurt everywhere, but especially in his left leg.

The inside of his mouth was so dry that he could hardly swallow. Bodie summoned all of his strength and raised up on his knees. A fiery stream of pain lanced through his left leg, making his head spin. The ground felt like it was rolling beneath him.

He managed to get to a sitting position, then he crawled to the side of a building and used the wall to work his way to his feet.

He stumbled his way between lampposts and had gone less than half a block when he started to feel faint. He wrapped his arms around a lamppost and eased himself to the ground. Two carriages passed by, going in opposite directions. Bodie raised a hand and tried to call out, but the carriages were soon out of sight.

Suddenly the big clock in the tower of Bruton's department store on Park Avenue began to chime. Bodie counted the strokes. Eight o'clock.

He thought of Jared. The place in the alley where Jared, Susan, and Nathan lived was little more than a block away. Jared always finished his work at Koehler's store by six o'clock; they would be in the alley by now. I can make it that far, he thought.

Jared had stayed late at the store to help Mr. Koehler do inventory. Susan and Nathan watched them while munching on sandwiches Mrs. Koehler had made for their supper.

When the big clock on Bruton's department store clanged out nine chimes, Oscar Koehler closed his notebook and sighed. "Okay, Jared, that's it. I can place the order for new goods in the morning."

Jared nodded, then turned to his sister and brother. "You two ready to go home?"

They stood up without reply and moved to where Jared stood.

To the store owner, Jared said, "Tell Mrs. Koehler thanks again for feeding us, sir. We'll see you tomorrow afternoon."

↑

Susan and Nathan pressed close to their older brother as the three made their way toward their alley "home." They saw lights going out in apartment windows on both sides of the street, and there was little traffic.

They were within a block of their alley when they saw a policeman standing under a street lamp, talking to two men. As the children drew near, the men thanked the officer and walked away.

"It's Officer Ryan," Susan said.

"Hi, kids," burly Sean Ryan said, twirling a nightstick in one hand. His badge reflected the dull light of the lantern overhead. "Aren't you on the street a bit late?"

"Yes, sir," Jared said. "We were helping Mr. Koehler do inventory. We just got done."

"I see. Well, I'll walk you to your alley. There's a lot of meanness on these streets at night."

"Thank you," Jared said.

Soon Ryan slowed his pace. "Well, here's your alley. You kids take care of yourselves."

"Thank you, Officer Ryan."

Jared took hold of Susie's and Nathan's hands as he led them into the alley. This particular block had been occupied only by them, but Jared had not ruled out that other street urchins might show up. So far, they hadn't.

They were almost to their boxes when they heard a moan.

Jared pulled Susan and Nathan to a stop. "You two wait here. I'll check—"

"Jared," a hoarse voice cut in. "It's me…Bodie."

"Bodie!" Jared knelt beside the dark form. "What's wrong, Bodie? Are you hurt?"

Bodie worked his tongue against the dryness in his mouth. "I think my left leg is broken."

Jared bent close, squinting. "Is that blood on your head?" He jumped to his feet. "I'll get Officer Ryan! He can't be far away. Susie, you and Nathan stay here with Bodie!"

Officer Ryan was walking his beat, making sure the doors of the stores and shops along the street were securely locked, when he heard a voice calling, "Officer Ryan! Officer Ryan!"

He was surprised to see Jared Hamilton again so soon. "Why, hello, Jared."

Jared was panting hard. "You know...my friend, Bodie...Brolin, sir."

"Yes."

"Somebody beat him up...real bad. He's in our alley. Will you come?"

"I sure will, son. Let's go."

Moments later, Officer Ryan knelt beside Bodie with the Hamilton children at his side. He wrapped his bandanna around Bodie's head and said, "Let me get this bleeding under control, then I'll go for an ambulance. Who did this to you?"

"It was Mike McDuff and his hoodlums, Officer Ryan," Susan said. "Bodie told Nathan and me."

"McDuff, eh? No-good hooligan. How many did he have with him?"

"Six," Bodie said.

"Will you arrest them?" Jared asked.

"Wouldn't do any good."

"Why not?"

"They'd deny it. It'd just be Bodie's word against theirs. Without proof or eyewitnesses, the judge wouldn't be able to prosecute them. Is there bad blood between you and those no-goods, Bodie?"

"Yes. They...they never have liked me...and I don't like them. They make it tough on those of us...on the streets...who work for a living. A few weeks ago...when McDuff and his pals were beating up on Jared...I—"

"He jumped in to help me," Jared interrupted. "Made those dirty bullies mad. They've just been waiting for a chance to get Bodie alone and do this to him."

"I just wish someone had seen this happen tonight," Ryan said. "I'd love to put those hoodlums behind bars." He knotted the bandanna. "There. That should slow the bleeding. I'm going after an ambulance."

"Could we go along, Officer Ryan?" Jared asked.

"I'm afraid not, son. Only family can ride in an ambulance."

"But how will we know how Bodie is?" Susan asked.

"There's no way you can know, kids," Ryan said. "If I was going along, I would see to it you were given word on Bodie's condition. Since I can't leave my beat, I won't know either."

When he saw their expressions in the dim light, he took a deep breath and sighed. "Okay, here's what I'll do. I'm sure Bodie will have to be in the hospital for a day or two, at least. Before I come on duty tomorrow afternoon, I'll stop by the hospital and see about Bodie. You find me tomorrow, and I'll let you know how he's doing."

On Tuesday morning, May 9, Jared was on his usual corner at Thirty-eighth and Broadway, selling papers. Susan and Nathan sat on the curb nearby, speaking to people who had become accustomed to seeing them with Jared.

A well-dressed man in his early thirties reached into his pocket and smiled. "I'll take one of your papers, there, lad."

"Yes, sir!" Jared said, folding the paper and handing it to him. The man dropped a silver dollar in Jared's palm, thanked him, and walked away.

"Just a minute, sir," Jared said. "Your change. I owe you ninety-five cents."

The man stopped, made a half turn, and said, "You may keep the change, son."

Susan and Nathan looked on, rising to their feet.

"Well, thank you, sir!" Jared called after him.

The man nodded and proceeded up the street. Another well-dressed man, one of Jared's regular customers, was passing Jared's benefactor. He smiled at the man and said, "Good morning, Mr. Rockefeller."

"Good morning, Mr. Emerson," came the reply.

Laird Emerson stopped in front of Jared and saw him showing his sister and brother the shiny silver dollar. Their eyes were wide at the sight of it.

Jared let Susan hold the dollar as he handed a folded paper to Mr. Emerson, a banker. "Morning, Jared," the banker said warmly, reaching in his pocket.

"Good morning, sir."

Emerson glanced at the silver coin in Susan's hand as he handed Jared a nickel. "You probably don't see one of those very often, do you, Jared?"

"This is the first time, Mr. Emerson," Jared replied. "I see lots of quarters, and a few fifty-cent pieces, but I've never had anyone buy a paper with a silver dollar before. Is that man rich?"

Emerson chuckled. "Well, he sure isn't poor. He and some partners established an oil refinery about eight years ago in

Ohio. Last year they organized the Standard Oil Company of Ohio. They just put an office here, so he'll be coming here quite often. His name is John D. Rockefeller. He's the president of the company, and he's only thirty-two years old. Some accomplishment, wouldn't you say?"

Jared figured thirty-two was pretty old, but didn't contradict Mr. Emerson. "Yes, sir. It sure is."

When Emerson was gone, Jared turned back to Susan and Nathan, who were still eyeing the silver dollar with awe. "Tell you what, kids. Since we made an extra ninety-five cents today, we're going to have us a feast. You know that café over on Park Avenue?"

Both siblings nodded.

"Well, when all the papers are sold, we're going to eat at the New Yorker Café before we go to work at the grocery store!"

Susan and Nathan clapped their hands and hugged their big brother.

It was almost 11:30 when Jared sold his last paper. As the customer walked away, Jared smiled at his siblings. "Well, kids, by the time we get to the café, it'll be almost noon. Let's go."

"Look!" Susan said, "It's Bodie!"

Bodie Brolin hobbled toward them on crutches. He wore a white bandage around his head. A tuft of coal-black hair bounced on his forehead as he moved, and his left leg dangled from his hip like a length of rope.

"Hi," Bodie said, as he stopped beside them, breathing hard.

The three Hamiltons returned the greeting, then Jared said, "Officer Ryan told us Saturday afternoon that you had to have eight stitches in your head, Bodie."

"Yeah."

"And that your kneecap was shattered, and your leg is broken in four places between the knee and the ankle."

"That's right."

"So what do the doctors say about it?"

"Well, they were able to set the leg, so the bone will heal all right, but my knee is permanently damaged. They say I'll be able to walk on it eventually, but I'll never be able to run again, and I'll always limp."

Jared's eyes flashed fire and his face darkened. "That dirty Mike McDuff and his scummy friends! I wish I could break every one of their legs and smash every one of their kneecaps!"

Bodie was about to comment when he saw a carriage round the corner off Thirty-eighth Street. The carriage pulled up to the curb on Broadway, and Reverend Brace told his driver to stop. There were three pitiful-looking children sitting together on the rear seat.

He alighted from the carriage and greeted Jared, then ran his gaze over the faces of the others. "And who are these children, Jared?"

"This is my sister, Susie, sir. My brother, Nathan. And this is my best friend, Bodie Brolin."

"Well, I'm glad to finally meet you Susie and Nathan. Jared has told me about you. And you, Bodie, did you have an accident?"

"No, sir," Bodie said. "I—"

"He got beat up by some dirty thugs, Reverend," Jared cut in. "And it was all because he came to my rescue a few weeks ago when those thugs were beating up on me. They cut his head real bad, broke his leg, and smashed his knee so he won't ever walk right again."

"Oh, Bodie, I'm so sorry," Brace said, laying a firm hand on

Bodie's shoulder. "Do you live on the streets?"

"No, sir. I live with my father."

"Well, that's good." Brace turned to Jared. "I haven't seen you for a while, son. How's your mother doing?"

"She died, sir. It'll be three weeks tomorrow."

"Oh, Jared, I'm so sorry. Do you children have a place to live?"

"We...we live in an alley, sir."

"This is not good, Jared." Reverend Brace bent down to Jared's height. "Son, you know about my orphan trains that take homeless children out West to be adopted by farm and ranch families..."

"Yes, sir."

"Our society has placed hundreds of children in homes out there. I could send all three of you on one of the trains. You would be adopted, and you wouldn't have to live like this anymore. How about it?"

A tight knot formed in Jared's stomach. "Thank you very much for the offer, Reverend, but we want to stay here."

"Well, I can understand that Manhattan is home to you, son, but I hate to see you living in an alley when you could go out West and have a real home."

"It's very nice of you to offer, sir," Jared said politely, "but we really want to stay here."

Brace patted the boy's shoulder. "Well, if you change your mind, let me know. Our office is at 19 East Fourth Street."

"Yes, sir. Thank you, sir."

Brace bid the children good-bye, climbed in the carriage, and rode away.

Bodie's dark eyes looked at his best friend with a soft expression. "You're afraid the three of you would be separated, aren't you?"

"I've read in the paper about how so many brothers and sisters on those orphan trains are adopted by different families out there in the West and never see each other again. I'd rather live here like we are than be separated."

"I can understand that," Bodie said. "Well, I've got to go pick up my matches and toothpicks and get back to work."

"Okay. See you later, Bodie."

As Bodie hobbled away, Jared called after him

"Yes?"

"I'm sorry for what happened to you because of me."

"It wasn't your fault. Don't be blaming yourself. We're best friends, right?"

"We sure are."

When Bodie had left, Jared said, "Kids, I'm afraid if we try to go to the New Yorker Café now, we'll be late getting to the store. I sure don't want Mr. Koehler to be unhappy with me."

"It's all right," Susan said. "How about if we just stop and buy some sandwiches from the vendor over on Thirty-sixth Street? We've never had enough money to buy from him before."

As they walked, Susan said, "Jared, what are we going to do when winter comes? We can't stay in the alley; we'll freeze to death."

"I know," Jared said. "I'll figure something out before then."

It was midafternoon when Jared was sweeping the boardwalk in front of Koehler's Grocery. Susan and Nathan remained inside the store. Nathan wasn't feeling well, and Susan was watching over him.

Jared greeted people on the street while he swept. What was wrong with Nathan? He had been fine up until about an hour ago.

Jared was almost finished sweeping when Oscar Koehler came out the door. "Jared, Nathan's throwing up, and now Susie's getting sick."

Jared sat in the waiting room at the doctor's office, fretful over his sister and brother. Soon Dr. Weiss emerged from the examining room and said, "It's food poisoning, son. Susan and Nathan are not in any danger of dying, but they will have to be hospitalized in order to have the proper care."

"Yes, sir," Jared said, rising to his feet. "You mean they ate bad food, sir?"

"That's right. They told me you bought lunch from a vendor."

"Yes, sir."

"And they both ate fish sandwiches, but you had a bologna sandwich."

"Yes, sir."

"And you're feeling all right?"

"Yes, sir."

"Then they probably got spoiled fish. I've ordered an ambulance to take them to the hospital. You'll need to go with them so you can make financial arrangements for the hospital bill."

"Yes, sir."

"How did you get here?"

"My employer, Mr. Koehler, got us a taxi."

"I see. My receptionist tells me you will pay the bill for my services on a weekly basis."

"Yes, sir."

"You'll have to make the same kind of arrangements with the hospital."

Jared nodded. "How much is your bill, sir?"

"Well, usually it would be ten dollars for two patients, but I'll cut it in half. You owe me five dollars."

"I'll pay it off as soon as I can, sir."

The next day after Jared sold all his papers, he walked the nineteen blocks to the hospital. He had made arrangements with Mr. Koehler to work later in the afternoon so that he could look in on Susan and Nathan.

Jared went to the children's ward and found them feeling somewhat better, but they would have to stay for two more days.

Jared was leaving the ward to head for the grocery store when he heard a familiar voice behind him say, "Hello, Jared."

"Oh. Hello, Reverend Brace."

"You visiting someone in there?"

"Yes, sir. My sister and brother. They got food poisoning yesterday, and I took them to Dr. Jacob Weiss. He put them in here."

"Are they going to be all right?"

"Yes, sir. The nurse just told me they will have to stay two more days."

Brace frowned and stroked his beard. "How are you paying for this?"

"They've been real nice. They're going to let me pay the bill a little bit each week. Dr. Weiss is letting me do that with his bill, too."

"I see. Do you know how much the doctor's bill is?"

"Yes, sir. It's five dollars."

"And what about the hospital bill?"

"I don't know for sure, Reverend. It will probably be at least thirty dollars. Maybe more."

"And how much will you be able to pay both the doctor and the hospital each week?"

"I don't know," Jared said, looking at the floor. "Probably about…about twenty cents a week to each. Then when I get the doctor paid, I can put forty cents a week on the hospital bill."

Brace leaned over and looked into Jared's eyes. "Have you any idea how long it will take you to pay the hospital bill at forty cents a week?"

"Well, quite a while, sir, but that's all I can do."

"And that forty cents will have to come out of your food money won't it?"

"I'll just eat less."

Tears filmed Charles Brace's eyes. "Tell you what I'm going to do, son. I'll pay what you owe to Dr. Weiss in full today. I will also go to the office here at the hospital and tell them that I will pay your bill when they release Susan and Nathan."

It was Jared's turn to blink back the tears. "Sir, I…I don't know what to say. How can I ever thank you?"

"There's one way you can thank me, Jared."

"Yes, sir?"

"Let me put you, Susan, and Nathan on one of my orphan trains and send you out West for adoption."

With lower lip quivering, Jared said, "Reverend Brace, I…I…well, sir, Manhattan is home to us, and—"

"All right, but my offer still stands, son. If you ever change your mind, you children have a place on an orphan train."

"I will sure let you know if I change my mind, sir. Thank you, again, for doing this for us. Thank you from the bottom of my heart."

14

ON SATURDAY MORNING, MAY 6, Dr. Lyle Goodwin and his wife, Martha, were in their spacious back yard, working on their rock garden. Martha carried small rocks from one spot to another, trying to find the best place for them, while Lyle dug in the soil, preparing it for the flower seeds they would plant later in the day.

Martha glanced at the small cottage at the rear of the property, which was home to Breanna Baylor. Lyle noticed the longing look in his wife's eyes. "You miss her, don't you?"

"I sure do," Martha said with a sigh. "I couldn't love Breanna more if she were my own daughter."

"Me, too," he said. "Precious girl."

"Any idea when we'll see her?"

"Nope. But don't worry. She'll let us know when she's done at Abilene and ready to come home. She's always wired when she was returning from an assignment so I could have somebody meet her at the station."

"I sure hope she doesn't forget to do it this time. Mayor Collins will need a full day before she gets here to have everything ready."

"She won't forget, Martha dear. You're a worrywart."

"I'm *not* a worrywart, Lyle," she said. "It's just that I want this big reception to be all it should be for that sweet, brave girl."

"Ah, there you are, Dr. Goodwin!" came a male voice.

Both Goodwins turned to see Morey Jardine, the Western Union messenger.

"I have a wire here from Nurse Baylor," Morey told them.

Thank You, Lord, Martha said in her heart.

Dr. Goodwin signed for the telegram, gave Morey a tip, and thanked him. Instead of hurrying away, Morey said, "Mind if I wait and see if it's what I think it is?"

The good doctor laughed as he broke the seal on the envelope. "Not at all."

He read it quickly and smiled at Martha. "She'll be home Tuesday on the eleven o'clock train."

"Oh, wonderful! And what a reception that girl's going to get!"

"And she wants me to let John know her time of arrival if he's in town." I'd better go see if I can find him. He won't want to miss the big day, that's for sure!"

Breanna sat on the left side of the coach and pressed her cheek against the window so she could see the majestic Rocky Mountains. The sun was near its apex in the heavens, and its brilliance enhanced the snow-capped peaks.

The coach was no more than half-occupied, and Breanna sat alone. At the first sign of Denver's outline against the backdrop of the foothills, her heart skipped a beat. "Please be there, John darling," she whispered. "I've missed you so."

As the prairie breeze carried black smoke from the smokestack past the window, Breanna's attention was drawn to a small herd of antelope running about a hundred yards away.

She smiled at them and said, "Racing the iron horse to Denver, are you?"

Moments later, the herd dipped into a low spot and disappeared.

Breanna pressed her cheek to the glass again, and fixed her gaze on Denver's skyline. So far, the tallest buildings in town were the two fancy hotels, each boasting four stories.

The sound of the coach door opening drew Breanna's attention. "Denver, twenty minutes! Twenty minutes to Denver, the mile high city and gateway to the Rockies!"

The other passengers were talking excitedly and preparing for arrival at Denver's Union Station as Breanna reached under the seat in front of her and picked up her purse. She started to slide across the seat, but the man who had placed her overnight bag in the rack at Abilene rose from his seat and said, "I'll get it for you, Miss."

"Oh, thank you," she said. "You've been very kind." Her mind flashed to Davis Claymore and Cleve Holden in Abilene.

Breanna scooted back toward the window. Her mind ran back over the things that had happened while she was in Abilene—the attempted assassination of President Grant and the privilege of getting to know him and the lovely first lady; the deaths of the assassins; the pleasure of meeting the famous lawman, Wild Bill Hickok. But most pleasurable was the joy of leading Bonnie Rand and Myra Dupree to Christ. In her mind's eye, she relived each of those experiences.

Breanna's reverie was interrupted when a boy near the front of the coach shouted excitedly, "Oh, look, Mama! Papa! There's a big crowd at the depot! See all the flags and banners? Oh! And look! There's a brass band!"

Breanna leaned against the window and her eyes widened when she saw a huge white banner stretched across the station's entrance, declaring with large red letters: WELCOME HOME, BREANNA BAYLOR, OUR COUNTRY'S BRAVEST ANGEL OF MERCY.

"Oh, no!" she gasped.

The band struck up the "Star Spangled Banner," and the crowd began cheering and waving red, white, and blue flags.

Now everyone in the coach was peering through the windows at the gala sight.

"Oh, no," Breanna moaned again, shaking her head.

The man across the aisle leaned toward her. "Young lady, are you all right?"

She looked at him with wide eyes and barely whispered, "I...ah...well, not exactly. Those banners...it's just that I—"

A broad smile captured his face. "Oh, I get it. *You* are this Breanna Baylor." He turned to his wife and said, "Myrna, you know who this lady is? She's the one who saved the president's life last month in Abilene! Sure, I should've recognized her! Her face has been on the front page of every newspaper in the country."

The other passengers in the coach suddenly converged on Breanna, repeating her name.

She managed a smile and said, "Really, folks, I didn't do that much. Really, I—"

The train chugged to a stop, wheels squealing, and the engine gave a final hiss. The excited passengers in Breanna's car picked up their belongings and started filing out.

Breanna swallowed hard when she looked out the window and saw Mayor Jess Collins standing with his wife in front of the blaring band. Beside them were her pastor, Robert Bayless, and his wife, Breanna's sister Dottie, nephew James, niece Molly Kate, brother-in-law and chief administrator of Mile High Hospital, Dr. Matthew Carroll, Dr. and Mrs. Lyle

Goodwin, and Sheriff Curt Langan and his wife, Stefanie. Next to Matt Carroll was Chief U.S. Marshal Solomon Duvall, and leaving Duvall's side at that very instant was a tall man dressed in black, who towered over the rest of the crowd.

Breanna felt frozen to her seat as she saw John talk to the conductor, who was helping Union Station personnel guide the passengers to one side of the excited crowd.

Suddenly, the tall man with the twin scars on his right cheek walked through the door of the coach. He smiled broadly and moved to where she was still glued to the seat.

"Hello, sweetheart," he said. "I sure have missed you. I just got into town on Thursday. That was some wonderful thing you did in Abilene! The whole country's talking about you!"

Breanna reached out a trembling hand. "Oh, John, help me! I...I can't go out there!"

John bent over and planted a kiss on her nervous lips. "I love you, sweetheart," he said.

"I love you, too, darling. Now, help me get off this train without facing that crowd."

"Oh, no you don't," he said, and chuckled. "Credit must be given where credit is due. The people of this town are so proud of you they can hardly contain themselves. You must let them pour their adulation on you."

Breanna's brow furrowed. "Some other time?"

"Nope. Now!"

As he spoke, John lifted her from the seat. "Come on, honey. Let me escort my wife-to-be to meet her subjects. I'll send someone in here to pick up your bag."

Breanna's whole body trembled. "John, I didn't tackle President Grant with this kind of thing in mind. I just didn't want him to get shot."

"We all know that. The whole story was in the papers. I was

clear down in southern New Mexico Territory and read about it. C'mon. Let these people have their day."

Breanna allowed John to lead her onto the platform, where Denver's Mayor Jess Collins greeted her. He then turned toward the cheering, shouting, whistling crowd and the loud band, and raised his hands for silence. Breanna held onto John's hand and looked out over the crowd.

The local news people were there, along with photographers, who were ready to take pictures as soon as the ceremony was over.

When the mayor introduced Breanna to the crowd of at least four thousand, he let them cheer and applaud, then said, "Ladies and gentlemen, as mayor of this fair city, I hereby declare Tuesday, May 9, 1871, Breanna Baylor Day in Denver!"

The crowd went wild.

After a few minutes, the mayor raised his hands once again for silence, and turned to Breanna. "We read in our newspaper that President Grant said some powerful things about you to the people of Abilene only moments after the assassination attempt. Well, Miss Breanna, from what I've just learned, the president is going to say some more words about you, only this time it will take place before the Congress of the United States!"

Breanna blinked. "What?"

The mayor gestured toward Chief U.S. Marshal Solomon Duvall. "Chief Duvall, will you come and tell the people of this city about the telegram you hold in your hand?"

Breanna turned to John. "What's this all about?"

"I don't know. I wasn't aware of the telegram."

Duvall smiled at Breanna and then turned to the crowd. "Ladies and gentlemen, this telegram came to my office yesterday. It was directed to me, telling me to pass it on to Miss Breanna and our friend, John Stranger. It's from President Grant, himself.

"Instead of reading it to you, I'll simply tell you what it says. President Grant is asking both John and Breanna to come to Washington at the government's expense. He wants to give Breanna a special presidential commendation before a joint session of Congress. This will take place on Wednesday, May 17. He also wants to meet with John about a special assignment for him."

There was another rousing cheer, then Duvall said, "John, Breanna, President Grant asks for a reply from you today."

"I'll take care of it," Stranger said with a grin.

The mayor spoke again. "Breanna, I also have a telegram. This one is from Colorado's Governor Allen Domire, who is in Washington right now. Governor Domire and Lieutenant Governor Howard Channing both congratulate you, saying they wish they could be here. However, in their absence, Governor Domire has directed me to preside at a special luncheon in your honor at the Grandview Hotel, which is being prepared at this moment."

Breanna smiled her pleasure.

"Furthermore, I've taken the liberty, dear lady, of inviting your sister and her family, along with your pastor and his wife, Sheriff and Mrs. Langan, Dr. and Mrs. Lyle Goodwin, and Chief Duvall to your luncheon. Oh, yes. John can come, too!"

The crowd laughed and applauded and gave Breanna a lengthy ovation. When they were quiet again, Collins said, "Ladies and gentlemen, I believe it would be fitting before we go our separate ways to thank Almighty God for using our own Breanna Baylor to save the life of our beloved president, *and* to thank Him for sparing Breanna's life as well.

"Reverend Robert Bayless, would you please come, sir, and lead us in that prayer of thanks?"

James and Molly Kate clung to their Aunt Breanna and "Uncle" John as they headed for Matt and Dottie Carroll's carriage, where Sheriff Langan and Stefanie were waiting for them.

Matt and Dottie waited until the Langans were finished greeting Breanna, then Dottie put her arms around her sister and whispered, "I'm so proud to have such a wonderful sister!"

Stranger leaned close to Dr. Carroll. "Matt, we'll need to stop at the Western Union office on our way to the hotel so I can reply to the president's telegram."

"Will do," Carroll said.

James and Molly Kate each made sure they sat beside their aunt in the carriage.

On Saturday, May 13, the sky was overcast in New York City and a cool wind was blowing off the Hudson River.

Jared Hamilton had four papers left to sell, and it was already going on eleven o'clock. Susan and Nathan sat on the curb, playing a game they had invented to help pass the time. They would guess how many vehicles would turn the corner while one of them silently counted to a hundred. The other one would count the vehicles. The one who came closest was the winner.

Susan was in the middle of a count when Nathan spotted Bodie Brolin hobbling toward them on his crutches.

"Jared," Nathan said, "here comes Bodie."

Jared turned to look as his best friend and noted his sad countenance.

"Hello, Bodie," Jared said, frowning. "What's wrong?"

"My dad died in a drunken stupor last night. He never cared much about me. His drinking made my life miserable, but he was my father. I loved him. And now he's gone."

Susan put a hand on Bodie's arm. "Bodie, we know what it's like to lose both parents. We understand. And…we love you."

"We sure do," Jared said. "I'm so sorry about your loss."

"Me, too," Nathan said.

Bodie sniffed and wiped tears from his cheeks. "The rent was paid two days ago, so I have five days to stay in the apartment. Then I'll have to get out."

"Well, when your time runs out, you can come live with us in our alley," Jared said.

Bodie nodded. "That's what I'm planning to do." He sniffed again and said, "Since I've got five days to be in the apartment, I'd like for all of you to come and stay with me. When the five days are past, we'll move to the alley together."

"Hey, that would be great!" Nathan said. "It would be real good to sleep inside for a few nights!"

Jared turned to his sister. "Would you like to do that, Susie?"

"Oh, yes!"

"Okay, Bodie," Jared said. "We'll take you up on it."

"Good! Now I've got to pick up some more matches and toothpicks from my distributor. I sold out already this morning."

"Oh, that's good, Bodie," Jared said. "Hey, I know you live on Thirty-fifth Street, but I don't know the number."

"It's 314 East Thirty-fifth. Big brick building. I'm in apartment 3-B."

"Okay. We'll see you about five o'clock."

✦

Mike McDuff and his three pals were huddled in a doorway on Thirty-eighth Street near the corner where Jared and Bodie were talking. McDuff could hardly take his eyes off the two boys.

"Hey, Mike," Truxtun said, "you really are holdin' a grudge against that English kid."

"He was gonna tell old man Koehler 'bout that stuff we stole, and I hate him for it. He's gotta pay."

At that moment, Bodie left the Hamilton children and hobbled down the street.

"Why don't we just stomp Jared into the ground like we did Bodie?" Marty said. "Maybe break both his legs?"

McDuff spit, wiped his mouth, and said, "I want to be more imaginative when I make Jared pay. We'll follow 'em from the store to their alley this afternoon. I'll think of somethin' real bad to do to him by then. That kid's gonna be sorry he ever considered blabbin' his mouth off to old man Koehler."

Late that afternoon McDuff and his cohorts waited at the corner a few doors from the grocery, watching as they saw Oscar Koehler walk the three Hamilton children to the door. As usual, Koehler flipped the "Open" sign at the window to "Closed" and told the Hamilton three goodnight.

"Somethin's strange, Mike," Truxtun said. "Them kids are carryin' blankets and pillows. They ain't never done that before."

"Well, maybe ol' man Koehler washed 'em for 'em."

"Maybe."

"C'mon. Let's follow 'em to their alley. Then I'll decide what we're gonna do to Jared."

180

The hoodlums were surprised to see the Hamilton children walk by their alley.

"See what I mean?" Truxtun asked. "Them kids are goin' somewhere different."

"Well, we'll just stick with 'em and find out where they're goin'."

As Jared, Susan, and Nathan turned onto Thirty-fifth Street, Marty said, "You don't suppose they're movin' in with Bodie?"

"Could be."

Moments later, when Jared led his sister and brother into the tenement at 314 East Thirty-fifth Street, Mike McDuff swore. "They're movin' in with Bodie and his old man!"

When the Hamilton trio disappeared through the front door, Marty said, "Hey, Mike. See those two guys out front?"

"Yeah."

"I know 'em. They live in that tenement, too."

"How well do you know 'em? They friends of yours?"

"I'd say so."

"Well, let's go see if they know anything about them Hamiltons movin' in."

Marty spoke to Mel Ralston and Eric Chase, and introduced them to Mike and the others.

"What we were wantin' to know, fellas," Mike said, "is if you're aware of some new kids movin' in with Bodie Brolin and his old man."

"Don't know anything about kids movin' in," Ralston replied, "but I'll guarantee you it ain't with Bodie and his old man 'cause his old man died last night."

Mike rubbed his chin, thinking. To Ralston and Chase, he said, "I suppose you guys are good friends with Bodie."

"Naw, we can't stand 'im. He's not like us. He won't steal or anythin'."

"Well, if it turns out those three kids who just walked past you are movin' in with Bodie, I wanna fix 'em real good."

"They do somethin' to you?" Mel asked.

"The oldest one did. I've got a score to settle with him. Would you guys help me?"

"Sure," Eric said. "Any friend of Marty's is a friend of ours."

"You got a good idea, huh, Mike?" Truxtun asked.

A wicked grin curled McDuff's lips. "Yeah. A *real* good idea."

15

AFTER DARK, MIKE MCDUFF knocked on the door of apartment 7-B in Bodie's tenement. A burly, unshaven man with the smell of whiskey on his breath opened the door. He scowled at the four toughs.

"Is Mel in, Mr. Ralston?" Mike asked.

"I ain't Mr. Ralston!" The man then turned and shouted, "Hey, Mel! Somebody out here to see you!" With that, he walked away and disappeared into another room, leaving the door open.

Mel smiled when he saw Mike McDuff and Marty Lukacher. McDuff introduced Tony Hillaker and Doug Furlow, who had been in on the attack on Bodie, then said, "Mel, we were gonna be over here this mornin' to see if we could catch sight of them Hamilton kids around the place. Couldn't make it. Did you see 'em around?"

"Yeah. I found out by listenin' that they've moved in with Bodie, like you figured."

Mike looked at his friends and grinned. "Do you know if Eric's home?"

"Was fifteen minutes ago."

"I need to talk to both of you in private."

"Sure."

"Say, who's the big ugly guy? I called him Mr. Ralston and he almost bit my head off."

"He's my step-dad. We don't get along real good."

"I can see why. Well, let's go over to Eric's apartment. If he's still home, we'll have our little talk. If you boys can do what I ask of you, my revenge on Jared Hamilton will be full and sweet."

The next afternoon, Tony Hillaker and Doug Furlow picked a busy shopping time to enter Koehler's Grocery to browse among the shelves. Tony and Doug knew Jared Hamilton by sight. They eyed him furtively now as he stood behind the counter with Oscar Koehler and helped pack groceries for the customers. Susan and Nathan were in the storeroom, unpacking a shipment of staple goods.

Hillaker and Furlow were seasoned thieves. They wore light jackets and stuffed one item after another inside their shirts without being detected. After making a couple of small legitimate purchases, they left the store. Moments later, they slipped between two buildings a half-block from Koehler's where Mike McDuff waited for them.

"Everything go all right?" Mike asked.

"Sure," Tony said. "You think you're dealin' with amateurs?"

Mike laughed. "So what did you get?"

They moved farther into the shadows, and Doug and Tony unloaded their stolen items.

Mike's eyes danced as he took inventory. "Well, let's see, here…pocket knife, bag of marbles, package of pencils, candy canes, and three apples. You guys did good!"

"We thought you'd be happy," Doug said.

"Okay, boys, let's go meet up with our spies and see if the

coast is clear. If Bodie is havin' a normal day, he'll be on the street another couple of hours."

It was almost six o'clock when Mike McDuff watched Oscar Koehler walk the Hamilton children to the front door of his store. McDuff watched them turn the corner and pass from view. Then he backed a little farther into the shadows and fixed his attention on the windows of Koehler's apartment above the store.

He had timed how long it took to walk from Koehler's Grocery to Bodie's place. He waited for that much time to elapse, then crossed the street and climbed the creaky stairs behind the store to knock on Koehler's door.

Oscar Koehler recognized the youth immediately and frowned. "Oh, it's you. What do you want?"

McDuff lowered his head in a show of humility, and said, "Mr. Koehler, I want you to know that I'm ashamed for having stolen from you, and I'm sorry about it. You'll never have to worry about me or my pals stealin' from you again. We've changed our ways."

"I hope you have," Koehler said. "But I'm sure you didn't climb these stairs to tell me that."

"Well, uh…no, sir, but it's related to what I just told you."

"Yes?"

"Well, a little while ago, I ran into Jared Hamilton and his brother and sister. They were goin' home after leavin' here."

Koehler nodded impatiently.

"Well, sir, I was surprised when they told me they're livin' with Bodie Brolin now, instead of in the alley. Did you know about their move?"

"Of course. Jared told me. And they'll be moving back to

the alley when Bodie's rent runs out on Saturday."

McDuff masked his surprise as he said, "Yeah. That's what they told me. I...I guess Bodie don't make enough money to be able to stay there, now that his old m— uh...his pa died."

There were a few seconds of dead silence.

"Well anyway, Mr. Koehler, what I came here for was to tell you that Jared and those two kids have been stealin' from you. They been takin' stuff right out from under your nose."

Koehler's body stiffened. "You're lying, McDuff. Get out of here!"

"I ain't lyin', Mr. Koehler! I'm tellin' you the pure truth. Why would I want to make up a story like that? I feel bad the way me and my pals have stolen from you, and now I hate to see stealin' goin' on, especially when it's you they're stealin' from."

"I don't know what your game is," Koehler said, "but Jared Hamilton is a good, hardworking boy. He's no thief."

"If he ain't no thief, why'd he brag that he and his brother and sister just stole stuff from you before they left for the day? Jared was braggin' how they been puttin' it over on *old man Koehler* for a long time. He said you're a real sucker."

Koehler's expression hardened. "I don't believe it."

"Well, that's too bad," McDuff said. "As long as you're so blind to what Jared and those little kids really are, they'll just keep on stealin' from you."

"I've heard enough," Koehler said, and started to close the door.

"Wait a minute! I can prove it!"

Koehler stopped. "How?"

"Let me ask you somethin' first. Did Jared buy anything from you before they left a little while ago?"

"No. Why?"

"'Cause they pulled stuff outta their pockets and showed me what they stole! Some of it was even stuffed under Nathan's shirt."

"Like what?"

"Like…uh…a pocket knife. And three apples. Some candy canes. Ah…a package of pencils. You know, three in a pack like for school. And…ah…a bag of marbles."

Koehler looked a little less sure.

"Why don't you call a policeman and have him go over there to Brolin's apartment and see what he finds? Then you can apologize for callin' me a liar."

Bodie Brolin and the Hamilton children were just finishing supper when they heard a knock at the door.

"I'll get it," Bodie said, shoving his chair back and picking up his crutches.

There was a second knock before Bodie was halfway to the door. "Coming!" he called.

It was Officer Dean Farone.

"Hello, Bodie," Farone said. "I understand Jared Hamilton and his brother and sister are living with you now."

"Yes, sir."

"I need to talk to them."

"All right," Bodie said, backing up to let Farone in.

Bodie hopped around the officer, saying, "We've just finished supper; they're in the kitchen."

"Hello, Officer Farone," Jared said with a smile, leaving his chair. "Did I hear you say you wanted to talk to us?"

"Yes. I…well, Jared, you've been accused of stealing goods from Mr. Koehler's store. An eyewitness says he saw you with the goods."

Susan and Nathan exchanged blank looks, then set their eyes on their older brother. Jared blinked in disbelief. "Me, sir?"

"All three of you."

"Who's saying this?"

"Mike McDuff. I know the two of you have had run-ins before, Jared, but he told Mr. Koehler he saw you with the stolen goods on your way home from work today."

"He's lying, sir," Jared said. "He hates me, and he's just wanting to get me into trouble. He's the one who broke Bodie's leg and crippled his knee."

"I know that's what Bodie said, and I have no reason to doubt him. But McDuff swears he saw you, Susan, and Nathan with stolen goods just after you left the store today and that you bragged that you've been stealing from Mr. Koehler all along."

A mottled flush crossed Jared's face. "That's a lie, too! I would never steal from Mr. Koehler, or anybody else! Neither would Susan or Nathan. Mr. Koehler doesn't believe him, does he?"

"Of course not, and he told McDuff that he didn't. McDuff threw up a bluff that if Mr. Koehler sent a policeman over here to the apartment and searched it, he would find the stolen goods."

Bodie laughed. "That's crazy!"

"Mind if I search so that I can shut McDuff's mouth?" Farone asked.

"Of course not," Bodie said.

Officer Farone went through all the kitchen cupboards. From there he went into the larger of the two bedrooms and searched the drawers of a bureau and a dresser, and looked in the closet. He struck a match and looked under the bed as the four young people looked on.

"Well, nothing in here," he said with a smile. He moved to the small bedroom and looked around by the light of the gas lamp on the wall. "No dresser or bureau in here?"

"No, sir."

Farone lit another match, knelt down, and looked under the bed. He shook out the match and rose to his feet. "Well, all that's left is the closet."

"What's in the trunk, Bodie?"

"Just some old things that belonged to my pa."

The officer dragged the trunk into the light and flipped open the lid.

Bodie saw Farone's body stiffen. "What's the matter?" he asked.

The Hamiltons drew closer when Farone said, "Take a look."

Bodie's eyes bulged. "Wha—?"

Jared shoved past Bodie to look inside the trunk. There, on top of an old picture album, some old letters, and a faded yellow wedding veil, were three red apples, a pocket knife, a small netted bag of marbles, a package of pencils, and six candy canes.

Jared gasped.

"What is it?" Susan said, pressing closer.

Nathan sucked in a sharp breath. "How did those get in there?" he asked.

"I don't know," Jared said, and turned to the policeman. "That's the truth, Officer Farone. I have no idea how those things got in there. Susie, Nathan, and I did not steal them. I swear it."

Officer Farone shook his head. "Jared, you had me fooled. I thought you were being honest with me. Unless Bodie stole these items and hid them here, who else could it be but you?"

"It wasn't Bodie!" Jared cried. "Bodie wouldn't do such a thing!"

"And neither would you, Jared," Bodie said.

Officer Farone put his hands on his hips. "So you boys are telling me these things just walked in here all by themselves? Jared, why would you do such a thing? Mr. Koehler has been awfully good to you."

Jared's lips quivered and tears glistened in his eyes. "I didn't do it!" he cried. "Somebody else did! And it was probably Mike McDuff!"

"And just how would he do it? Does he have a key to this place? The door does lock doesn't it?"

"It locks, sir," Bodie said.

Jared looked around. "How about the windows? Could somebody have come in through them?"

Farone checked the windows and found them secure. He rubbed his jaw. "Jared, I had so hoped the liar was Mike McDuff. It really grieves me to find out the liar is you. And that you've included your little sister and brother in your scheme."

Tears spilled down Jared's cheeks, and his voice shook as he said, "Officer Farone, I'm not lying."

"Tell you what, son. If you'll take what you stole back to Mr. Koehler and apologize to him, I'll try to talk him into not pressing charges against you."

Jared knew it would do no good to declare his innocence any further. He put the stolen items in a paper bag and went with Officer Farone to talk with Oscar Koehler.

"How can I believe you, Jared?" Oscar Koehler said, throwing up his hands. "Only you and Bodie have keys to the apartment. You not only stole from me, but you stand there and lie about it."

"Jared," Officer Farone said, "I think that if you come clean, Mr. Koehler won't press charges."

"I'll agree to that," Koehler said. "Jared, if you'll admit your larceny and apologize for stealing from me, I won't press charges. Your job is gone, but at least you won't have to spend time behind bars."

Jared drew in a shuddering breath. "Mr. Koehler," he said, "I did not steal from you. Please don't take my job away from me. I can't provide for my little sister and brother without the job. Ple-e-ase!"

Koehler looked at the officer and sighed. "Tell you what, Officer Farone. Loss of his job is punishment enough. At least this way he can look for another one. Susan and Nathan need him."

"Okay," Farone said. He looked at Jared and said, "If you're going to stay around this neighborhood, you'd better watch your *P*s and *Q*s. Get out of line just once, and you're a jailbird!"

Without another word, Jared Hamilton turned and walked out the door.

The next morning, while eating a meager breakfast of three-day-old bread spread with marmalade, Bodie Brolin and the Hamilton children sat around the table barely saying a word. When they were almost finished with breakfast, Jared finally said, "Susie, Nathan, since we're not living in the alley right now, I want you to stay here in the apartment while I sell my papers and look for more work this afternoon. You'll be more comfortable here."

Sister and brother nodded miserably.

Bodie looked at his best friend with compassionate eyes. "Jared, I wish I could get you a job with Mr. Morgan but he already has enough boys."

191

"That's okay," Jared said. "I'll find more work. First thing I'll do is go back to the merchants and shop owners I used to do occasional work for. The firehouse, too. Maybe I'll get enough work to make up for losing the job with Mr. Koehler. If not, I'll try some new places."

Bodie swallowed his last bite of bread and said, "How do you suppose Mike got in this apartment?"

"I can't imagine, but we know he did."

"Or he had someone else do it for him."

"The door was locked when we got here yesterday afternoon. Does the landlord have a key?"

"Yes, but he wouldn't let anybody use it."

"Could somebody use it without him knowing?"

"No. He keeps all his spare keys in a safe that only he can open."

Jared sighed. "I guess we'll never know how Mike did it."

Bodie eyed the old clock on the wall. "Oh-oh. Time to go."

"I'll clean up here," Susan said.

Bodie draped his cloth sack of matches and toothpicks over his neck, picked up his crutches, and hobbled to the door. Jared told his siblings he would see them later, and the two friends left together.

At dusk a dejected Jared Hamilton headed for Thirty-fifth Street. Peter Stillman, the owner of Stillman's Clothing Store, had flat told him to get out and never come back. A boy named Truxtun Gowen had come in and told Stillman about Jared stealing from Oscar Koehler, and Officer Farone would back up his story. It had gone the same with Luigi Olivetti. Jared was told never to darken the door of the Manhattan Shoe Repair shop again. When Jared stopped at the fire station, he was told he was no longer welcome.

And so it had gone at the other places where Jared had done odd jobs in the past. Mike McDuff had seen to it that Jared's name was blackened at every place he had ever worked.

As he turned onto Thirty-fifth Street, Jared saw McDuff and his usual pals. They were waiting for him.

Traffic was heavy on Thirty-fifth as Jared moved toward them without breaking his stride. Anger darkened his features as he said, "I don't know how you got the stuff into Bodie's apartment, McDuff, but sooner or later you're going to dig yourself a hole and fall in it."

McDuff grinned. "Find a new job, Jared?"

"I will."

"Not in Manhattan, you won't."

"I'll find someplace where you and your cronies haven't been."

"No, you won't. You're gonna have to resort to stealin' just like the rest of us."

"That I'll never do. And in spite of you, I *will* get a job."

McDuff and his friends laughed.

"When you and your little brother and sister get hungry enough, you'll start stealin'," Marty Lukacher said.

Jared ignored Marty's words and started up the front steps of the tenement.

McDuff called after him, "I'll fix you at the *Tribune,* too, Hamilton! When I get done, you won't even be able to sell papers in this town!"

Jared's mind was whirling from what he'd just heard. McDuff wasn't bluffing. He *would* go to the newspaper and libel him. They would be living back in the alley in three days. Even if he didn't lose his newspaper job, there wouldn't be enough money for the shoes and clothing all three of them needed, let alone enough for food.

Bodie was already home when Jared walked into the apartment. Susan was cooking supper, and Nathan was putting plates and glasses on the table. All three turned to look at Jared as he entered the kitchen.

"Oh, Jared," Susan said, leaving the stove to take his hand, "what happened? You look like it's the end of the world!"

"It may be the end of our world, Susie," Jared replied.

16

SUSAN AND NATHAN WEPT as Jared told them he'd been turned down for work at every place he'd asked.

"Well, there is one bright side," Bodie said, trying to sound cheerful. "At least you still have your job with the *Tribune*. That'll keep you in food, won't it?"

"Just barely. Only I'm about to lose that job, too."

"How do you know?" Susan asked.

"McDuff and his pals were waiting for me when I got here. The last thing McDuff said was that he would fix me at the *Tribune*, too."

"Maybe it was just a bluff," Bodie said.

"It's no bluff. He'll probably be there first thing in the morning. He means to fix me so I'll have to steal like he does to take care of the three of us."

Nathan began to sob. "We're gonna starve to death! That's what's gonna happen! We're gonna starve to death!"

Jared patted his little brother's shoulder. "No, we won't. I'll find a job in spite of McDuff."

"Nathan," Bodie said, "you won't go hungry as long as I have a nickel in my pocket. I'll share what I make on my job with all of you."

Susan shook her head as she wiped at her eyes. "That's

195

sweet of you, Bodie, but it's not right that you work to support us. Besides, we're all three about to walk out of our shoes. And look at our clothes. Soon we'll have to replace them. Not only that, but Jared and Nathan need haircuts. We've got to do something before things get worse."

"Like what, Susie?" Jared asked.

She looked at the floor and then met Jared's gaze. "There's always the orphan trains."

Bodie broke the silence by saying, "What about you three staying together?"

"I don't want to be separated, Bodie," Susan said, "but it would be better than having no clothes to wear and starving to death. And, you know, there's a chance that some family would want all three of us. Jared...have you ever asked Reverend Brace about the chances of us getting adopted by the same family?"

"No."

"Well, why don't we go over to his office and ask him?"

Nathan had stopped crying and was studying his big brother's face. There was a trace of a smile on Jared's lips as he said, "I was thinking about Reverend Brace just before I came in. Sure wouldn't hurt to talk to him."

Bodie sighed. "If Reverend Brace says he won't let you be split up, and you go on an orphan train, I'd sure like to go with you."

"Oh, we'd love that, Bodie!" Susan said.

A sad look passed over Bodie's young face. "I don't know if they'd let me go. From what you've told me, Jared, those people out West adopt kids for farm and ranch work. Who'd want me?"

"I'll ask Reverend Brace about it tomorrow," Jared said. "See what he says."

✦

The sun was barely up in downtown Manhattan when Jared and his siblings waited on the corner of Thirty-eighth and Broadway.

"Here comes Mr. Morton, Jared," Susan said, pointing down the street.

The wagon drew up with bright red lettering on its sides, advertising that it was owned by the *New York Tribune*. Elmer Morton set the brake and smiled down at them. "Morning, kids. He twisted on the wagon seat, picked up a bundle of newspapers from behind him, and handed it down to Jared. "There you go, boy. See you tomorrow."

Jared wondered if that were true. If Mike McDuff paid the *Tribune* office a visit, Jared wouldn't be selling papers anywhere.

Charles Loring Brace's attention was so intent on the papers before him that he jerked when the knock came at his office door. "Come in!" he called.

It was Charlie Fry, the Society's Emigration agent. Fry's job was to travel West and break ground in new territory where they might take the orphan trains. When he found interest in western towns, he set up local committees to make preparations for the train's arrival. Fry supplied the town preprinted posters announcing the coming of the train and its purpose. There was a blank spot on the posters to fill in the date the train would arrive in the selected town. The committees also placed advertisements in local newspapers many weeks in advance of the train's arrival.

Brace rose from his desk. "So! You're ready to head west again."

"Yes, sir," Fry said. "Just thought I'd tell you good-bye, and that I'll see you in a couple of months."

Brace shook Fry's hand. "You're doing a marvelous job, Charlie. We all appreciate you around here."

"Thank you, Reverend. This job has its special rewards. Just to know that all those precious children are off the streets of New York and happy in real homes out West gives me joy. I'm honored to have a part in it."

"We sure couldn't do it without you, Charlie."

Fry smiled, gave a little wave, and started out the door. "Whoops!" he said, almost running into Laura Welton, Brace's secretary.

"Hello, Charlie," she said, dodging him. "Good-bye, Charlie."

Fry disappeared, and Brace waited for Laura to state her business.

"Reverend," she said, "there are three children out here asking to see you. They say you know them. Jared, Susan, and Nathan Hamilton."

A broad smile spread across Brace's face. "Of course. Bring them in."

Brace shook hands with the boys and bowed to Susan. To Jared he said, "And to what do I owe this pleasure?"

"We'd like to talk to you, sir."

"All right. Let's pull up some chairs in front of my desk."

Laura arranged the chairs, then excused herself and closed the door behind her. Brace leaned his elbows on top of his desk and looked at Jared expectantly. "All right," he said, "what can I do for you?"

"First of all, sir, I would like to ask a question."

Brace nodded.

"I read in the *Tribune* that many times when you take

brothers and sisters to be adopted out West, they are separated. Is that true?"

"Yes, it is. But sometimes they are adopted by the same family."

"Sometimes?"

"Let me say this, Jared. If, say, you, Susan, and Nathan wanted to go on one of our orphan trains, but you said you wouldn't go if there was a chance you would be adopted into different families, I could put a stipulation that the three of you have to be adopted together or not at all."

"You could?"

"Of course. I've done it several times. Now, you would have to understand that such a stipulation might mean you have to make a number of trips west before someone would adopt you. That's because most families just can't accommodate three children all of a sudden. At least you would be well fed, have comfortable beds, and nice clothing. Even making a hundred trips before you were adopted would be better than living the way you do now."

Jared looked at Susan and Nathan, who nodded their agreement.

"Let's get down to specifics, here," Brace said. "Are we actually talking about the Hamilton orphans?"

"Yes, sir," Jared said. "You see, sir, things have gone really bad for us."

While sister and brother looked on and Reverend Brace listened intently, Jared told him the story of why he had lost his job at Koehler's Grocery and was denied jobs around town.

"Please believe me, sir, I didn't steal those things from Mr. Koehler."

"I do believe you, Jared. I'm sorry that Officer Farone and Mr. Koehler didn't. It's enough for me to know something about the McDuff boy's delinquency record. I know you're telling me the truth. Any boy who would work the way you have to care for your mother while she was alive, and to provide for Susan and Nathan, isn't a thief."

Jared felt an enormous burden leave his shoulders. "Thank you, sir," he said with dignity.

Brace smiled. "So, with my stipulation that you must be adopted by the same family or not at all, do you want to go?"

Jared looked at Susan and Nathan again. "What about it, you two?"

"Do *you* want to, Jared?" Susan asked.

"We've lived in that alley long enough. And besides, I promised that I'd think of something before winter comes. This way, we'll either be in a nice home out West or still riding the train."

"And we'll have real meals, too!" Nathan said.

"And nice clothes, didn't you say, Reverend?" Susan asked.

"Yes, honey. They're like uniforms. All the boys dress the same way, and so do the girls. You'll be given three outfits so you can wear a clean one every day while the others are being washed and ironed by the ladies on the trains, who are also your chaperones. Some of the women who work for the society have husbands who chaperone the boys."

"It sounds wonderful!" Susan said.

"So you're all in agreement?" the director asked.

"Looks like it," Jared said, and smiled.

"Good! Tell you what. We've got a train pulling out tomorrow morning. There's room for you."

"Oh!" Jared said. "I need to ask you something else, sir. You remember our friend Bodie Brolin?"

"The boy with the broken leg?"

"Yes, sir. Bodie said that if we decided to go on the orphan train, he wants to go with us."

"Well, there's room for him, too."

"Even though he's on crutches? Bodie's afraid you might not want to take him…you know, since he won't be able to do farm or ranch work like boys with two good legs."

"I'm not going to say it will be easy, son, but I'm willing to try if Bodie's willing to come along. Maybe there'll be some family who is childless and isn't really looking for a worker."

"Oh, I know he'll be willing, sir. So if we're going to leave tomorrow, when do you want us here?"

Brace looked up at the clock. "Let's see, it's almost two o'clock. Let's take one of the carriages and go after Bodie right now. The first thing we'll do when we get back here is measure you for sizes. Then all three of you boys will get haircuts. If I remember correctly, Bodie's hair was getting a little shaggy."

"It's about like mine and Nathan's," Jared said.

"Mm-hmm. Shaggy. All of you will get a nice hot bath and new clothes from the skin out. Shall we go?"

"Yes, sir. And could you run me by the *Tribune* building so I can tell my distributor I won't be selling papers anymore?"

Jared was only inside the *Tribune* building for a few minutes. When he came out and climbed into the buggy, he said, "McDuff has been here, and I was just told I couldn't sell their papers anymore."

"So who cares?" Susan asked.

"Well, not me," Jared said. "I've got a new life ahead of me!"

"Yeah!" Nathan said. "We're gonna go out West and punch cattle!"

"I sure hope the cattle don't punch back," Susan said with a giggle.

Bodie was on the corner of Thirty-sixth Street and Park Avenue when Brace told him the Hamilton children were boarding the orphan train tomorrow morning and that Bodie was welcome to come, too. He shouted for joy and almost leaped into the carriage.

They stopped at the tenement so Bodie could pick up what personal things he wanted to take with him, and within minutes they were on their way to the Children's Aid Society building.

Brace explained to Bodie that they would be fed a good supper at the Society's dining hall, and a good breakfast before the train pulled out in the morning. They would sleep on bunks in the Society's dormitory tonight.

"Let me tell you a little about the chaperones," Brace said. "There are husbands and wives and some single ladies who are known as our 'Placing Out Committee.' They take care of the children on the trip, and they oversee the adoptions in the towns.

"Sometimes the children and their chaperones are provided with a meal by the townspeople. This depends upon the time of arrival in each town. When the meal is served, the prospective adoptive parents move around, looking the children over. At other times, the children simply line up at the depot, or sometimes in the town hall or a schoolhouse or even a church building, and are chosen for adoption."

"How many children will be on our train?" Bodie asked.

"We don't send a train until we have at least 100 children. As of noon today, we had 114. Unless others have been added this afternoon, there'll be a 118, including you four."

"Does the train travel at night, sir?" Susan asked.

"No, and there are several reasons for that. The most important is that every morning we want you to get some exercise. It's pretty hard for kids your age to stay cooped up in a railroad car for so many hours a day. This way, we let you blow off some steam before starting the next leg of the trip."

"Reverend Brace," Jared said, "do you know what towns we'll stop at?"

"Four of them are in western Nebraska, and the other two are Cheyenne City, Wyoming, and Denver, Colorado. The four Nebraska towns are North Platte, Ogallala, Sidney, and Kimball."

"This is so exciting, Jared!" Susan said.

"I wonder which town we'll get adopted in," Nathan said.

At the Children's Aid Society headquarters, Reverend Brace led the children into his office and seated them. Laura Welton entered and formally met all the children.

"Mrs. Welton will ask you some questions," Brace said. "While she's doing that, I'll make arrangements for you to stay in the dormitories tonight, and make sure there are places at the supper table for you."

"Thank you, sir," Jared said.

"The pleasure is mine, son." Before he left the office, Brace turned to Laura. "Have we had any more children brought in this afternoon?"

"No, sir. With these four, we'll have 118 on the train tomorrow."

"Fine. Keep them here till I get back. I'll take them to their dorms when I return."

When Reverend Brace was gone, Laura opened her notebook and said, "I need what we call some vital statistics on each of you—your birth dates, parents' names, places of birth…"

At supper, Reverend Brace stood up before all the children and said, "Boys and girls, here at the Children's Aid Society, we always give thanks to the Lord for our food. Please bow your heads and close your eyes while I pray."

Bodie had been around people who prayed, but this was the first time Jared, Susan, and Nathan had ever heard or seen someone pray. Nathan stole a peek around him. When his eyes met those of a redheaded girl behind him, he quickly faced forward and squeezed his eyelids shut.

During supper, Bodie and the Hamiltons met some of the other children and were amazed at how friendly everyone was. The food was the best they had eaten in a long time.

In the girls' dormitory, Susan was given a cot next to a ten-year-old girl from the Bronx, named Cleora Coffield. They both were a little frightened and pushed their cots together to hold hands after the lights went out.

The next morning, all sixty-four girls and fifty-four boys were given brand-new clothing. The boys wore navy blue knickers, white collarless shirts, black suspenders, black socks, and black high-top shoes.

The girls wore frilly white petticoats and pantaloons, navy blue cotton dresses, white pinafores, black stockings, and sturdy high-top black shoes that laced above the ankles.

The chaperones were there to help the girls dress and fix their hair. Each girl wore either a red or a white ribbon in her hair.

Miss Ellie Voss, who now helped Cleora and Susan with their hair ribbons, had dedicated her life to the work of the orphan trains. She was tall for a woman and wore her mouse-colored hair pulled straight back into a bun. Despite her spinsterish appearance, Ellie made every child that came her way feel special, and each one blossomed under her care.

Now she told Susan and Cleora that they would ride in coach number two, which was always where Ellie's girls rode. There would be boys in the car, too.

✦

At breakfast Reverend Brace talked to the children and wished them well as he told them good-bye.

Afterwards, the children and their chaperones were transported by carriages to Grand Central Station on Manhattan's East Side. The orphan train, with its engine, coal car, and four coaches, stood ready for boarding at the far end of the depot. Engineer Boris Myers, fireman Wally Hicks, and cook Hezekiah Washington, stood by the coal car and waved their greetings to the children as they lined up to board the train.

When Ellie Voss lined up her girls beside coach number two, Susan was glad to see her brothers and Bodie in line for the same coach. She introduced them to Cleora.

As each child boarded, a small name tag was pinned to his or her shoulder.

In coach number two, Jared and Nathan sat directly across the aisle from Susan and Cleora. Just behind Jared and Nathan, Bodie sat with a nine-year-old boy from Yonkers.

As the engine whistle let out a long, shrill blast and the train chugged out of the station, the 118 children—who ranged in age from five to fifteen—were both frightened and excited. Most of them had never been outside the New York slums, much less to the wild and wooly West. Out there in that mysterious land lay their new life. Who would adopt them? What would life be like where there were savage Indians, great herds of buffalo, and thousands of cattle dotting the prairies?

As the train left the city behind, spellbound children pressed their noses to the windows and watched the landscape fly by. When lunch time came, they ate in shifts in the dining car and hurried back to their seats to see what the countryside looked like.

When darkness fell, the train pulled into a small Pennsylvania town for the night, chugging to a stop on a side track.

17

ON MONDAY, MAY 15, John Stranger and Breanna Baylor were leaving the train at Washington's Union Station when a well-dressed man approached them.

"Mr. Stranger? Miss Baylor?"

"Yes," John said, turning back to give Breanna his hand as she stepped off the platform.

"I'm Edward Hatch. I'm here from President Grant's office to escort you to the White House. May I say, sir, that I've heard of your prowess in tracking and catching criminals. It is an honor to have you here."

"Thank you," John said, as he shook his hand.

Hatch then bowed slightly to Breanna. "I speak for all of the president's staff, Miss Baylor, when I say that your name has become a household word in the White House. We, as well as the rest of this nation, are in your debt."

After Hatch made arrangements to have the luggage delivered, he escorted John and Breanna to the official carriage. When the carriage started moving, Hatch asked John about Chief U.S. Marshal Solomon Duvall, with whom he had fought in the same army unit in the Mexican War. John assured Hatch that Duvall was fine and in good health, and he would give Duvall his greetings.

The carriage turned onto Pennsylvania Avenue, and the White House came into view.

"If I remember my U.S. history correctly," John said, "wasn't it George Washington who chose the site for the presidential mansion?"

"Yes," Hatch said. "Construction began in 1792, but it wasn't completed until 1797, when John Adams was president."

"And it was burned in 1814 by British spies, right?"

"That's right."

"John," Breanna said, "for not being American-born, you really know a lot about this country."

Hatch looked at John inquisitively. "What country are you from, sir?" he asked.

"Oh! There it is!" John said, as the White House came into view. "Hard to believe it's almost eighty years old, isn't it, Breanna? How large is the property?"

"Eighteen acres, sir," Hatch replied.

"Look at the cherry trees, Breanna," John said.

"Oh, they're lovely! I hope we can see them up close later."

John and Breanna craned their necks to take it all in. On the north front, forming the main entrance, was a portico of Ionic columns reaching from ground to roof pediment. As the carriage swung toward the west gate, they saw that the columns at the front of the structure were balanced on the south by a semicircular colonnaded balcony. The lawn was greening up from winter's tawny color, and the shrubbery was in bud.

Guards recognized the carriage and swung open the west gate. As the carriage pulled up to the front portico, Hatch said, "Mrs. Grant gave us orders to alert her as soon as you arrive. She wants to personally escort you to your rooms. The president said he would see both of you at dinner this evening.

Actually, the entire White House staff has been invited."

In a few moments Julia Grant came out and embraced Breanna, then offered her hand to the tall man in black. John bowed and kissed her hand, and Julia giggled like a schoolgirl. She dismissed Hatch, saying she would see him at dinner.

That evening, when John Stranger answered the knock at his door, he found Edward Hatch in the hall with a gracious silver-haired lady beside him.

"President and Mrs. Grant asked that we escort you and Miss Baylor to the dining room, sir. May I present my wife, Pearl? Honey, this is the famous John Stranger."

Pearl Hatch was impressed with John's towering height and rugged good looks. She smiled and offered him her hand as she said, "I am honored to meet you, Mr. Stranger." She wondered what his real name was as he took her hand and inclined his head.

The trio walked a short way to Breanna's room. When she opened the door, her beauty took John's breath away. Her hair was done in a stunning upsweep, crowned at the top with tiny ringlets. The velvet bodice of her floor-length dress was royal blue. The shirred puffed sleeves and skirt were a creamy taffeta elaborately flocked in darker blue velvet. At her graceful neck was a ruffle of the same creamy fabric as the skirt. She wore sparkling sapphire eardrops that caught the light as she turned her head.

After introductions, they proceeded to the closed doors of the White House dining room where the rest of the president's staff was gathered in the hallway. Edward Hatch nodded at a distinguished-looking couple, who hastened to meet the guests of honor. Hatch introduced John and Breanna to Vice

President and Mrs. Schuyler Colfax.

Colfax was about to take the couple around and introduce them to the rest of the White House staff when someone whispered, "The president and Mrs. Grant!"

The staff cleared a path to John and Breanna, and all eyes turned toward the Grants as they descended the spiral staircase. Julia was stunning in a black faille dress, a black onyx brooch pinned to the high collar, and fluted ruching at her wrists.

Grant smiled pleasantly at John, while Breanna and Julia exchanged some words. "John Stranger, I presume?" he said.

John took Grant's hand in his solid grip and smiled. "Yes, sir. President Ulysses S. Grant, I presume."

Grant laughed heartily. "Yes, Mr. Stranger!"

The president turned to Breanna and said, "Hello, brave lady."

Breanna curtsied gracefully.

When everyone was seated at their places in the dining room, President Grant introduced Breanna and John to his staff. First he spoke of John Stranger's impressive record in tracking and capturing the worst outlaws in the West, under the authority of the U.S. Marshal's Office in Denver. He then told the story of how the lovely nurse, seated next to Julia, had risked her life to save his own at Abilene, Kansas, on April 22.

The small crowd began to clap, and Grant urged her to stand. The applause grew louder as the White House staff stood and gave her an ovation that lasted for two full minutes. John knew that Breanna probably felt like hiding under the table, but he only winked encouragement at her and continued to applaud with the rest of them.

After a time, the president turned the conversation to why

he had invited John Stranger to Washington. He had a job for him to do, if he would agree to it. "I'd like to meet with you in the Oval Office at ten o'clock tomorrow morning, Mr. Stranger, if that's acceptable to you."

"Fine, sir."

"Julia has plans to entertain Miss Baylor for lunch with some of the senators' wives. On Wednesday at eleven, Miss Baylor, you will receive your presidential commendation before a joint session of Congress."

Breanna's stomach did a flip-flop.

On Tuesday morning, John entered the Oval Office in the company of the president's personal secretary, Wilson Campbell.

When he was seated, the president moved behind his desk and sat down.

"I asked Miss Baylor if your last name was really Stranger," he said, "and she politely evaded giving me an answer. I suppose if I ask you the identical question, you'll do the same."

"We had a beautiful sunrise this morning, didn't we, sir?" John said.

Grant shrugged. "Oh, well. I guess there are some things that even the president of the United States can't know."

John smiled and confirmed the president's statement with his silence.

"Well!" Grant said. "Let's talk about this job I have in mind for you."

"Yes, sir."

"First, let me say that you will be well paid for your services, Mr. Stranger."

"You can call me John, sir."

"All right. And you can call me Ulysses."

"Yes, Mr. President."

Grant chuckled, and shook his head.

"And as far as my being paid, Mr. President," John said, "I decline. I'll do whatever you ask of me gratis, for my country, even as I do now under the direction of my good friend Solomon Duvall."

"John, this is highly irregular. The government has funds allotted in the budget for—"

"It isn't necessary, Mr. President. All my bills are paid, and I'm doing fine financially. Now, what can I do for you?"

"This world could use about a million men like you, John."

Stranger grinned. "You could get some votes against that."

"No doubt," the president said. "Well, let me say first that I have often received information from Chief Duvall about your success in capturing outlaws. Impressive to say the least."

"Thank you, sir."

"I have also received information from other sources of your expertise in handling Indians."

"I've had some experience along those lines, sir. It seems the Lord has given me a keen understanding of the Indian mind."

Grant nodded. "Well, John, a serious problem has developed in Dakota Territory between the Sioux and the government Indian agency at Bismarck. If something isn't done, there's going to be bloodshed. I need a man with your experience and ability to go there and handle it."

"I'll do my best, sir. Are we talking about Sitting Bull?"

"He's at the core of it, but so far he's had his Hunkpapa sub-chiefs give the agency headaches. The man in charge of the agency is a half-breed Comanche. Name's Perez Tamerlane."

"Some name for a half-breed," John said. "This may be the core of your problem, sir. The Sioux may not like to deal with a half-breed—which is an abomination to them—especially a half-breed Comanche."

"Sounds like you're already onto it. Can you leave for Dakota Territory right away?"

"How about if I take the first train west after Breanna receives her commendation before Congress tomorrow?"

"Excellent! My secretary will give you the money for your travel expenses before you leave this office."

John threw up his hands. "Not necessary, sir."

"As you say. Now, Julia has a special luncheon planned for your Breanna on Thursday, so she probably won't be heading west until Friday. Is that all right?"

"Of course."

"All right, then. When you get to Bismarck, John, feel free to wire me with any questions you might have, and please wire me when you have this Sioux situation in hand."

"I'll do it, sir."

"I don't know how to thank you for this," Grant said.

"No need for that. I'm glad to help."

"Well, you and I are to have lunch with the two most beautiful women in the world in about fifteen minutes. Shall we mosey that way?"

The large Congressional Hall was beginning to fill up with chattering senators and representatives. Breanna nervously waited with John and Wilson Campbell in a side room while the president conversed at the door with two men of his cabinet.

"John" Breanna whispered, "I've never been so scared in all my life."

"Even when you dashed up those steps on the presidential

213

coach, knowing bullets would fly any second?"

"This is worse, John. It's planned."

John put an arm around Breanna as Wilson Campbell said, "You'll do fine out there, Miss Baylor. Anyone with your kind of grit will find this a breeze. Just smile and let Mr. Grant brag on you for a while."

The president finished his conversation at the door and closed it. He turned around and glanced at the clock on the wall, and said, "All right, Wilson. You take John and get seated out there. My usual entourage is waiting for me down the hall. Miss Baylor will stay with me and sit on the platform."

When the president made his entrance with Breanna at his side, the crowd stood to their feet and applauded. It helped Breanna to see John out there smiling at her.

Vice President Colfax called the meeting to order and introduced President Ulysses S. Grant. The president waited until the applause had faded and the congressmen had taken their seats, then began telling of the attempted assassination.

When Grant finished the story by saying he had been on many a battlefield and had observed great deeds of valor, but none compared with the valor displayed by Miss Breanna Baylor, the men of Congress broke in on his final words by leaping to their feet and cheering.

The president then led Breanna to the podium. The roar intensified, and Grant let it go on for a long moment, then motioned for quiet.

When everyone was seated, the president presented Breanna with the Presidential Commendation of Courage and Valor. There was another standing ovation as Breanna graciously received it from the president's hand and he kissed her cheek.

While the crowd continued to voice its approval, the president asked Breanna to say a few words. For a brief moment, Breanna thought she might faint, but when the place grew quiet and she stepped to the podium, a calmness came over her.

"Gentlemen of the United States Congress, first lady, and guests...I will be brief. In the Gospel of John, the Lord Jesus Christ said, 'This is my commandment, that ye love one another as I have loved you. Greater love hath no man than this, that a man lay down his life for his friends.' I consider this great president of the United States my friend. What I did in Abilene that day was only a natural thing because I love my president. There is no love that can match the love Jesus showed when He died to provide a way of salvation for sinners like you and me. Let it be said that what Breanna Baylor did for her president at Abilene is because she learned the principle from her Lord Jesus Christ at Calvary. Thank you."

The crowd surged to its feet once more, applauding and cheering, while John Stranger wiped tears from his cheeks.

That afternoon, Breanna kissed John good-bye at the railroad station, saying she would ask the Lord to give him wisdom in Dakota Territory.

When the train was out of sight, Julia Grant put an arm around Breanna, and they walked slowly back to the carriage. "All right, honey," Julia said, "let's go back to the White House and have some tea."

When Breanna later boarded the train at Washington's Union Station to return to Denver, both Julia and Breanna wept. A deep friendship had sprung up between the women, and they knew it might be a long time, or never, before they met again.

As the train rolled westward, Breanna laid her head back and closed her eyes and thought of John. She had kept a frenetic pace in Washington, and she was worn out. Soon, the rhythm of the clacking wheels and the steady sway of the coach lulled her to sleep.

At midday on Monday, May 22, Breanna was reading her Bible when the train slowed, then chuffed to a stop in a small Nebraska town. The conductor had come through the car only moments before, announcing to the passengers that at Lexington they would need to take on coal and water. The stop would last about fifty minutes.

As the train squealed to a halt, Breanna placed her Bible in her overnight bag. She looked forward to getting off the train and stretching her legs. She glanced out the window and noticed a smaller train parked on a side track. Several children—all dressed in navy blue and white—played in an open area next to the parked train. Two women and a man were watching them.

Breanna wondered if this was one of the New York Children's Aid Society trains she had read about. There were no markings on the train to indicate that it belonged to the Society, but the sight of the children dressed alike made her almost certain this was an orphan train.

Breanna made a quick count and tallied up twenty-six boys and girls—not as many as she'd read usually traveled together.

To satisfy her curiosity, Breanna left the coach and crossed the tracks toward the children. The adults who watched the children smiled as she approached.

"Hello," Breanna said. "My name is Breanna Baylor. I'm on

that train over there on my way to Denver, Colorado. I saw these children dressed in uniforms and just wondered if this is one of the famous orphan trains out of New York City."

"Sure is," the man said. "May I introduce my wife, Nora Egelston, and Miss Ellie Voss? I am Harold Egelston."

"I'm glad to meet you," Breanna said.

Ellie Voss frowned slightly. There was something familiar about the name *Breanna Baylor*. Where had she heard it before?

Harold Egelston continued to speak. "The three of us are part of the train's Placing Out Committee, Miss—it is Miss Baylor?"

"Yes. I've read a good deal about your work. You and other adults are on the train to oversee the adoptions, aren't you?"

"Yes, ma'am. Right now, though, we have a serious problem. There are 118 children on the train, and several of them are sick. We've put them in the rear coach. The unaffected ones are either in town right now with the other members of the committee or are here with us, as you can see."

Breanna's ears pricked at mention of the sick children. "Do you know what the sickness is?" she asked.

"Influenza. We weren't scheduled to stop here in Lexington, but we wanted to have a doctor check the children as soon as possible. They only have one doctor, and he diagnosed the influenza and quarantined them in coach four, then he had to get back to his office.

"At the moment, Dr. Drennan has his nurse at the Western Union office, trying to find a qualified nurse in some nearby town who could join the train and care for the sick children so the train can stay on schedule. Prospective adoptive families travel great distances from their farms and ranches to meet our trains. If this one gets off schedule, it'll work a hardship for many people."

"I can understand that," Breanna said. "I haven't told you yet, but I'm a certified medical nurse. I work out of Dr. Lyle Goodwin's office in Denver. I've had a great deal of experience with influenza. If you'll accept my services, I'll gladly travel with you. I'm headed for Denver, anyway."

"We would consider you an answer to prayer, Miss Baylor!" Egelston said.

Suddenly Ellie's eyes lit up. "Yes! I knew I recognized your name, and now I recognize your face from the newspapers! Breanna Baylor! You're the nurse who saved President Grant's life in Abilene, Kansas, last month!"

18

"MISS BAYLOR, WE'RE HONORED to be in the presence of such a celebrity!" Nora Egelston said.

"I'm not a celebrity," Breanna said shyly. "Just an American citizen who did her duty. Since you've accepted my offer to join the train, could somebody help me with my baggage? I have a small trunk in the baggage coach."

"Of course," Egelston said. "I'll get it for you."

"Thank you. Since it's checked to Denver, I'll come along and tell them I'm getting off here. I have an overnight bag at my seat, too. Is anyone with the sick children at the moment?"

"Yes," Nora said. "Chaperones like the rest of us."

"All right. Mr. Egelston, I'll need you to take me to Dr....Drennan, did you say? I'll need as much salicylic acid as possible to take with us. It's the only medication used successfully to treat influenza. It brings the fever down and keeps it in check."

Movement at the engine caught Harold Egelston's eye. "Here's the engineer and fireman. I'll get them to take care of your luggage, Miss Baylor, and we can go to Dr. Drennan's office immediately."

Ellie headed for the Western Union office to stop any more telegrams going out requesting a nurse, and Nora went to coach number four to tell the women there what was happening.

Thirty minutes later, Harold Egelston was carrying a box containing a good supply of salicylic acid, thermometers, and some bottles of wood alcohol, as he and Breanna walked briskly toward the railroad station.

"Oh!" Breanna said, as they approached the Western Union office. "Mr. Egelston, I need to send a wire to Dr. Goodwin in Denver to tell him what I'm doing."

Before the orphan train pulled out of the station, Egelston gathered the entire Placing Out Committee and introduced Breanna, explaining that she had volunteered to ride the train for the rest of the trip and care for the sick children.

While Breanna proceeded to coach number four, the men of the Committee fulfilled her request for water in wooden barrels, tin cups, and a sufficient number of blankets.

Inside the coach, children lay on the seats and the floor between the seats, leaving the aisle clear. Breanna moved slowly along the aisle, telling the children that she was a nurse and would help them get well.

As the whistle blew and the orphan train pulled out of Lexington, Breanna was already making the children as comfortable as possible. She was glad they had identification tags so she could call them by name.

Breanna had worked her way through about half of the children when a knock came at the front door of the coach. It was Ellie.

"Oh, hello. What can I do for you?"

"I came to see what I can do for you, Miss Baylor. The two ladies who stayed with the sick children while the train was stopped in Lexington said you told them to go on back to their husbands."

"Yes, I didn't want them exposed any more than they already have been."

"I appreciate that, Miss Baylor, but—"

"Breanna."

"I appreciate that, Breanna, but twenty-seven sick children are an awful lot for one person to handle. I'm here to help if you need me."

"Ellie, I appreciate your offer, but adults can get influenza as easily as children."

"Well, if you're willing to take the risk, why can't I?"

Breanna smiled. "You can. Come on in."

When the door was shut and the loud sound of the wheels muffled, Ellie said, "Before we get started, could I ask you something?"

"Certainly."

"The papers quoted you as giving thanks to God that neither the president nor you were hit. Then they quoted you as saying that you're a born-again Christian."

Breanna smiled. "So you want to know if the quotation is accurate."

"Yes."

"Ellie, I'm a blood-washed, born-again child of God, with my faith in the precious Lord Jesus Christ and Him alone for my salvation."

"Praise the Lord! So am I!"

"Well, Ellie, it'll be wonderful having a Christian work with me. Let's get started. The water barrels are there, and the tin cups. See the teaspoon? The salicylic acid is in those cloth sacks. Two level teaspoons to a half-cup of water. Mix it good with the spoon. And while you're doing that, I'll finish making the children as comfortable as possible, then I'll begin taking temperatures. Those children who have high fevers will get a double dose."

Before they could start their tasks, there was another knock at the door. Breanna looked down at a blond girl with big blue eyes.

"Miss Baylor, I'm Cleora Coffield. I'd like to know how my friend is doing."

"Well, honey," Breanna said, "I haven't examined the children yet. I'll let you know as soon as I can. What's her name?"

"Susie Hamilton. Her two brothers are in this car, too. Could I come back in an hour or so and see how they are?"

"Cleora," Ellie said, stepping close, "you shouldn't be here, honey."

The door of the adjoining coach opened, and Nora Egelston appeared. "Cleora, here you are! You're not supposed to leave your coach!"

The child looked as if she might cry. "I just wanted to know how Susie and Jared and Nathan are, Mrs. Egelston."

"But it's dangerous to move between the cars when the train is in motion." Nora touched Cleora's shoulder. "You go back to your seat, honey. I'll keep close check with Nurse Baylor and I'll let you know about your friends as soon as possible."

"All right. Thank you, ma'am."

The rear door of the adjoining coach opened again. This time a dark-haired youth on crutches appeared.

"Bodie, you're not supposed to be moving between the cars, either," Nora said.

"I was wondering about Jared, Susie, and Nathan Hamilton, ma'am. I didn't mean to break any rules."

Breanna looked at Nora, then Ellie. "I'll say one thing—the Hamilton children sure have some good friends."

Cleora and Bodie smiled at each other.

"You two get back to your seats, now," Nora said. "I'll come back later and check with Miss Baylor about your friends."

Both children thanked her, then Bodie looked at Breanna and said, "Thank you for joining the train to take care of us, Miss Baylor."

"I'm glad I can do it, Bodie. What's your last name?"

"Brolin, ma'am."

"Well, Bodie Brolin and Cleora Coffield, I am very happy to meet you. Are you both feeling all right?"

They assured her they were, and Nora Egelston ushered them back to the other car.

When Breanna closed the door, she turned to Ellie and asked, "When did these children start showing signs of illness?"

"On Saturday. It came on ten of them quite suddenly, and almost exactly at the same time. The rest of the twenty-seven got sick yesterday. None of us knew for sure what it was until Dr. Drennan confirmed it. We were afraid it might be one of those European plagues or something. Saturday morning, the ten I spoke of began complaining of muscle pains, with soreness in their chests, heads, and abdomens. Then came the fever and the chills. Worked the same way with the other seventeen yesterday."

"Influenza does come on rather quickly," Breanna said. "Ordinarily it doesn't last long. The acute phase of the infection is usually over in three or four days."

"Is it life-threatening?" Ellie asked.

"The mortality rate is quite low, actually, but it's very important that we keep the children warm."

Breanna had noticed two boys and a girl near the rear of the coach who kept raising their heads when Cleora and Bodie were at the door. She moved close to the sandy-haired boys and the girl with the long dark-brown hair. "Something tells me you three are the Hamiltons," she said.

The children acknowledged that they were.

"Oh, I love your British accents," Breanna said, tucking the blankets tightly under their chins. "Where in Great Britain are you from?"

Jared told her they were from Wales, and that both their parents had died since they came to New York.

"I'm so sorry about your parents," Breanna said. "You lie still and relax now. I'll get to you as soon as I can to take your temperatures."

As the train rolled westward, Ellie followed Breanna as she took temperatures and gave instructions one by one on how much of the salicylic mixture to administer.

As Breanna knelt over a little boy who was coughing, she glanced over her shoulder and said, "Ellie, don't let them sneeze or cough directly at you. The influenza infection is transmitted through the respiratory tract."

Ellie carefully observed Breanna's bedside manner and was impressed with the tenderness she showed as she spoke to her young patients.

Soon Breanna came upon a set of identical twin girls who identified themselves as Bessie and Tessie Spaulding. They told her they were from Brooklyn. Their parents had died in a tenement fire while the twins were staying all night with some friends.

Breanna soothed them with her hands and words, and after taking their temperatures, told Ellie to give them each a half-cup of the mixture. When Breanna moved on, the girls were looking at her with adoring eyes.

"Breanna," Ellie said, "you certainly have found your calling in life. The Lord created you to be a nurse. You have such a marvelous way with your patients, and I can tell you have a deep love for children."

"Comes naturally," Breanna said with a grin. "I used to be a child. Anyone could see that you love children, too. You make your living taking these precious ones west so they can have real homes and meaningful lives. Were you working with children before you went to work for the Society?"

"Not for a living. I was a maid in a hotel. Reverend Brace and I went to the same church. I was a Sunday school teacher there, and he said no one teaches children in Sunday school unless they love them. He offered me this job, and I jumped at it."

"And I'm sure you find the work very rewarding."

"There's no way to describe it, Breanna. You show children love, and they'll give it back a hundredfold." Ellie paused for a moment, then added, "The job has one real tough part, though."

"Oh?"

"I get so attached to the little darlings on these long trips that I hate to give them up."

"I can understand that. It's so easy to get attached to children. I often think of how much Jesus loved children when He was on earth—how He took them in His arms and showed them His love."

Breanna paused to read a thermometer, then said, "Remember what the Bible says in Mark 10, when people were bringing little children to Jesus so that He could touch them and His disciples rebuked them?"

Ellie nodded. "And Jesus let those guys know real quickly how much He loved children."

"A half cup of medicine here, Ellie. Oh, and I love the way He put it: 'Suffer the little children to come unto me, and forbid them not: for of such is the kingdom of God.' And then

He took them in His arms and put His hands on them and blessed them."

Sunshine spilling through the coach windows reflected in Breanna's tears as she looked at her newfound friend and said, "Ellie, some glorious day I'm going to put my arms around Jesus and thank Him for going to the cross for me so that He could give me eternal life and make me a child of God."

Some of the children looked on as tears flowed from Ellie's eyes, too. "You'll have to get in line, honey!" she said, smiling. "I'm going to get to Him first!"

The two women laughed together for joy at the thought.

There was a knock at the door, and Ellie opened it to find Lucille Paddock, another chaperone of the Committee, with a small boy.

"This is Billy Ames, Miss Ellie," Lucille said. "He's getting sick."

Ellie put her hand on top of Billy's head. "Come in, darlin'. We'll get some medicine in you right away. Thank you, Lucille."

"I'm afraid I'll be bringing more," Lucille said.

Ellie put Billy Ames on the floor between two occupied seats and covered him with a blanket. Breanna told Ellie to go ahead and give him a half-cup of the medicine.

Moments later, Breanna reached the Hamilton children and placed thermometers in their mouths. "Keep your mouths closed," she said, as she had done with all the others. "Just nod to answer my question. Did you come down with the influenza Saturday?"

All three nodded.

She brushed hair from Susan's forehead. "Then you only have a couple more days till the worst is over. The medicine Miss Ellie gives you will make you feel better within an hour or so."

She read the thermometers one by one, then said, "Ellie, when you get to these three, Susie will need three-quarters of a cup. The boys will do fine on half cups."

Ellie nodded. "I've got to mix up some more. Be there shortly."

"Miss Baylor…"

"Yes, Jared?"

"I sold papers for the *New York Tribune*. I saw your picture on the front page with President and Mrs. Grant. You saved his life, didn't you?"

"Mm-hmm."

"When I saw the picture, I thought you were pretty, but you're even prettier in person."

"Thank you, Jared. You're very kind. I imagine as a newsboy you've met a lot of interesting people."

"I sure have, ma'am."

"I'd like to hear about them sometime."

"Jared did lots of other kinds of jobs, too, Miss Baylor," Susan said. "After Papa died, he worked very hard to take care of Mother and us kids. He's the best big brother in all the world."

"And I'm the best *little* brother in all the world, huh, Susie?" Nathan said.

"Of course," she replied, giving him a wan smile.

Nathan looked up at Breanna. "I didn't like living in the alley."

"You children lived in an alley?"

"Yes," Jared said. "After Mother died, we had to move out of our apartment. We had nowhere else to go."

Breanna stroked Nathan's brow. "Well, you won't ever have to live in an alley again. There are some nice people out there ahead of us who will adopt you and give you a nice house to live in."

"Reverend Brace fixed it so nobody can adopt just one or two of us," Jared said. "They have to take all three, or they can't adopt any of us."

Breanna smiled. "That's good. I've read about many of the orphan children being adopted out and separated from their brothers and sisters."

"We won't be separated," Nathan said. "Reverend Brace promised."

Breanna nodded. "Well, I have to move on. Miss Ellie will be here in a few minutes to give you your medicine."

Breanna worked steadily, moving from child to child. The last child was a dark-eyed little girl whose name tag identified her as Antonia Alberghetti.

"Hello, Antonia," Breanna said. "Will you hold your mouth closed over this thermometer until I take it out?"

"Yes, ma'am." Antonia suddenly began to cough, her chest heaving painfully. When Antonia had stopped coughing, Breanna placed the thermometer in her mouth.

There was something immensely appealing about this little girl that stirred Breanna's heart. She was a cameo in miniature, with porcelain features, dark expressive eyes, and black wavy hair.

Breanna could tell that Antonia's fever was high, even before reading the thermometer. When she took it from the child's mouth and read 103.8, she turned to Ellie, who was right behind her. "This little girl will need a cup and a half. I think she may already have pneumonia."

As she spoke, Breanna pressed an ear to Antonia's chest and said, "Start giving her the mixture now. I'm going to get my medical bag."

Breanna took out her stethoscope and listened to Antonia's lungs. Ellie watched Breanna's eyes and knew before she spoke that it wasn't good.

"It's pneumonia, all right," Breanna said. "I assume she was one of the first to become ill."

"Yes. In fact, Antonia was the very first to complain of not feeling well."

Breanna nodded. "Even then, I'm surprised that her lungs could be full so quickly. Antonia..."

"Yes, ma'am?"

"Have you had pneumonia before?"

"I've been sick like this before, but I don't know what it was."

"Ellie, do they have any health records on these children?"

"No. They're all street urchins."

Breanna pulled up the blanket around Antonia's chin and rose to her feet. "Go ahead and give her the other half cup, Ellie, then start at the front and give water to each child. They must have water continually so they don't dehydrate. I'll be back shortly."

As Breanna headed toward the front of the coach, Ellie called, "Where are you going?"

"To speak to the cook. I'll explain when I come back."

Breanna hastened across the platforms between the second and third coaches. In number two she spotted Cleora Coffield and Bodie Brolin and paused to tell them the Hamiltons were doing as well as could be expected. They would be fine in a few days.

When she entered car number one and darted up the aisle toward the front door, Nora Egelston intercepted her. "You look upset, Miss Baylor. Is something wrong?"

"Little Antonia Alberghetti has pneumonia. I'm on my way to the dining car to ask the cook to make a poultice."

By this time, other committee members had gathered.

"Miss Baylor," said a short, bald man, "I'm Gil Kingman.

This is my wife, Doris. Antonia's in our group. Is this pneumonia serious?"

"*Very* serious, folks. I think she's had pneumonia before, which has left her lungs weak. The only way I can save her is to make an onion poultice. Time is of the essence. I must hurry."

"Of course," Kingman said. "May God bless your efforts."

"I'm praying that He will," she said, and plunged through the door.

Ten minutes later, Ellie Voss looked up from her task of distributing water to the children as Breanna entered the car, carrying a cloth fragrant with onions.

While placing the poultice on Antonia's chest and wrapping it with gauze to hold it in place, Breanna said, "I hope this will break up her congestion. I'm going to listen to the chests of the other children. If any are getting pneumonia, I want to catch it early."

At sunset the train began to slow. They had arrived in North Platte, the first stop for the children to go on display for adoption.

In the other coaches, ninety excited and apprehensive children got ready to walk to the town hall. They would eat supper while the townspeople looked them over. When the meal was done, the prospective parents would make their choices.

Ellie explained to Breanna that the committee members would talk with the people to make sure they understood the rules of adoption. The committee members would also ask questions about their homes. If they were satisfied with the answers, the adoption would proceed.

In some cases, the orphans would be taken in as foster children. The rules for foster parents were the same as for those who adopted the children.

Breanna was satisfied that none of the other children showed signs of pneumonia, but while the train was stopped, she wanted to pick up some more onions for Antonia. She wished she could get mustard seeds, which worked even better than onions, but she doubted they would be available in this small town.

19

BODIE LEANED PAST CLEORA to look out the window as the train pulled into North Platte.

"Wondering if this will be your new home, Bodie?" Cleora asked.

"Might be yours," he said, sitting back again. "You're not going to have a problem being adopted. I'm the one nobody's going to adopt."

"Bodie, don't worry," Cleora said. "You're a very nice boy, and there's lots of things you can do, even if your knee is bad."

A large crowd of farmers, ranchers, and townspeople converged on the cars to get a closer look as the children emerged. The children had been told that most of the people in the crowd would be there to gawk. Only a few would be looking for children to adopt.

The North Platte town council chairman greeted the Placing Out Committee and presented three of their town's pastors and their wives. Breanna glanced at the crowd for a few moments, then went back to her patients.

As Bodie slowly made his way down the platform steps, he felt the eyes of the crowd on him. Cleora stayed at his side as they joined the line of uniformed orphans.

"I might as well have stayed on the train, Cleora. Do you

see how those people are staring at me?"

Cleora smiled up at Bodie. "Just ignore them, Bodie. If not here, you'll find your family in some other town. Besides, you have to get off the train to get your supper."

While the meal was in progress at the town hall, prospective parents inspected the orphans. When the meal was over, the children were lined up so the people could get a closer look.

When the evening was over, seventeen orphans left the train to go to their new homes. The committee spoke cheerfully to the remaining children, telling them there were five more stops. Most likely, by the time the choosing was done at Denver, all of them would have new homes.

"See, Bodie?" Cleora said. "I didn't get picked either."

A little six-year-old boy walking in front of them was crying quietly. Bodie hopped up beside him and said, "Hey, Charlie, there are plenty more towns ahead. I bet there'll be a nice family in one of them who'll adopt you."

Charlie Harper had been a street waif on Manhattan's lower East Side for over two years. His parents had abandoned him on the doorstep of a tenement building. From time to time, people in the tenement had fed him, but he had slept in a storage space under a staircase until just a month ago, when new owners of the building ran him off. Reverend Brace found him wandering the streets, begging for food, and took him to the Society's dormitory.

"Promise, Bodie?" Charlie said.

"Well, I can't really promise, but I bet there will be. Everything's going to be all right."

A smile broke over the little boy's face, and he skipped on ahead.

Cleora looked up at Bodie with a smile on her face. "You just did a wonderful thing, Bodie," she said.

↑

When Ellie Voss returned to the quarantine car, she learned that Hezekiah Washington had provided what little food the sick children could eat, and a good meal for Breanna.

Gil Kingman and Harold Egelston had talked to the local grocer, who came up with a small sack of mustard seeds. The onion poultice hadn't worked. Now Breanna quickly made a mustard seed poultice and put it on Antonia's chest, praying that the Lord would spare Antonia's life.

In the middle of the night, as the other children and Ellie Voss lay asleep, Breanna sat beside little Antonia, listening to each rattling breath. A single lantern burned low at the ceiling, midway in the coach.

Breanna held Antonia's tiny hand and spoke just above a whisper. "Dear God, I ask you in Jesus' name to spare this sweet child's life. I've gone as far as I can. It's now up to You. She's had more than her share of bumps in life. I pray that You will clear up the pneumonia and let her live to find a good home and a happy life. I'm asking that she will be raised in a Christian home. You are a great big wonderful God, and I know I can ask big things of you."

While Breanna continued to pray, Jared Hamilton lay a few feet away, listening to every word. He had never heard anyone pray until that first day at the Children's Aid Society. These people on the train prayed and thanked God before every meal! As he listened to Breanna, he realized she believed that not only was God interested in people thanking Him for the food He provided, He also cared about making sick children well.

When Breanna closed her prayer in the name of Jesus, Jared remembered songs he had heard people sing at Christmas time about baby Jesus in the manger. He knew the songs were about

God's Son, but that was where his knowledge ended. He was touched by Breanna's prayer for Antonia, and he felt something warm flow through his heart.

The next morning, after the children ate breakfast, the chaperones took them to a field nearby and let them run off some energy before starting the day's journey. While the shouts and squeals of children drifted through the open windows in the isolation coach, a weary Breanna Baylor and Ellie Voss rejoiced. The mustard poultice had worked, and from the sound of little Antonia's cough, it was evident the congestion was breaking up.

Jared Hamilton looked on and smiled as the two women openly praised the Lord. He decided that God really did hear Miss Baylor's prayer.

The train pulled out at midmorning and continued its westward journey. The children in the first two coaches pressed their noses to the windows at the sight of a great herd of buffalo. Engineer Boris Myers slowed the train so they could get a good look at the huge beasts. In the isolation car, some of the children, including Jared, Susan, and Nathan, were feeling much better. With help from Breanna and Ellie, they were able to get a look at the buffalo, too.

Bessie and Tessie Spaulding were feeling so much better that they were sitting up now. When they politely asked Ellie and Breanna if they could have something to eat, the ladies smiled at each other.

When the twins finished eating, Breanna stopped to pick up their dishes and eating utensils. As she was placing them on the tray, Tessie said, "Miss Baylor, Bessie and I are really scared."

"About what, honey?"

"Being adopted by different families. Look at how Donnie and Kathy Marsh were separated yesterday. I would just die if Bessie was taken away from me."

"So would I," Bessie said.

"Well, I know Reverend Brace made a stipulation concerning the Hamilton children. Didn't he do the same thing for you?"

"Not that we know of," Tessie said.

"I'll check on that with Mr. Egelston," Breanna said.

Harold Egelston was by the back door, talking with Luther Wiggins, when Breanna entered the car.

"Hello, Miss Baylor," Egelston said. "Ellie told us of the improvement you're seeing in some of the children. Glad to know Antonia has passed the crisis."

"Yes," Breanna said with a sigh. "She gave me a real scare."

"Is there something we can do for you, ma'am?" Wiggins asked.

"I have a question concerning the Spaulding twins."

"Are they worse?" Wiggins asked.

"No, a few minutes ago they told me they were afraid the same thing that happened to the Marshes could happen to them."

"Oh, I see," Wiggins said, rubbing his chin. "I guess it could."

"Are you sure? The Hamilton children told me Reverend Brace made a stipulation that they can't be separated. All three must be adopted by the same family. Certainly he would have made such a stipulation for identical twins."

"I don't think so," Wiggins said, "but let's check the records."

Egelston turned to the overhead rack, opened a valise, and pulled out the folder marked "Spaulding." He studied the documents for a moment, then shook his head. "No such stipulation here."

"Surely you can make such a stipulation," Breanna said.

"No, we can't. Only Reverend Brace has that power, Miss Baylor. If it wasn't done before we left New York, it can't be done now."

"Mr. Wiggins, it was hard enough for Bessie and Tessie to be orphaned and become street waifs, but to be torn apart at this young age could be very harmful to them. Wouldn't Reverend Brace understand that?"

Wiggins and Egelston exchanged glances.

"I'm sure our director does understand," Egelston said. "It could be that it was an oversight, or it could be that in his mind the most important thing was to get them off the streets, even if they had to be separated."

Breanna thought on it a moment, then said, "I understand, gentlemen. But it *is* definite that the stipulation is in there for the Hamiltons?"

It took only seconds for Egelston to pull out the Hamilton folder and check. "Yes, ma'am. It's written right here."

Breanna sat down with the twins in the isolation car and told them the situation.

"Oh, Miss Baylor," Tessie said, "we'd rather go back to Brooklyn than be separated."

"You're not going to be separated," Breanna said. "I'm going to pray that the Lord won't let that happen. He cares about you, and He answers prayer. I'm going to pray right now. Will you bow your heads and close your eyes while I pray?"

The twins were amazed at Miss Baylor's confidence as they bowed their heads. Breanna asked the Lord to keep His hand on the eleven-year-old girls and give them a family together. When she finished praying, the twins hugged her and said, "We love you, Miss Baylor."

"And I love both of you," Breanna said.

As they eased back on the seat, Breanna said, "Do you girls know who Jesus is?"

"He's God's Son, Miss Baylor," Bessie said.

"And He died on a cross," Tessie added.

"Do you know *why* Jesus died on a cross?"

The twins looked at each other blankly, then Bessie said, "I guess we don't know."

"Do you girls know what the Bible is?"

"It's a book from God," Tessie said.

"That's right. I'll get my Bible and—"

"I'll get it for you," Ellie said from behind Breanna. "It's in your overnight bag, isn't it?"

"Why, yes. Thank you, Ellie."

After Ellie handed the Bible to Breanna, she went back to her work. She smiled to herself, knowing what was about to happen.

Breanna carefully read passage after passage of Scripture to the twins about salvation, making sure they understood. When it was clear in their minds and hearts, both girls were eager to have their sins forgiven and gladly opened their hearts to Jesus. Ellie had her own praise service going on as Breanna prayed with the twins.

Late in the afternoon, the train pulled into Ogallala. None of the children in the isolation car were well enough yet to eat supper with the others or to be in the lineup. Hezekiah Washington provided soup for them, and even little Antonia Alberghetti was feeling well enough to swallow a small portion of it.

The other children were recovering well, and Breanna told those who had come down with the influenza on Saturday that by the day after tomorrow they could travel in the other cars and stand in the lineup. Those who had taken ill on Sunday would be ready the day after that.

The turnout of prospective parents was small at Ogallala. Only nine orphans were chosen. When the children were back on the train, Cleora Coffield tried to cheer up both Bodie Brolin and little Charlie Harper by reminding them there were four more stops.

At bedtime, Ellie snuffed all the lanterns except the usual one in the center of the isolation coach and began helping Breanna make the rounds.

When Breanna came to the Hamiltons, Jared said, "Miss Breanna, I heard you praying for Antonia last night. Would you help me to understand more about praying to God?"

"You haven't learned to pray?" Breanna asked.

Both Susan and Jared shook their heads.

"Do you know who Jesus Christ is?"

"He was a baby who was born in a barn in Pennsylvania," Jared said.

"Pennsylvania?"

"Uh-huh. A town called Bethlehem. It's in Pennsylvania, I'm pretty sure."

Breanna smiled inwardly. "It was a different Bethlehem that baby Jesus was born in, Jared. We'll talk more about it tomorrow, okay? Right now, you need to go to sleep."

As Breanna turned away, Jared said, "Miss Breanna…"

"Yes, Jared?"

"I love you."

"I love you, too," she said in a half-whisper, and moved on.

20

THE NEXT MORNING, no more children had come down with the grippe. And the last few who had were on their way to recovery. Some of the children in the isolation car would be able to eat with the rest and stand in the lineup when they stopped at Kimball.

By late morning, Breanna was able to sit down with the Hamilton children. It was evident that little Nathan didn't grasp most of what Breanna told him about God and Jesus and salvation, but Breanna was pleased at how quickly the other two understood. She read many passages of Scripture to them, starting with the crucifixion story in the gospels. After they could tell her why Jesus had to die on the cross, she took them to passages that pointed out what sin is.

When Jared and Susan acknowledged they were sinners in need of forgiveness and salvation, Breanna said, "You think on it for the rest of the day, and we'll talk about it tomorrow."

The train arrived in Sidney with ninety-two children. This time, Nora Egelston and Helen Wiggins stayed with the children in the isolation car so that Breanna could watch the adoption process.

The meal and the lineup were in a local church's fellowship hall. As the lineup began, Breanna looked on with interest, her eyes straying to Bodie, Cleora, and little Charlie Harper, who stood together. They smiled at the adults who passed by.

Suddenly, loud voices drew Breanna's attention. Two men were arguing in front of a husky boy of fifteen about who should get him.

"Gentlemen! Gentlemen!" Harold Egelston said, holding up his hand. "Now, I know Byron is a muscular boy, and no doubt is capable of producing a good day's work. Since you both want him but only one of you can have him, will you accept a coin toss?"

Gerald Mossberg and Frank Stanton looked at each other.

"Coin toss is fair enough," Stanton said. Mossberg nodded.

Egelston produced a silver dollar and let both men examine it. "Okay," he said, "Mr. Mossberg, you call it." He flipped the coin in the air and caught it in his right fist.

"Heads," Mossberg said.

Egelston slapped the coin onto the back of his left hand. "Tails," he said.

"Well, Byron," Stanton said, "looks like Rose and I are going to be your new ma and pa!" Byron let the shadow of a smile show on his lips.

The Stantons walked to the tables with their new son to fill out the adoption papers, leaving the Mossbergs to stand dejectedly looking after them. Suddenly, little Charlie Harper left the line, dashed to the Mossbergs, and wrapped his arms around Gerald's leg. "I'll be your son, mister!" he said. "Please adopt me! I'll work hard and—"

"Get away from me!" Mossberg jerked his leg free from the boy's grasp. "I don't want a scrawny little wart like you! We need a boy who can do some real work."

Charlie looked as if he'd been slapped. Breanna dashed to the little boy and picked him up.

"It's all right, Charlie," she said. "There'll be somebody in one of the other towns who will want you."

Charlie leaned back and looked at her through his tears. "Would you adopt me?" he asked.

A lump lodged in Breanna's throat. "Charlie…I…I can't adopt you. I'm not even married. I travel most of the time, and I wouldn't be there to be a mother to you. Besides, you need a daddy and—"

"Charlie…" It was Ellie Voss. The little boy looked up and waited for Ellie to speak. "Honey, listen. Miss Baylor can't adopt you any more than I can. But I'm sure some nice people will adopt you before this trip is over."

The boy wrapped his arms tight around Breanna's neck. "I want to go home with *her!*"

It took a few minutes to calm the disappointed child. When he stopped crying, they convinced him to reenter the line.

"Ellie, I wish I could adopt every one of them," Breanna said.

Ellie nodded. "Now you know what I go through on every trip."

When the choosing was over, twenty-one orphans had found families, and seventy-one orphans boarded the train. Among them were Cleora Coffield, Charlie Harper, and Bodie Brolin.

Breanna, who had seen the dejected look on Bodie's face, said, "Don't get discouraged, Bodie. God has your new parents all picked out for you."

Bodie didn't know much more about God than the Hamilton children. He raised his eyebrows and said, "You mean God cares what happens to me…or any of the rest of us?"

"He sure does. Don't you give up, all right?"

"Yes, ma'am."

As Breanna hurried on to the isolation car, Cleora didn't say anything, but the nurse's words had given her hope.

The next morning, the twelve children who had been in the isolation car the longest were sent to the other cars. All except for Antonia Alberghetti. Although she was much improved, she wasn't yet ready to be up and about.

At midafternoon, Breanna went to find the Hamilton children. They greeted her with adoring eyes as she sat down and pulled Nathan onto her lap.

"Jared, Susan, have you been thinking about the conversation we had yesterday?"

They both nodded their heads enthusiastically and told her they had been waiting for her to come. "Miss Breanna," Jared said. "Susie and I have talked about it a lot all day. We want to be saved."

"Nathan doesn't understand it," Susan said.

"He will when he gets a little older," Breanna said, and reached around Nathan to open her Bible. "All right, let's see if you two can tell me why Jesus came to die on the cross and who he came to die for?"

"Praise the Lord!" Ellie Voss cried when Breanna told her what had just happened. "Jared and Susie are such sweet kids. We need to pray that a Christian couple will adopt them."

At 5:15, the train pulled into Kimball. The meal was scheduled for 6:30 in the town hall, and the lineup would begin at 7:30. Again Breanna was relieved of duty so she could go with the children. As she watched the potential parents walk slowly along the line, Breanna thought of the Spaulding twins. Tomorrow evening they would be in the line. She breathed a paryer, asking the Lord, again, to please let them be adopted by the same family.

Breanna noticed a couple approach Bodie Brolin and introduce themselves as Foster and Myrtle Twine. Cleora and little Charlie were standing on either side of Bodie. At the same time, a well-dressed couple began to show interest in Cleora. They had a girl with them who was a little older than Cleora.

Myrtle, who had a nose like an owl's beak and dark, piercing eyes, fixed Bodie with a stare and said, "I suppose you're on them crutches because you injured your leg, right? I mean, you ain't a lifelong cripple, are you?"

"It's an injury, ma'am," Bodie replied.

"Well, is it permanent?"

"The leg was broken in several places below the knee, ma'am. It's healing, but my knee will never be the same."

"Busted up good, eh?"

"Yes, but I can still do most anything that's needed for farm or ranch work," he said rapidly.

"But the knee will always be bad?"

Bodie started to tremble. "That's what the doctor in Manhattan told me, ma'am."

Myrtle screwed up her face. "Which one of these people is responsible for you?"

"My chaperones are Mr. and Mrs. Paddock, ma'am," Bodie said. "I don't see Mr. Paddock right now; Mrs. Paddock is the lady in the green dress talking with the couple at the adoption table."

Myrtle whipped her head around and called, "Hey, you there in the green dress!"

Lucille Paddock excused herself to the couple and stepped toward Myrtle Twine, forcing a smile on her face. "Yes? May I help you, ma'am?"

"Question."

"Yes?"

"Whatcha got this here cripple in the lineup for?"

The woman's loud voice had everybody's attention now, including Breanna Baylor's.

Lucille felt her scalp tingle. "Ma'am, Bodie's here because—"

"How dare you people bring in misfits like this! You're tryin' to palm him off on decent people who need workers for our farms…tryin' to play on our sympathy, ain't you?"

Breanna saw the pain in Bodie's eyes and felt her blood heat up.

Lucille fought her own anger as she continued to speak in a low and level tone. "Ma'am, our society picks up all the homeless and destitute children we can off the streets of New York. We—"

"You figure to get some poor sucker to feel sorry for the kid and adopt him so's you can get him off your own hands! What earthly good is he?"

Breanna's face was flushed as she rushed toward the woman who was tearing Bodie's heart out.

"But, ma'am!" Lucille said, "you don't understand. We—"

"You ain't foolin' me!" Myrtle said. "I know—"

"You don't know what you're talking about!" Breanna said.

"Now, lookee here, I—"

"You look here!" Breanna said. "Who do you think you are, coming in here and ripping at this boy's heart with your unmerciful tirade! Mrs. Paddock has tried to be kind and reasonable with you, but you can't shut your mouth long enough to let her speak! Nobody's trying to palm Bodie off on you, and nobody's trying to play on your sympathy!"

"Well, I—"

"These children are orphans who have lived half-starved and half-frozen in the slums of New York City. The people of this Society have the kindness and decency to do something about it. Bodie needs a home as much as the other children do, and just because he's got a knee that will never work perfectly again, doesn't mean he's helpless or useless. If you don't like what you see here, the same door that let you in will let you out!"

Myrtle Twine's lips moved but no sound came out. Finally she gasped, "Well, I never—!"

"And you never will again, either!" Breanna said.

"Come on, Foster!" Myrtle choked out. "Let's get out of here!"

Foster snorted at Breanna as he followed after his wife. Breanna ignored him and turned to Bodie. When the door shut behind the Twines, Committee members, prospective adoptive parents, and children broke into applause.

"Thank you for standing up for me, Miss Breanna," Bodie said.

"Yes, thank you, Miss Baylor," Lucille Paddock said.

"It isn't often that I lose my temper, but that woman—"

"Had it coming," Harold Egelston finished for her. "You had every right to tell her off."

Children and committee members alike gathered around Bodie, speaking words of encouragement. It was then that Bodie noticed Cleora was no longer at his side. He saw her at one of the desks across the room, standing by a girl about her age and a couple in their late thirties. Cleora was looking at him, waiting for some of the crowd to move away so she could see him. When their eyes met, she threaded her way through the people to his side.

Cleora touched Bodie's arm and said, "I'm sorry for what that woman said about you. None of it was true. God bless Miss Baylor for the way she told her off. Bodie..."

"Mm-hmm?"

"I just got adopted."

Bodie forced himself to smile and said, "I'm so glad for you! I knew it would happen pretty soon."

"They're a real nice family, Bodie. And...and they have a daughter who's eleven. So, I'll not only have a home, I'll have a sister!"

"Hey, that's wonderful," Bodie said. "Know what?"

"What?"

"I've...well, I've sorta been thinking of you as my little sister."

She touched his arm again. "I'm glad to hear you say that, because I've sorta been thinking of you as my big brother."

Cleora's adoptive parents caught her eye, and the mother called, "Cleora, honey. We're all through with the paperwork. We need to be going."

"Be right there," Cleora said, and turned back to Bodie. "You'll always be my big brother. Will you always keep me in your heart as your little sister?"

Bodie swallowed with difficulty and nodded. Cleora raised up on tiptoe and kissed his cheek, then she walked quickly away. She stopped long enough to tell Breanna good-bye, then hurried out the door with her new family.

Breanna watched Cleora for a moment, then turned back to the scene before her. A Mr. and Mrs. Dawson were telling Harold Egelston about their desire to adopt Jared Hamilton. Breanna stood silently as Egelston explained the condition Reverend Brace had placed on the adoption of the Hamilton children.

"We just can't afford to adopt all three," Dawson said. "We

came here looking for a boy just like Jared."

The Hamilton siblings pressed closer to each other and glanced at Breanna, who gave them a reassuring smile.

"I'm sorry, sir," Egelston said, "but it's all or none with these three. There are a couple of other boys Jared's age a little farther down the line. They have no brothers or sisters. Why don't you take a look at them? Here, I'll go with you."

When the choosing was over, twenty-four children had been adopted, leaving forty-seven on the train. All but five would be in the lineup at Cheyenne City.

When the children were back on the train for the night and preparing for bed, Jared saw the sad look on Bodie's face.

"Still bothering you what that woman said?" he asked.

"Hmm?" Bodie said, his mind preoccupied. "Oh. No. Miss Baylor helped me feel better about that."

"Oh, I know. You miss Cleora."

"Yeah. She's like my little sister, you know."

"I know. It's sort of like when someone you love is about to die. You know it's going to happen, but no matter what you do to prepare yourself, it's still hard when it happens."

"Yeah. This was a lot like that. And...and I don't know what's going to happen to me."

Susan spoke up. "I'll ask Miss Breanna to pray that you get adopted by a real nice family. Her prayers get answered."

"She has a lot of faith in God, doesn't she?"

"She does," Jared said. "She also knows how to show a person from the Bible how to be saved and have all their sins forgiven. She showed Susie and me how to ask Jesus to come into our hearts and save us. We did that, and now we know we're going to heaven when we die."

"You know it? I thought nobody could know whether they were going to heaven or hell till they died. You know, they'd have to stand before God and see whether they did more good things than bad."

"That's not how it works, Bodie," Jared said. "Jesus died on the cross and paid for our sins so that if we have faith in Him, we're forgiven and made clean and will go to heaven when we die."

"She showed you that in the Bible? Do you suppose she would show me?"

"I know she would," Jared said with a grin. "I'll see if Mr. Egelston will tell Miss Breanna you'd like to see her."

That night, while most of the people on the train were fast asleep, Jared and Susan stayed awake and watched Breanna lead Bodie to Jesus.

After exercise time the next morning, the orphan train was once again on its westward journey. Since none of the infected children were contagious now, they were scattered throughout all three cars.

In car number three, Breanna sat beside little Antonia, with Jared, Susan, Nathan, the Spaulding twins, and Bodie Brolin in adjacent seats. The newly saved children were full of questions, and it delighted Breanna to answer them.

Nathan was still on Breanna's lap. Suddenly he wrapped his arms about her neck and said, "Miss Breanna, I wish you could adopt us."

"Me, too," Tessie Spaulding said.

"*Could* you adopt us, Miss Breanna?" Antonia asked, her dark eyes looking into Breanna's.

Breanna caressed her cheek. "I can't, Antonia. I'm not married yet. And the Children's Aid Society only wants husbands and wives to adopt their children."

"Are you going to get married?" Susan asked.

"Well, yes, someday."

"Are you engaged?" Bodie asked.

"Yes, as a matter of fact."

"What's his name?"

"John."

"When are you and Mr. John going to get married?" Jared asked.

"Well, we don't have a date set, but I think it won't be long now."

"Maybe we could live with somebody else till you get married, then you could adopt us. That would work, wouldn't it?"

Fourteen eager eyes riveted on Breanna's face. She ran her soft gaze over them, letting it stop on Jared, and smiled warmly.

"It wouldn't work, Jared, because of my occupation as a visiting nurse, and because of what Mr. John does. We both travel much of the time, and we couldn't be home to take care of you. The work we do is what the Lord wants us to do. I hope you children understand." A sweet smile graced Breanna's lips. "Believe me, in my heart I would love to adopt every one of you."

21

BREANNA STOOD CLOSE BY JARED, Susan, and Nathan in Cheyenne City's town hall as the ranchers and townspeople moved up and down the line of children. Some of the men felt the boys' arms to see how muscular they were.

Now that he was a Christian and knew how to pray, Bodie whispered, "Please, Lord, bring somebody who will want me. All that's left after here is Denver. I want a home and family. Please don't let me ride the train all the way back to New York."

The Spaulding twins were not far down the line from where Breanna stood. From time to time she cast a glance toward Bessie and Tessie, especially when people stopped to look them over.

Suddenly she noticed that a well-dressed couple had stopped in front of the twins. By their dress, they appeared to be city folk. The couple began to talk to Luther Wiggins about the twins. Breanna was close enough to overhear the man introduce himself as Reverend Paul Hayden, pastor of Cheyenne City's Calvary Community Church.

As the conversation continued, Breanna learned that their only child, a daughter, had died a few weeks previously at eleven years of age. They had come to the town hall with the prayer that God would lead them to a girl the same age.

Breanna prayed that the Lord would let this young preacher and his wife adopt the twins. Then she heard Hayden say that they could only afford to feed and clothe one child.

Hayden turned to his wife and said, "Lois, I can see in your eyes that you'd like to take both girls, and I would too. But you know we can't afford it. So which one shall we take?"

Lois looked uncertain. "Maybe we shouldn't separate them, Paul."

"We asked the Lord to lead us to an eleven-year-old girl, like Sally, and these are the only eleven-year-old girls here. I mean, look at it this way, Lois. If we don't take one, somebody else will come along and separate them. At least we know we'll be giving one of these girls a good Christian home."

The twins clung to each other as tears slid down their cheeks.

Breanna could refrain no longer. "Pardon me," she said. "I couldn't help overhear your conversation. Pastor and Mrs. Hayden, my name is Breanna Baylor. I'm a certified medical nurse. I've been riding this orphan train since Lexington, Nebraska, caring for several of the children who came down with the grippe.

"Bessie and Tessie were among the sick children I took care of, and I had the joy of leading them to the Lord. I've been teaching them about living the Christian life. One of the things I've told them is to walk by faith and trust the Lord for His leadership in their lives, and to trust Him to supply their needs."

Hayden smiled and nodded.

"Pastor and Mrs. Hayden, the Lord made these girls in their mother's womb and created a special bond between them. He also knew they would be on this orphan train, and that you dear people would be here to find an eleven-year-old girl to adopt. Surely you can see what a terrible thing it would be to separate them."

Paul Hayden and his wife exchanged glances, then he said, "My reasoning, dear sister in Christ, was that it was unlikely that someone would come along and take them both. So if we could give even one of them a good Christian home, it would be the right thing to do. We really would love to adopt both of them, but we can't afford it on my salary."

"Your comment brings me to my main point, pastor. Are you certain the Lord wants you to adopt one of these girls?"

Again the Haydens exchanged glances, then nodded yes.

"Don't you, as a man of God, have enough faith in your Lord to believe Him for the money to provide for *two* new lives in your home? Could it be that you're supposed to trust the Lord to supply your needs so that these precious Christian girls can grow up together?"

Lois's eyes were brimming with tears. "Paul, she's right."

Hayden looked down, then at Breanna. "Miss Baylor, if I were to enter a preaching contest against you, you would win hands down!" Then he turned to the twins and said, "Bessie, Tessie, your friend, Miss Baylor, has just taught Mrs. Hayden and me a valuable lesson. We were limiting our limitless God. We're going to trust Him to supply our needs and adopt both of you."

The twins' tears quickly turned to tears of joy, and they embraced each other and then their new parents.

Breanna returned to the line and watched children being chosen and led away to the tables. Then a nicely dressed couple in their late twenties approached the Hamilton children. Harold Egelston introduced himself and learned their names were Jack and Corinne West. He offered to answer any questions they might have. Breanna moved closer to listen.

After a few minutes, Jack said, "We would like to adopt Susan and Nathan, Mr. Egelston. We've been married seven years and are still childless. We agreed that we would adopt a boy and a girl who were no older than ten. Can we get started with the paperwork?"

Egelston sighed. "I'm sorry, Mr. West, but our director set a stipulation on these three children. They cannot be split up. All three must be adopted, or none of them."

When the Wests heard this, they turned away in frustration and disappointment. Then Corinne's eyes fell on a little girl named Lila Lee. "Wait a minute, Jack." She stepped close to the blond little girl. "How old are you?"

"Eight, ma'am."

Corinne looked at her husband, who now stood beside her, and said, "She's two years younger than Susan, but she's a pretty little thing."

"Mm-hmm," Jack said, taking one last glance at Susan and Nathan. He then bent low, laid a hand on top of Lila's head and said, "Would you like to come home with us and be our little girl?"

"Yes, sir," Lila said with a smile.

"Okay, Corinne. Maybe next time one of these trains comes through we can find us the right little boy."

"I'm the same age as Nathan, sir!" came Charlie Harper's voice.

The Wests turned to look at him.

Charlie was smaller than Nathan, and quite thin. "I can do all kinds of work. I've been taught about farms and ranches, and I know I can clean barns and chicken sheds. I can hoe weeds. I can do dishes and sweep floors, too. I can—"

"I'm sorry. You're just too small and skinny, son," West said, then turned back to his wife and Lila.

Harold Egelston, who had remained close by, said, "We can go over the rules of adoption and draw up the papers now, Mr. West. Bring Lila and come over to the table." Corinne took Lila by the hand and the Wests started to walk away.

Little Charlie left the line and dashed after them. "Please, mister! Take me, too!"

West read the name tag on Charlie's shirt and said, "Charlie, we've decided to wait till another time to adopt a boy."

"Please, sir," Charlie said, wrapping his arms around the man's leg. "Let me be your little boy! Ple-e-ase, sir!"

Breanna thought her heart would break when Jack West patted Charlie's head and said, "There'll be someone else who will adopt you, little fella." He broke the boy's hold on his leg and said, "You get back in line, now." Then he followed his wife to the table to fill out the papers for Lila.

Breanna ran to Charlie and swooped him up in her arms.

Charlie wrapped his arms around Breanna's neck and sobbed out the words, "Nobody wants me! My mommy and daddy threw me away, an' nobody wants me!"

"Hush, now, Charlie. There will be someone in Denver who will not only want you, they'll love you a whole bunch, too!"

"Those people want Lila! They love her! Why don't they want me? Why don't they love me?"

Corinne still had Lila's hand in her own when she stopped abruptly in the middle of the room and looked at her husband through a film of tears. Jack looked as if he'd been stabbed in the heart. He nodded at his wife and headed back toward Breanna and Charlie.

"We, uh…we've changed our minds, ma'am," West said, on

the verge of tears. "We want Charlie as our son."

Breanna didn't know whether to laugh or cry as she handed the weeping child to his adoptive father. Charlie continued to sob as Jack held him and patted his back. "We do want you, Charlie, and we do love you," West said.

Corinne left Lila for a moment and went to caress Charlie's tear-stained face. "I love you, son," she said. "And you can call me Mommy!"

The train pulled out of Cheyenne City at 9:30 the next morning with twenty-one children on board. As coach number two rocked and swayed on its southern journey toward Denver, Breanna sat with Antonia and Susan on the right side of the car, pointing out the Rocky Mountains to the west. In the seat behind them were Jared, Nathan, and Bodie.

"Miss Breanna," Jared said, "I'm glad we haven't been adopted yet."

"Why do you say that?"

"Because the Lord has answered my prayers. Since I got saved I've been praying that the Lord would let us be adopted by a family near Denver. That way, we can see you often."

Breanna grinned and said, "You're a conniver, Mr. Hamilton."

"What's a conniver?" Antonia asked.

"Somebody who works secretly to bring about their own plans, honey," Breanna said.

"Oh."

"I like your plans, big brother," Susan said.

"Me too," Nathan said. "I wanna live real close to Miss Breanna so I can hug her lots of times!"

Bodie was silent, thinking about how much he had prayed

for someone to adopt him so he wouldn't have to make the trip back to New York and start all over again. Had the Lord heard him at all?

It was just past noon when the orphan train chugged into Denver's Union Station to find a large crowd waiting. Many ranchers and farmers and townspeople were there. Some were interested in adoption, while others were there just to observe.

When Breanna alighted from the train with Ellie Voss by her side, her sister, Dottie, and nephew and niece, James and Molly Kate, and a great host of her friends surged toward her. Among them was Dr. Lyle Goodwin.

"Hello, Dr. Goodwin," Breanna said, and smiled, as he gave her a fatherly embrace. "Is Martha with you?"

"Yes, but she said to tell you she'd hug you later when you're not so swamped. I wanted to tell you that a telegram came from John three days ago. He thought you'd be home by then. He said to tell you he's still in Dakota Territory and won't be home for a while."

"All right," Breanna said, feeling a bit disappointed. "Thank you for letting me know."

The silver-haired physician smiled. "Breanna, why don't you wait a couple of days before coming in to work. I'm sure you're tired. Get some rest."

"All right, sir. Thank you."

"Good girl," Goodwin said, patting her arm. "Martha and I will see you at the church."

This time the orphans were directed to carriages outside the depot. They would ride to the First Baptist Church for a meal and their last chance to be adopted on this trip.

Luther Wiggins stood at the carriage that held the

Hamiltons, Antonia, and Bodie, and told Breanna she could ride with them. Harold Egelston and the carriage driver were bringing Breanna's luggage from the train and would arrange to have it delivered to her home.

Dottie touched Breanna's arm and said, "I assume you're going on to the church."

"Yes. I want to be there when these five get adopted. They've become very special to me."

"Well, I'm helping with the meal, so you can introduce them to us there. I'll see you there."

As Dottie and her children walked away, the Langans stepped up. "I'm helping with the meal at church, too," Stefanie said, running her gaze over the faces of the five children in the carriage. "Are these special friends of yours, Breanna?"

"I've grown very close to these precious children. Let me introduce them."

Jared felt overwhelmed to be in the presence of a real live western lawman. He looked from the big Colt .45 on Curt's hip to the shiny badge on his chest.

Breanna chuckled. "I think you've got an admirer, Sheriff."

"How many bad guys have you shot with that gun, Sheriff Langan?" Jared asked.

"I really haven't kept count," Curt said with a grin.

"I'd sure like to hear some stories about bad guys you've killed and captured."

Bodie looked on with interest. "I would, too, Sheriff," he said.

"Tell you what," Curt said, "Steve's still over there at the depot talking to some of his friends. I'll have him watch the office while I spend the afternoon with these kids."

On the way to the church, Curt told Jared and Bodie some

stories about outlaws he had tracked and captured and bad guys he had killed in all kinds of gunfights. Breanna wasn't sure how much was fact and how much was fiction, but the children were entranced.

That evening, Pastor Bayless made sure everyone was well fed by the ladies of his church. Breanna noticed a young couple who were members standing among those considering adopting a child.

She smiled and greeted them. "Rex…Eileen, are you observing or looking?"

"We're looking, Breanna."

The Johnsons had lost both their children the year before, when Indians attacked the stagecoach they were riding.

"How many do you want to adopt?" Breanna asked.

"Just one," Rex said. "We're not ready for more at this point."

"We've been praying about it and agreed the Lord would have us adopt a girl first. That one over there is so pretty," Eileen said.

Breanna smiled when she realized they were talking about Antonia. She told them the little girl had been through a rough time with influenza and pneumonia, but assured Eileen that she was on the mend and would be fine.

Eileen looked at Rex with a longing in her eyes. He smiled his approval. Moments later, when the line was formed and the official adoptions began, the Johnsons were at the tables with little Antonia in Rex's arms. Breanna thanked the Lord for answered prayer. Not only had Antonia been adopted by Christians, but Breanna would get to see her often.

As the evening progressed, two families showed interest in

the Hamilton children, but neither was willing to adopt all three. Breanna and the Langans stayed close to them as more prospective parents walked slowly by.

Jared was about to tell Breanna that her prayers hadn't been answered when a couple in their early thirties walked by the Hamilton children for the third time, eyeing them closely.

The man said to Harold Egelston, "We like the looks of these three children. You told us earlier that they can't be separated."

"That's right, sir," Egelston said.

"Well, we've decided to adopt them."

"Oh, boy!" Nathan said. "We're gonna live in a house again!"

Ward and Maudie McLander introduced themselves to the Hamilton children and told them they lived on a farm some forty-five miles east of Denver. Jared asked if they could come into town periodically and see Miss Breanna. Both McLanders assured him they came to town at least once a month. They would be happy to allow the children to visit Miss Breanna.

Both Harold Egelston and Breanna questioned the McLanders about their home. Breanna asked if they were Christians, and she was pleased to find out they were and that they attended church in a small community near their farm.

Bodie watched with envy as the Hamiltons waited at a table while the adoption paperwork was completed. Curt and Stefanie Langan came up to the table and hugged each of the three children. Curt and Stefanie asked them to also come and see them when they were in town.

"Just think of it," Jared said, "now our last name is McLander!"

Big Ward McLander put an arm around Jared's shoulder and said, "And we're mighty proud to have you as our very own kids!"

Maudie hugged all three and said, "All right, sons and daughter, let's go home!"

It was hard to let them go. Breanna hugged and kissed Jared, Susan, and Nathan, saying she would see them soon. She thanked the McLanders for adopting them, and they said it was their pleasure.

Jared and Susan turned toward Bodie, who was one of only four children left, and people were looking with interest at the other three.

Breanna's heart was heavy for Bodie. She waited while the Hamiltons told him a tearful good-bye, then she put her arms around him. He clung to her and wept as the last three children in the line were chosen and led to the tables.

It was more than Bodie could bear. He pulled back to look into Breanna's eyes. "Doesn't God care about me at all, Miss Breanna?" he asked.

"Oh, yes, Bodie...He does!" Breanna beseeched the Lord for just the right words. Before she could speak again, a deep male voice said, "Pardon us."

Breanna and Bodie turned to find a man and woman Breanna had noticed in the crowd earlier in the evening. The man's face was familiar.

"I'm Cliff Walker, Miss Baylor. Do you remember me?"

"I know I've seen you somewhere, Mr. Walker, I—"

"Santa Fe? About a year-and-a-half ago? Smallpox epidemic? You saved my life along with the lives of many Indians and other whites."

"Oh, yes, of course. Cliff Walker! And I remember you received the Lord Jesus as your Saviour."

"Yes, and thank God that your knowledge of the Word broke this rock-hard heart of mine and brought me to Jesus. This is my wife, Mary, Miss Baylor. I asked her to marry me at least a half-dozen times, but she kept turning me down because I wasn't a Christian. When I went home from Santa Fe, we got married."

"That's wonderful, Cliff," Breanna said. "Mary, I'm so happy to meet you."

"And I'm delighted to finally meet the nurse who saved Cliff's life and led him to the Lord," Mary said.

"Was there something you wanted?" Breanna asked.

"We've been watching Bodie all evening," Miss Baylor, "and we want to adopt him."

22

BODIE'S HEART THUDDED IN HIS CHEST, and he stood speechless as Breanna stammered, "You...you want to adopt Bodie?"

"Yes, ma'am," Mary Walker said. "All evening we've been watching him to see how he related to the other children and with prospective parents. You can't fake a kind heart, Miss Baylor. And we know Bodie's been put to the test by waiting all this time for a family. We want him to be our son."

Bodie's eyes misted over again, and a smile of pure joy broke across his face.

"Mary and I own a small ranch about fifty miles west of Denver," Cliff said. "We just happened to be in town today and heard people talking about the orphan train coming in. We've known about the orphan trains for some time and decided to come and see how it all works. You know...just as spectators."

Mary smiled at Bodie. "As we watched this precious boy being passed by, we decided the Lord would have us adopt him...that is, if he would like to be a part of this family."

"We don't have a lot of money, Bodie," Cliff said, "but Jesus is the center of our home, and we have plenty of love to give."

Bodie wiped his tears and drew a shaky breath. "Yes! Oh,

yes, I want to be part of your family."

The Walkers embraced Bodie and assured him he would be well taken care of and would be very happy as their son.

At the adoption table, Breanna waited with Bodie as Cliff and Mary signed the adoption agreement.

"Miss Breanna," Bodie said, "you told me this would happen. I shouldn't have gotten so discouraged…and I shouldn't have doubted the Lord."

When the final paper was signed, Bodie said, "Fifty miles isn't so far, Miss Breanna. I'll come and see you whenever my parents will let me. Thank you for everything you've done for me. Especially for showing me how to be saved."

Breanna was still wiping her tears when Cliff, Mary, and Bodie Walker left to go home. Suddenly she felt an arm around her shoulder and turned to see Ellie Voss.

"Oh, Ellie," Breanna said. "I don't know how you stand it, riding one train after the other. Each child is so precious. It's a good thing John and I aren't married yet, or he might have become daddy to a set of twin girls, a crippled boy, a little Italian beauty, and three sweet kids named Jared, Susan, and Nathan!"

Ward McLander's face was purple with rage as he stood over Susan and bellowed, "Why don't you do your work like Maudie tells you? You've been down in the cellar for two whole days, and now I'm told you still don't have it cleaned up!"

Maudie stood with her hands on her hips, glaring angrily at Susan. Jared and Nathan watched from the kitchen door. Fear lodged in their hearts as their sister shook with terror and said, "Those wooden crates she told me to move and sweep under are heavy, Papa. I—"

"Don't call me *Papa* when I'm mad at you, girl!"

"Y-yes, sir."

This was the fifteenth day since the McLanders had adopted them. By the third day the children realized the McLanders had lied about everything. All three had been pushed harder than their bodies could stand, and when they didn't produce according to the McLanders's expectations, the boys had been whipped with Ward's belt. Susan had been cuffed and slapped a few times.

When Jared saw Ward unbuckle his belt as Susan cowered, it was all he could take. He burst into the kitchen and stood between Ward and Susan. "Don't beat her! Susie's not strong enough to move those heavy boxes! I was down there. I saw how heavy they are!"

Ward's eyes pinched back until they seemed almost hidden behind the lids. There was acid in his voice as he said. "You're gettin' the first beatin', kid. And your sister's next!"

That night in their bedroom, Jared limped to the window. "Okay," he said, "let's go. I'll crawl out the window and help you both. Susie, you come first."

Susan could hardly walk. The belt had lacerated the backs of her legs. Blood trickled over great purple welts. Nathan helped Susan to the window while Jared went over the sill and dropped to the ground.

When all three were on the ground, Jared lifted Susan in his arms and carried her through the shadows with Nathan on his heels. As soon as they were behind the barn, Jared said in a low voice, "Let me rest for a moment."

"Jared, I can walk," Susan said. "It's too hard for you to carry me."

"No, I know what kind of pain you're going through."

The half-moon gave enough light for Jared to see the bruise on his little brother's face. Nathan had begged Ward McLander to stop beating Jared, and his reward was a vicious slap. Nathan had been unconscious for about a minute. When he came to, Maudie railed at him for daring to interfere.

"How long before we get to Denver, Jared?" Susan asked.

"Probably three or four days. We won't be able to move very fast, and we don't dare to go on the road. Ward will be looking for us."

"Do you think Sheriff Langan will put the McLanders in jail?" Nathan asked.

"I don't know. But I'll tell you one thing, he's going to be real mad when he finds out what they've been doing to us."

"Miss Breanna will be mad, too," Susan said.

"Yeah," Nathan said. "An' we've seen her mad. She'll probably whip up on both of 'em!"

"Okay," Jared said. "Let's head across that field."

Sheriff Langan was looking forward to Stefanie's cooking at the end of a hard day. He unsaddled his horse at the small barn behind the house and hung up the bridle. As he stepped onto the back porch, he could hear what sounded like weeping. He moved quickly into the kitchen to find Stefanie sitting at the table with her head in her hands. Her whole body shook as she sobbed.

"Stefanie...honey...what's wrong?"

Stefanie sat up and said shakily, "Remember I had an appointment with Dr. Carroll after my shift at the hospital?"

"Yes. Did he find out what was causing the pain?"

Stefanie drew in a sharp breath and nodded. "It's another infection."

"Bad?"

"Dr. Carroll says I...I will never be able to give you children." Her last words came out in a rush, and she couldn't look at him for a moment. When she did look at him, she got a vivid impression of someone who had just been hit in the midsection with a battering ram.

"After Dr. Carroll examined me today, he said the scar tissue on my ovaries from the other infections had sealed off my tubes and would prevent me from ever conceiving."

Curt's legs felt a bit shaky, and he sat down at the table. He and Stefanie had planned to start their family soon. Even though she loved her job at Mile High Hospital, she wanted to be a mother more than anything.

Curt reached for her and pulled her close. "Darling," he said, "our lives are in the Lord's hands. He has allowed this, so we must trust Him through it."

"You're not upset with me?"

"How could I be upset with you? It's no fault of yours."

"But it's natural for a man to want his own children and—"

"Hush, now," Curt said, touching her lips with his fingertips. "Tell you what. The next time an orphan train comes to town, we'll adopt a little boy or girl."

"Oh, Curt...you mean it?"

"Of course I do."

"Oh, thank you! Why don't we send a wire to the Children's Aid Society in New York and ask them when the next train is coming?"

"I'll do it tomorrow."

Jared could carry Susan for only a half mile or so before he had to put her down. After a brief rest, they moved on. The going was slow, but at least they knew they were headed toward safety.

"Jared," Susan said, "are we going to try to find Miss Breanna first?"

"I don't know what time of day we'll get to Denver, Susie," Jared said. "If it's daytime, we'll ask someone how to find Sheriff Langan's office. He'll know where to find Miss Breanna. If we get there at night, we'll see if we can find the hospital."

When Jared's strength was almost gone, they stopped under a tall cottonwood beside a stream. Jared eased Susan to the ground so she could sit with her back against the tree.

"Jared," Nathan said, "will we have to go back to New York?"

"The train we came on is gone, Nathan. I don't know what we'll do."

"Maybe we can stay with Miss Breanna till the next train comes," Susan said.

"I would love that," Nathan said. "I wish she and Mr. John would get married and adopt us."

No one spoke until Susan said, "Maybe Sheriff Langan will make us go back and live with those awful people. They did adopt us, you know. They're our parents now."

Jared shook his head passionately. "I can't believe he would make us go back and live with them. When he sees our bruises, he'll be real mad at those people."

"If we don't have to return to them, can we change our name back to Hamilton?" she asked.

"I don't know. I sure don't want the name *McLander* anymore." Jared took a deep breath and rose to his feet. "Well, let's keep moving."

"We're not gonna walk all night, are we, Jared?" Nathan asked.

"No." Jared grunted as he tried to lift Susan in his arms.

"We'll keep going for about another hour or so, then look for a good spot to get some rest."

"Jared," Susan said, "let me walk now—I think I'll be okay.

"Well, if you're sure…"

"What are we gonna eat?" Nathan asked.

"Nothing until we get to Denver," Jared said.

"You said it would take us three or four days. How are we gonna keep walkin' without somethin' to eat?"

"We have to. We don't have a choice."

The meadowlarks woke Jared at dawn. He moved his sore legs, and streamers of pain shot upward and spread across his back. Nathan was still asleep, but Susan was looking at him.

"How long have you been awake?" Jared asked.

"Since we lay down. My legs and my back hurt too much."

"I'm sorry, Susie. Once we get to Miss Breanna or Miss Stefanie, they can take care of us."

Nathan stirred.

"Come on, little brother," Jared said, ruffling Nathan's hair. "Time to get a move on."

As the orphans walked across open fields, dipping into gullies and ditches, they looked back frequently for any sign of Ward McLander. The road was more than two miles to their right, and only now and then did they see a rider or wagon.

At midmorning they climbed a grassy rise and were surprised to see a farmer behind his plow. The man spotted them, stopped the horses, and headed their way.

"Jared, what should we do?" Susan asked. "Maybe he's a friend of Ward McLander and will make us go back."

"Let me do the talking," Jared said.

"Howdy, kids," the farmer said as he drew up. "What on earth are you doin' out here all by yourselves?"

Sheriff Curt Langan and his deputy looked at the bruises and lacerations on Susan as Breanna and Dr. Carroll applied salve. In the next stall of the children's ward, two nurses were giving the same care to Jared. Nathan sat on a chair next to Jared and waited.

"Steve and I are going out to the McLander place and arrest them," Curt said, when Breanna had finished.

Susan looked up from the table. "Sheriff Langan..."

"Yes, honey?"

"Are those bad people going to prison?"

"No, but they'll get a good taste of what it's like to be locked up in my jail for a while."

"When they get out, will they come after us?"

"They'll know better than to do that."

"Will they hurt Mr. Sheppard for bringing us here? He lives pretty close to them."

"No, they won't hurt Mr. Sheppard. I'll keep a tight leash on them, even after they get out of jail."

"Do we have to go back to New York?" Jared asked.

"Looks like it," Langan said. "I know there's an orphan train supposed to come here sometime in August. We'll have to figure out what to do with the three of you till then."

"They can stay at our house till the next train comes," Dr. Carroll said. "We've got plenty of room. James and Molly Kate would enjoy their company."

"I have a better idea," Breanna said. "Instead of your house, Matt, why not let them stay with me? Dottie's pretty well got her hands full. I know Martha would be glad to look after them when I'm at the clinic or the hospital. I just won't take any out-of-town jobs till the orphan train returns and things are settled for these three."

"Either way is fine with me," the doctor said.

"Then my house it is!"

Three small faces lit up.

Ward and Maudie McLander were in their wagon searching for the children when Sheriff Langan and Deputy Ridgeway arrested them. Langan and a federal judge in Denver would decide how long the two stayed behind bars.

As the days passed, the Langans spent a lot of time with the children. Curt and Jared were becoming quite close, and on several occasions, Curt took Jared to the office with him.

One night, when the Langans were at Breanna's cottage for supper, and Curt was telling more of his outlaw tales, Jared said, "Sheriff, you know what we talked about at your office a couple of days ago?"

"Yes?"

"Are you going to teach me?"

"Teach him what?" Stefanie asked.

Curt cleared his throat. "Well, Jared has become quite interested in guns and lawmen, as you can tell. In fact, he says when he grows up, he wants to be a lawman."

"That's an admirable goal," Breanna said, smiling at Jared.

"So, he asked if I would teach him how to handle a gun," Curt said.

Stefanie thought for a moment, then nodded her approval. "Since it would be you teaching him, Curt, I think it'd be all right."

"I agree," Breanna said. "Most fathers in the West start teaching their sons how to handle firearms at his age."

"Tell you what, Jared," Curt said. "We'll start you with a handgun. A .44 or a .45 is probably too big for you, so I'll get you a smaller caliber to start with."

"Curt," Breanna said, "I have one Jared can use. It's a .36 caliber Navy Colt that John bought for me. Jared can use it anytime you and he get together for shooting lessons."

"We'll just take you up on it," Curt said. "Okay, Jared?"

"Yes, sir! And thank you, Miss Breanna."

"You're welcome, Jared. How soon did you want to start, Curt?"

"How about nine o'clock tomorrow morning? I'll leave Steve in charge of the office, and we'll get Jared started."

"Could I see the gun, Miss Breanna?" Jared asked.

Susan grinned. "You're not very eager, are you big brother?"

"Looks to me like he is, Susie," Nathan said in a serious tone.

Everybody laughed.

Breanna headed toward the rear of the cottage and returned with a beautiful nickel-plated .36 caliber Navy Colt. Breanna broke it open with the muzzle pointed toward the floor, slipped out the five cartridges, and snapped the cylinder back in place. She handed it to Curt. "Think this is small enough for him?"

Curt hefted the gun. "It'll be fine, Breanna. Your hands and Jared's are just about the same size."

"Can I hold it?" Jared asked.

"Tomorrow," Curt said. "I want to start you off right by showing you exactly how to handle it. Even though you saw Miss Breanna unload the gun, the first thing I want you to learn is that you always treat a gun as if it's loaded, even if you know it's not. We'll go into all of that tomorrow. I'll do my best to give you an hour a day for the next few weeks, and we'll see how you do."

Day after day, Curt Langan kept his promise and spent an hour with Jared. The boy proved to be a natural with a gun. Stefanie and Breanna were pleased to see Jared so happy and Curt offering the boy such special attention.

On the last day of June, Stefanie had Breanna and the Hamilton children over for supper. As soon as the meal began, an excited Jared said, "Sheriff, did you tell Miss Stefanie about my shooting lesson today?"

"Not yet. Did you tell Miss Breanna and Susie and Nathan?"

"Huh-uh. I wanted them to hear it from you 'cause they probably won't believe me."

Curt laughed. "Well, I've told you all how Jared's improved his accuracy every day since we started practicing. Today I set up a target fifty feet away. The farthest it's been is forty. Jared's been drilling the bulls-eye dead-center at that distance for a week, without varying a quarter of an inch. Well, today, with the target a full ten feet farther away, he hit the bulls-eye dead-center fifteen times in a row."

"That's good!" Susan said.

"And listen to this," Curt continued. "You know we've also been working with *moving* targets—tin cans swinging on a string from a tree limb." Curt reached over and messed up Jared's hair. "Today this sharpshooter drilled every tin can I swung on the string on the very first shot. And guess how many times in a row he did it."

"Five!" Nathan said.

"More."

"Ten?" Susan asked.

"More."

Stefanie giggled. "Okay, Sheriff Langan. How many times in a row did your student drill the swinging tin cans?"

"Sixteen!"

"Then he missed?" Susan asked.

"No. Then we ran out of tin cans!"

There was a round of laughter and applause. Jared bowed and said, "Thank you, my friends! Thank you! I say this from the depths of my heart. I owe it all to Denver County's great Sheriff Curt Langan! Let's hear it for Sheriff La-a-ngan!"

More applause. More laughter. Breanna was thrilled to see the Hamilton children so superbly happy.

On a warm night in July, Breanna prayed with her three house-guests as usual and tucked them into bed. She had brought in military-type cots for the boys; Susan slept in Breanna's bed. Breanna slept on the overstuffed couch in the parlor.

When Breanna emerged from the bedroom, she felt sad and a bit depressed. The orphan train would be in Denver next month, and the children didn't want to go back to New York. She didn't want them to go either. When the children prayed that night, they had asked God for someone in Denver to adopt them.

The house was quiet as Breanna sat down at the kitchen table and opened her Bible. Soon she could hear the soft, even breathing of slumber coming from the bedroom.

After reading some of God's promises, Breanna closed the Bible, lowered her head, and said softly, "Dear Lord, I'm claiming the promises I just read here in Your Book. Those precious children have been through so much, and now they're living with the dread of having to go back to New York and start all over. I know You love them more than I ever could, because Your love capacity is bigger than mine. But I do love them an awful lot. You know I would adopt them myself, it if were possible. Please, Lord Jesus. Please let somebody right here in Denver—"

Breanna's prayer was interrupted by a knock at the door.

Probably one or both of the Goodwins, she thought. They always checked on her at bedtime to make sure she was all right. They were a little early tonight, but she appreciated their concern.

"Yes?" she said, with her hand on the doorknob.

Breanna was stunned to hear a male voice with a strong Southern drawl.

"Miss Baylor, my name's Davis Claymore. I have Cleve Holden with me. I think you will remember us. We met you in Abilene. Wanted to say hello. If we're callin' at too late an hour—"

"Oh, no, of course not!" Breanna said. She shoved back the dead bolt and opened the door. "Come in, gentlemen. It's so nice to see you. What brings you through Denver?"

Neither man replied until Breanna closed the door behind them. Then, with the swiftness of a cougar, Claymore seized Breanna and clamped a hand over her mouth, his other arm locking her in a powerful embrace. Breanna squirmed against his strength and let out a muffled scream.

"We've lived for this moment ever since you saved the stinkin' president's life, lady," Claymore said. "Took us awhile to find you, but here we are!"

Holden chuckled. "She's wonderin' why we're here, Davis. Well, honey, it's like this. We were backups in the assassination plot, but we couldn't get a shot at ol' Useless Grant because you knocked him flat on the train platform. You cost Monty Drake and Jake Brawmer their lives. Well, now you're gonna pay. We're gonna toss you in the Platte River while it's nice and dark. They'll fish you out downstream somewhere."

Breanna's first thought was for the sleeping children. If they woke up, they would come out to see what was going on. These hate-filled men would kill them, too!

Claymore held Breanna in his vise-like grip as Holden pulled several short lengths of cord from his hip pocket.

Suddenly a young voice said, "Let her go!"

Both men turned to see a twelve-year-old boy holding a nickel-plated .36 caliber Navy Colt. The hammer was cocked, and the boy's eyes were full of fire.

"I said, let her go!"

23

WRATH FLITTED ACROSS DAVIS CLAYMORE'S FACE. He dare not let go of the woman to go for his gun; one scream from her could bring help from the big house. He gritted out a terse, "Take care of the kid, Cleve."

Jared licked his lips and adjusted his feet firmly beneath him. "I said let go of her, mister! Both of you put your hands in the air!"

Cleve Holden laughed a quick explosive sound, easing his hand toward the butt of his revolver. "Hey, you're really somethin', kid! You don't really think you can handle two Civil War veterans, do you?"

When Holden's gun came out of the holster, the .36 caliber Navy Colt fired. Breanna ejected a muffled cry beneath Claymore's hand.

The bullet struck Cleve Holden's gun hand, and he howled and dropped the weapon. It clattered across the floor out of reach. As blood flowed from his hand, Holden lunged and said, "I'm gonna kill you, kid!"

"Don't move, mister! I'll shoot you again if I have to! And I can hit what I shoot at!"

Holden reached for Claymore's holstered gun with his good hand. The Navy Colt spit fire again, and Holden staggered back against the door with a bullet in his shoulder. When he made another attempt for Claymore's gun, Jared squeezed the trigger again, this time hitting Holden in the thigh. He dropped to the floor with a howl.

Breanna trembled in Claymore's grasp as Jared moved forward and stopped six feet from the tall man. He aimed the smoking Colt between Claymore's eyes and said, "Let go of her, mister, or I'll make you!"

The door flew open as Dr. Goodwin burst in with a Colt .45 in his hand. "What's going on here?" he demanded.

Breanna slipped from Claymore's grasp and relieved him of his gun. "These two men are just learning what it's like to go up against a boy who has the heart of a lion, Doctor."

On the following Sunday afternoon, Breanna and the Hamiltons rode home from church with the Goodwins. Martha had invited them for Sunday dinner.

While Martha, Breanna, and Susan worked in the kitchen, Dr. Goodwin and the boys sat on the front porch and discussed the men who had come to Denver to kill Breanna. Dr. Goodwin explained that Cleve Holden's wounds would keep him in the hospital for several weeks, then he would be transferred to jail.

"Are they going to prison, Dr. Goodwin?" Jared asked.

"I have no doubt they will, Jared. When Miss Breanna testifies in court that they were going to kill her, and you back it up, it's not going to look good for them in front of a judge and jury. Not only that, when Miss Breanna testifies that they told her they were part of the assassination plot against President Grant, that'll seal their doom for sure."

"Hey, look!" Nathan cried, pointing down the tree-shaded

street. "It's Sheriff Langan and Miss Stefanie!"

The boys jumped off the porch and ran to meet the Langan buggy as it pulled into the circular drive.

Nathan jumped up and down. "Are you eating dinner with us?" he asked.

"They sure are!" Goodwin said.

"Does Miss Breanna know?" Jared asked.

"No," the doctor said with a chuckle. "It's…well, it's sort of a surprise."

"It sure is!" Breanna said from inside the screen door. She looked between the Goodwins and the Langans and smelled a conspiracy. She grinned and said, "What's this all about?"

"Let's go inside and you'll soon find out," Goodwin said.

The Goodwin house was furnished and decorated in old Victorian style, with beautiful tapestries, elaborate draperies and sheers, and plush, colorful carpets. Martha led the Hamilton children to the bay window and pointed to a sculpted mahogany couch. "Jared, Susan, Nathan," she said, "I want you to sit together right here."

They looked puzzled, but obeyed, then gazed expectantly at the adults.

Curt took Stefanie's hand and led her to stand directly in front of the children. Breanna started to speak, but Martha touched her arm and winked.

"Jared, Susie, Nathan," Curt said, "Miss Stefanie and I have been talking to Jesus a lot about you. We found out from Dr. Carroll a few weeks ago that because of some problems Miss Stefanie has been having, we won't ever be able to have any children born into our home. So, we would like to ask you three if…well, if you would like to change your last name to Langan."

Breanna felt as if she might faint from happiness. Oh, thank

You, Lord! she said in her heart.

The children were speechless.

Curt continued. "Even though we haven't been married very long, Miss Stefanie and I are old enough to adopt children your age."

Martha took the silently weeping Breanna into her arms.

Jared found his voice first and spoke for his brother and sister when he said, "We love you and Miss Stefanie and...well, to tell you the truth, at night, after Miss Breanna has tucked us in and kissed us goodnight, we've had secret prayer meetings. We've been asking Jesus to help you and Miss Stefanie love us so much that you'd adopt us."

The Langans gathered all three children in a hug and wept. Curt prayed aloud, thanking the Lord for the way He had worked in all of their lives.

When he finished praying, Nathan said, "Sheriff..."

"Yes, Nathan?"

"Do we still have to call you Sheriff and Miss Stefanie now?"

"What do you want to call us?"

"I want to call you Mama and Papa."

"And you, Susan?"

"Daddy and Mother."

"And you, Jared?"

"I'd like to call you Dad. And I'd like to call her Mom."

"Well," Stefanie said, "from now on we're Papa, Daddy, and Dad...and Mama, Mother, and Mom!"

As the Goodwins joined the children and the soon-to-be-adoptive parents, Breanna stood slightly apart, marveling at the way God had orchestrated this moment.

She felt honored to be part of God's plan to gather the children to Himself and bless them, first through Reverend Brace and the Children's Aid Society, then through her nursing skills and her heart for witnessing, and finally through the love of people as dear as Curt and Stefanie Langan.

Breanna moved back into the circle of hugs and thanked the Lord that He had brought Jared, Susan, and Nathan out of their poverty and brutal mistreatment into the light of His love.

OTHER COMPELLING STORIES BY
AL LACY

Books in the Battles of Destiny series:

☞ A Promise Unbroken

Two couples battle jealousy and racial hatred amidst a war that would cripple America. From a prosperous Virginia plantation to a grim jail cell outside Lynchburg, follow the dramatic story of a love that could not be destroyed.

☞ A Heart Divided

Ryan McGraw—leader of the Confederate Sharpshooters—is nursed back to health by beautiful army nurse Dixie Quade. Their romance would survive the perils of war, but can it withstand the reappearance of a past love?

☞ Beloved Enemy

Young Jenny Jordan covers for her father's Confederate spy missions. But as she grows closer to Union soldier Buck Brownell, Jenny finds herself torn between devotion to the South and her feelings for the man she is forbidden to love.

☞ Shadowed Memories

Critically wounded on the field of battle and haunted by amnesia, one man struggles to regain his strength and the memories that have slipped away from him.

☞ Joy from Ashes

Major Layne Dalton made it through the horrors of the battle of Fredericksburg, but can he rise above his hatred toward the Heglund brothers who brutalized his wife and killed his unborn son?

☞ Season of Valor

Captain Shane Donovan was heroic in battle. Can he summon the courage to face the dark tragedy unfolding back home in Maine?

Books in the Battles of Destiny series (cont.):

☞ *Wings of the Wind*

God brings a young doctor and a nursing student together in this story of the Battle of Antietam.

Books in the Journeys of the Stranger series:

☞ *Legacy*

Can John Stranger bring Clay Austin back to the right side of the law...and restore the code of honor shared by the woman he loves?

☞ *Silent Abduction*

The mysterious man in black fights to defend a small town targeted by cattle rustlers and to rescue a young woman and child held captive by a local Indian tribe.

☞ *Blizzard*

When three murderers slated for hanging escape from the Colorado Territorial Prison, young U.S. Marshal Ridge Holloway and the mysterious John Stranger join together to track down the infamous convicts.

☞ *Tears of the Sun*

When John Stranger arrives in Apache Junction, Arizona, he finds himself caught up in a bitter war between sworn enemies: the Tonto Apaches and the Arizona Zunis.

☞ *Circle of Fire*

John Stranger must clear his name of the crimes committed by another mysterious—and murderous—"stranger" who has adopted his identity.

☞ *Quiet Thunder*

A Sioux warrior and a white army captain have been blood brothers since childhood. But when the two meet on the battlefield, which will win out—love or duty?

Books in the Journeys of the Stranger series (cont.):

☞ *Snow Ghost*

John Stranger must unravel the mystery of a murderer who appears to have come back from the grave to avenge his execution.

Books in the Angel of Mercy series:

☞ *A Promise for Breanna*

The man who broke Breanna's heart is back. But this time, he's after her life.

☞ *Faithful Heart*

Breanna and her sister Dottie find themselves in a desperate struggle to save a man they love, but can no longer trust.

☞ *Captive Set Free*

No one leaves Morgan's labor camp alive. Not even Breanna Baylor.

☞ *A Dream Fulfilled*

A tender story about one woman's healing from heartbreak and the fulfillment of her dreams.

Books in the Hannah of Fort Bridger series (co-authored with JoAnna Lacy):

☞ *Under the Distant Sky*

Follow the Cooper family as they travel West from Missouri in pursuit of their dream of a new life on the Wyoming frontier.

☞ *Consider the Lilies (available June 1997)*

Will Hannah Cooper and her children learn to trust God to provide when tragedy threatens to destroy their dream?

Available at your local Christian bookstore